AIR FORCE ONE HAS VANISHED!

DAVID H. BROWN

Deerfield Beach, Florida
800.889.0693

Published by TriMark Press, Inc., Deerfield Beach, Florida.

Library of Congress Cataloging-in-Publication Data

Air Force One has Vanished!
David H. Brown

p. cm.

ISBN: 978-0-9886145-4-3
Library of Congress Control Number: 2014936860

E14
10 9 8 7 6 5 4 3 2 1
First Edition, Fiction
Printed and Bound in the United States of America

A publication of TriMark Press, Inc.
368 South Military Trail
Deerfield Beach, FL 33442
800.889.0693
www.TriMarkPress.com

The Front Page

On March 8, 2014, a Malaysian B-777 carrying two-hundred thirty-nine crew and passgengers mysteriously disappeared on a flight from Kuala Lumpur to Beijing. All were presumed deceased.

Air Force One Has Vanished! was published a month later, but the timing is ***totally coincidental.*** I began writing this political novel over a year ago as a continuation of my previous book, *Next in Line to the Oval Office.* Both plots are unique.

This is my first experience with TriMark Press, recommended to me by the widely known political historian Professor Robert Watson, who has had books published by TriMark. As a result, I am grateful for the expertise and guidance provided by Barry Chesler, chief executive, and Penelope Love, publishing director.

Those who helped give birth to this novel include, in no special order:

Carl Stern – a personal friend and professional colleague of almost fifty years. As a correspondent for NBC/TV, he covered the Supreme Court and Department of Justice when I was assistant director of information for the DOJ. Ironically, he later became director of information for that agency. Afterward, he was a professor at George Washington University. He pointed me in the right legal direction, and his keen mind also helped correct factual errors.

Mark Brown – he just happens to be my son, but he never lets that stand in the way of sharp critiques. He is also an excellent writer and grammarian.

Dr. David B. Brown – he is my namesake cousin and a retired gastroenterologist, who saved me from medical mistakes. A budding screen writer, he also advised me on film potential for two of my novels.

Walt Wurfel – assistant White House press secretary during the President Carter administration. He kept me on the straight and narrow field of Oval Office media relations.

Doris Davidoff – an incredible editor, who made my drafts more readable and plausible.

And of course, Google – without which I could not do the necessary research.

Mea culpa. Although my charaters are usually fictional, I pattered one in this novel after a real person, although she does not know it. Dana Bash, chief congressional correspondent for CNN, is the inspiration for fictional Capitol Hill correspondent Diane Bana. Bash is a credible and unbiased reporter with amazing sources.

I have been fortunate in having a variety of professional experiences that have helped me with my non-fiction and fiction books. These include nearly fifteen years as an Ohio newspaper reporter; and twenty-four years as a public information officer for the Department of Justice, Federal Aviation Administration, Department of Transportation, and Government Printing Office. At the FAA, I was the press officer for the original Anti-skyjacking Task Force, and am the last remaining member of that group. A WWII combat veteran, I later received a commission in the Army Reserves. After twenty-eight years, including a mobilization designee assignment in the Pentagon, I retired as a lieutenant colonel.

David H. Brown

CHAPTER 1

"WHAT?!!!!!"

CHAPTER 2

The "Ice Queen" Melteth

No one had ever heard Alicia Rineheart raise her voice even once. After all, her nickname was the "Ice Queen."

The word reverberated off the wall of her West Wing first-floor congressional relations office in The White House, swept past the corner office of Chief of Staff Jared Winston, and stopped at the unoccupied Oval Office.

Her second outburst, in which she knocked over her chair, was only barely toned down:

> **"How in God's name can a plane the size of a B-747 with a crew of 26 that can carry up to 76 passengers 7,800 miles without refueling just . . .** *vanish?!!!!!"*

Deputy Press Secretary Greg Fountaineau, who made the call, waited until Alicia calmed down. Finally, as she took a deep breath and almost collapsed into her now up-righted chair, he continued: "That's as much as I know now. I tried to reach Winston, but he must be away from his desk."

Alicia thought she was beginning to hyperventilate, but she took more deep breaths and apologized, "I'm sorry, Greg." He waited another moment, cleared his throat, and said, "Alicia, I don't know how to say this in any other way, but Tim Anderson is one of those on board."

She almost dropped the phone. Greg had been Tim's boss at the television station, and he knew the relationship between the two. Alicia interrupted: "Did you just say Tim was on board Air Force One? He's the executive director of the Bardon Foundation, so it doesn't make any sense he would be flying with President Merriwether."

Greg continued: "So's my boss, Jorge Umberto. All I know is air traffic controllers at Miami lost contact with Air Force One on its way back from . . ."

She ended his sentence, "Puerto Rico."

"I know your phone will ring off the hook once the people on Capitol Hill get wind of this," he explained, "but there is one other piece of information you've got to keep to yourself for the time being."

She responded testily, "And, that is?"

Greg paused before saying in a hushed voice, "The last transmission from the plane was when it entered the Bermuda Triangle."

No sooner had the conversation ended than her phone lines lit up. The first one she answered was from The White House press corps' nemesis Bouchard, who had tipped off Greg. Just then, one of the Secret Service security detail burst into her office, his gun in hand. She put her hand over the mouthpiece on the phone and said, "I'm OK. I didn't mean to create a disturbance. Get me Whiz!"

He replied, "Ma'am, have you forgotten he's with the President?"

Alicia almost dropped the phone again.

"Andy Smollencoff is in charge," he explained. I'll get him."

She nodded, and apologized to Bouchard, who of course had heard the conversation. "Mr. Bouchard," she finally said, "you'll have to excuse me. I have another call. Please don't contact Greg again, and I promise we'll get back to you as quickly as possible."

Just then, the Chief of Staff burst into her office, a half-eaten sandwich in his hand. "What the hell is going on?!" Jared demanded in his booming voice.

Alicia quickly shared with him what little she knew about the missing Air Force One. "I was having a quick bite in the Executive Mess in the basement when my secretary told me to get to your office," he explained.

The two had known each other since President Merriwether was a congressman and Jared was his Chief of Staff, and she worked for Senator Michael Stafford. She always deferred to him, and he respected her. This relationship continued in The White House.

Throwing the rest of his sandwich in her waste basket, Jared said, "No one here is to respond to any inquiries just yet. I'm calling a meeting of those who would have input. Alicia, for the time being, I don't want you to call House Speaker Marshall Vance or Senate President pro tempore Christopher Cummings. Without a Vice President, they are the next two in line to the Oval Office. We'll meet one hour from now in the basement Situation Room because it's secure. I want you and Greg to be there, too."

As he left, Andy arrived. "I'm sorry I panicked about Air Force One," she apologized.

"Yeah, I just heard, too," he responded.

"I have to go to a meeting with Jared," she explained. "I'll get back to you as quickly as I can." He nodded and left.

When Jared returned to his office, he closed the door and unlocked a special drawer of his desk to retrieve a copy of the Air Force One manifest. He called Andy to put The White House security detail on alert with the only explanation "no one leaves or enters without my permission. Come to my office and I will give you a list of officials allowed in." He quickly explained the lockdown was necessary "because of a national security situation."

He then consulted his list of the heads of Cabinet departments, and added the Chairman and Deputy Chairman of the Joints Chiefs of Staff. He notified them to hurry to the White House basement's Situation Room "for an emergency national security meeting."

CHAPTER 3

Actions Speak Louder Than Words

THOSE ASSEMBLED KNEW the Situation Room normally is used for national and international crises. Usually, the monitoring of such events is done by a handful of Watch Teams, consisting of senior personnel from intelligence and military offices. So, they were surprised to see members of this new group. They were further taken aback when Jared arrived and called the meeting to order.

Jared was a no-nonsense executive who had been at President Merriwether's side ever since they were college dorm roommates. He did not waste any time with small talk. His 6-feet 4-inch stature was intimidating. Over the years, his black hair turned silver.

"Before the meeting officially begins, please take note there are two people here you may not know," he said. "Alicia Rineheart is head of congressional relations, because Capitol Hill will be affected. Greg Fountaineau, Deputy Press Secretary, is here because the news media will be affected. He also will take notes for historical purposes.

"We have a delicate situation involving national security." He paused, and then said evenly, "Air Force One has vanished!" There was an audible gasp. He continued: "Whatever is said in this secure room stays in this secure room. If someone on The Hill hears about our meeting, it will be easy to pinpoint the leaker."

"As you know, President Merriwether was on a well-publicized goodwill trip to Miami, and then on to Puerto Rico. It was on its return flight when the Miami Air Traffic Control Center lost communication with the plane. The last time it appeared on radar was when it entered the area often called the Bermuda Triangle. Do not jump to any conclusions because of that location. Until there is proof the President is dead, or cannot perform his sworn duties, there could be a dilemma about who is in charge of The White House. No one is going to pull an Al Haig, the former Secretary of State, who announced following the 1981 shooting of President Ronald Reagan that 'I am in control here,' mistakenly thinking he still was second line of succession, but forgetting this was changed in 1947. Normally, the Vice President would take over, but as you know, none has been nominated. There have been occasions in the past when either there was a delay in choosing a new Vice President, or as in the case of President Truman, there was none during his entire first term."

Admiral Haley Ridgely, Chairman of the Joint Chiefs of Staff, asserted, "There must be an immediate sea search of the area based on the last transmission!"

Air Force General Palmer Francene, added, "We certainly can make aircraft available."

Jared interjected, "If a significant sea and air search were to begin, that could raise unwarranted attention, given all the satellites floating around. Also, an increase in electronic traffic might tip our hand. Your invaluable collective experience is crucial. Admiral, you know from your naval career there is no such thing as the Bermuda Triangle, sometimes called the Devil's Triangle. The Board of Geographic Names does not recognize either designation. Even the Coast Guard questions its existence. But, the news media will no doubt refer to the area as the Bermuda Triangle once it becomes public. There is a triangle of sorts ranging from Puerto Rico to the Bahamas to, of course, Bermuda. The area has treacherous weather from time to time, and the Gulf Stream does run through it. The area ranges from 500,000 to 1.5 million square miles!"

General Francene interrupted, "You don't have to lecture us, Mr. Winston. On 5 December 1945, five Navy torpedo bombers designated Flight 19 were on a routine exercise in that area when they disappeared. There has been a host of theories over what happened – from an error in navigation of the lead plane to the aircraft running out of fuel. There also have been other incidents."

Secretary of Defense Jeremiah (Boz) Bosworth whispered to Admiral Ridgely, "He thinks he's the acting President who knows what he's doing."

Jared knew exactly what he was doing.

"Because time is of the essence," he continued, "I have already taken one immediate action."

* * * *

"This is Jared Winston, Chief of Staff to the President of the United States," the chief Miami air traffic controller heard on his phone. "After I am through, I will give you a special phone number to call back to verify I am who I say I am," Jared explained. "I speak for the President when I order you in turn to order every person under your jurisdiction to NOT CONTACT THE NEWS MEDIA OR ANY OTHER SOURCE WITH THE FACT THAT AIR FORCE ONE HAS DROPPED OFF YOUR RADAR. I EMPHASIZE THIS IN THE NAME OF NATIONAL SECURITY. ANY VIOLATION WILL BE TREATED HARSHLY. ARE YOU CLEAR ON THIS?!"

The chief controller recoiled at the terseness of the caller's voice. "Please give me the number, sir, and I will call you back immediately," he responded. In only minutes, the call was verified. The word was passed on to the current shift, with orders to be relayed to subsequent controllers.

"Who in the hell gave you authority to do that?!" Secretary of

Defense Jeremiah (Boz) Bosworth demanded. "You're just a presidential appointee who did not need Senate confirmation!"

"Sir, I felt it had to be done immediately," Jared explained. "I take full responsibility."

"You've got a lot of balls for someone who ranks below every one of us!" he thundered.

"Any other surprises, Mr. Winston?!" the Admiral added.

"No, sir," Jared replied stiffly. "May I continue?"

"You're on a short leash, Mr. Winston!" the Secretary asserted.

"For the record, I respectfully suggest you be known as the Emergency Situation Room Group, or 'E-SERG,'" Jared continued.

"Whatever, Mr. President," the Admiral snarled sarcastically.

Secretary Bosworth was not satisfied. "I'd like to know what right you have to even conduct this meeting, let alone issue orders to us?!" he insisted. "You are nothing more than a staff member who serves at the pleasure of the President! And, right now, he is missing!"

Jared carefully produced a document and explained, "Before we go on, I need to share the following with you:

"To whom it may concern: In the event of my temporary absence from The White House, Chief of Staff Jared Winston will conduct any and all business which does not require my signature. I invoke this special circumstance in the interest of security, national and international."

At his signal, Greg passed out copies of what Jared had read, which contained the President's actual signature (not an auto-pen version) and date.

Secretary Bosworth flung his copy across the table, and it fluttered to the floor. "This isn't worth the paper it's written on!" he thundered. "I'm not going to sit here and let you act as President when it is obvious he is missing and cannot conduct the duties of his Office!"

As the Secretary stood up, Jared also rose from his chair. "Mr. Secretary, you are privileged to do as you please," he began quietly.

"However, if it is learned that the President is able to conduct the duties of his Office as of this moment, and you refuse to accept his direct order, there could be consequences."

Bosworth's face turned beet red as he turned around to face Jared: "Who is the hell do you think you're talking you?!" he shouted. "You're the one who's going to face some consequences!"

Admiral Ridgely intervened by asking, "Mr. Winston, are you saying that while the President is not here, but is on the missing Air Force One, he is in fact able to conduct the duties of his Office?"

The group was surprised when Secretary of Homeland Security Paul Amato interjected: "In the interest of strategy, my feeling is that ordering a lot of ships and or planes to search the area has more negatives than positives. I suggest using an existing satellite program administered by the Coast Guard, which is part of my Department. If we can recess for a short time, I can have the Commandant, Admiral Roger Peckinpaugh, rush over here and explain its use. I believe a satellite will call less attention than ships or planes."

Jared looked around for further comment before asking, "How long would it take to have him here?"

"Half an hour at the most," the Secretary answered.

"If there is no objection, we reconvene in 30 minutes," Jared said.

* * * *

Back in his office, he again unlocked the desk drawer, withdrew a folder, scanned the contents, put it back, locked the drawer, and made the necessary call.

* * * *

As the meeting restarted, Secretary Amato introduced Admiral Peckinpaugh.

"Perhaps most of you never heard of an interagency satellite program we call SARSAT," the Admiral began. "That stands for Search and Rescue Satellite-Aided Tracking, as well as the international COSPAS-SARSAT. They have been able to rescue more than 22,000 persons. We are ready to implement SARSAT immediately."

Secretary Amato added, "If there are no objections, Admiral Peckinpaugh has to get this started." He departed quickly.

Jared stood up and said, "Before continuing, I have an announcement to make."

"You're resigning, I hope?" Secretary Bosworth snarled.

"In the interest of unity, and because I apparently have caused some friction, I would ask your approval of a new coordinator," he explained. He nodded to the guard to open the door. In walked a nearly 6-feet tall red-haired woman. Her high heels made her look even more than that.

"Members," Jared said, "This is Mary Ann McCormick. For those of you who may not have met her, she is the National Security Advisor to the President. Prior to that appointment, she was Director of the Women's Army Corps, and retired as a Major General."

Before anyone could say anything, he continued, "If there are no objections, I turn the meeting over to her."

His maneuver caught everyone off guard, including Alicia and Greg.

Not waiting for a comment, McCormick said, "Thank you, Jared. I'll try my best to keep things rolling. I understand you have been briefed by Admiral Peckpinpaugh about using a satellite to search for Air Force One. I could not agree more this was a wise decision."

The members still were in a state of shock and awe. She had taken control, and made it obvious she was not burdened with the connection to the now missing President that Jared has. The Group would be in for another shock.

"Prior to coming to this meeting, Mr. Winston revealed something that needs to be shared with all of you," she asserted.

"Thank you, General McCormick," he responded, clearly indicating how she wanted to be addressed. "To be blunt, the disappearance of Air Force One is about to become breaking news! Deputy Press Secretary Fountaineau will explain."

Greg began: "I received a call from White House correspondent Bouchard wanting comment on the disappearance of Air Force One. When I told him we did not have one, he said he heard the Coast Guard was about to begin a satellite search of the area where the last contact with the Miami Air Traffic Control Center was located. I could not ask him where he got his information, but he is itching to have an exclusive."

"How the hell did he find out something so fast?" Secretary Amato asked.

Greg hesitated before continuing: "He used to work for the Miami News before moving to Washington. I'm sure he has kept up with his contacts there. I'm guessing the original tip came from the Miami Air Traffic Control Center. Once he breaks the story, the media will play catch-up hard ball."

Jared was fuming. "I warned the Center not to say anything!" he declared. "Some heads will roll."

Secretary Amato interjected, "Mr. Winston, since the Federal Aviation Administration is part of my Department, I will see to that!"

Greg went on, "I know Bouchard's reputation. He is tenacious."

McCormick asked, "Can we ask him to delay it a bit?"

"General," Jared answered, "we can try, but we will need a good reason why. And, we would owe him a big favor."

"Greg," she continued, "does he know about our Group?"

"No, I'm sure he doesn't," he answered.

"Jared," McCormick said, "it's up to you to ask. Members, let's meet back in half an hour. Jared, call this Bouchard and have a talk with him. Let me know the outcome."

Group members did not realize they had not been asked for their views.

* * * *

Greg called Bouchard and asked him to come to Jared's office.

"Mr. Bouchard," Jared began, "Greg tells me you are on the verge of quite an exclusive."

"Yes," Bouchard answered curtly.

"When do you expect to release your story?" Jared asked.

"Hopefully, for tomorrow's morning edition," Bouchard answered.

"Would it be possible to hold off for 24 hours?" Jared asked.

"Why should I?!" Bouchard asked curtly.

"Would national security and perhaps international implications do?" Jared parried.

"Again, Mr. Winston, what would I gain by that?" Bouchard responded. "Some other reporter might find out what I did."

"Knowing your reputation, I doubt that," Jared replied. "But, let's stop playing games. In return for a 24-hour delay, I will be able to confirm for you – and you only – the facts about the Coast Guard satellite search. No one else will have that advantage."

Bouchard hesitated. No one had ever asked him to do this. Finally, he asked, "Why the 24 hours?"

"Are we off the record here?" Jared asked.

"For the time being," Bouchard answered.

"I'm sure you have figured out trying to find a missing airplane in an area so HUGE is almost an impossibility," he began to explain. "Let's give the satellite people a chance to locate Air Force One. If it is found, you'll have an exclusive. If it is not, you'll still have an exclusive. It's win-win for you."

Bouchard again hesitated before asking, "What if another reporter jumps the gun?"

Jared smiled, and answered: "I doubt anyone can be as resourceful as you are in 24 hours. If a reporter does call, we'll stall and I'll let you know. Besides . . . no one else will be able to be tipped off from the Miami Air Traffic Control Center anymore. That source has been shut down. You're home free."

Bouchard was surprised Jared found out about his source. He thought about what Jared had said, and finally responded, "I'm taking one helluva chance, Mr. Winston. If you're playing games with me, and another reporter beats me to the exclusive, I'm not one to take that lightly. On the other hand, I'm counting on you keeping your word."

"My word is my bond," Jared said, dredging up an old saying.

Bouchard stood up and said, "We have a deal. But, only for 24 hours."

* * * *

Bouchard often had been likened to Gene Shalit, the over-the-top film critic on NBC-TV's Today Show for many years. Like Shalit, he sported a thick mustache and wore dark-rimmed glasses. But Bouchard's hair in no way resembled the frizzy mop of Shalit.

Because of his real given first name of Sylvestro, Bouchard for his early years as a cub reporter had been teased with the nickname of "Silly." As a defense mechanism, he did act like a clown. One day he was assigned to do a story on a bullied teenage girl who later committed suicide. That changed his demeanor immediately. While he trimmed the mustache somewhat, he kept the owl-like framed glasses.

In 2006, The News was purchased by The McClain Company. Bouchard knew the new owner has a bureau in Washington, DC. He asked to be transferred there. As luck would have it, one of the senior editors there just retired. His transfer was approved. After making the move, he met with the bureau chief and made one request: If he were given a byline, he asked that it read S. Bouchard. The bureau chief agreed since he could not care less what his new arrival wanted to be known as.

Another piece of luck came his way. The bureau was entitled to a reporter at The White House. The person who held that job tragically was killed in an auto accident when his car was demolished by a drunk driver. Bouchard occasionally filled in for the regular reporter, and how he unashamedly asked for the assignment full time. The bureau chief admired what in Yiddish is called "chutzpah," or "boldness," and agreed to the change "on a temporary basis to start." Bouchard worked so hard to develop sources and to do solid reporting that the job became permanent after one year.

The tip on the missing Air Force One came to Bouchard from an air traffic controller who lived in the same Miami apartment building as he did. He quickly contacted Greg. Before responding, Greg conferred with Jared on what to say. Finally, Bouchard was talking with Jared.

"This is a very delicate situation, as I am sure you can understand," Winston began. "We certainly cannot tell you how to report what you were told, but this situation involves security at the highest levels. As you can imagine, the political implications are monumental."

He paused and Bouchard replied, "I'm listening, Mr. Winston."

Jared continued, "There is no question the aircraft is Air Force One. No use denying that. The President and Press Secretary have said you are very professional. You have not always agreed with past and present administrations, but you never have substituted personal feelings for unbiased news coverage. To our knowledge, you never have editorialized in your reporting. As Sergeant Friday used to say in his television series 'Dragnet,' 'Just the facts, ma'am.' We cannot favor you. Ask us a question and we will try to answer as truthfully as we can, all things considered. And, national security is one of those."

Bouchard knew his journalistic ego was being massaged, but he appreciated Jared's frankness. Yes, this could be called professional horse trading; however, he felt a sense of trust was evident on both sides.

"How long before you feel you have a new development?" Bouchard asked.

"A lot depends on when the aircraft is located, "Jared answered. "As I've said to others, the Bermuda Triangle alone is some 1 million square miles. I certainly hope the plane will be located sooner rather than later."

Bouchard asked, "Can you be more specific than that?"

Jared replied, "Hope springs eternal."

Bouchard said "I can live with that."

Jared quickly added, "I want to add one more thing, and please do not take this as game-playing. I have found in politics that patience and diligence uncover more than what seems on the surface. I'm sorry I can't give you any more time now. There are other pressures at work, and I cannot be in two places at the same time."

CHAPTER 4

The Scoop

Headline: AIR FORCE ONE HAS VANISHED!
Byline: By S. Bouchard

THE WHITE HOUSE HAS CONFIRMED that Air Force One, carrying President Lincoln A. Merriwether and some 100 other passengers, lost contact with the Miami Air Traffic Control Center after taking off from Ramey Air Force Base in Puerto Rico. Key members of Congress were notified early this morning.

Jared Winston, Chief of Staff, urged caution in drawing any conclusions. "This does not mean the plane has crashed into the Atlantic Ocean," he explained. "It is important to remember the only fact is that radar contact was lost."

The plane had originally stopped in Miami, and then went on to Puerto Rico. President Merriwether had planned the trip some time ago as a gesture to support a move for statehood not only for Puerto Rico but also the District of Columbia.

Among passengers are several members of the White House press corps. (Their names were listed.)

An intense search by the Coast Guard is underway for the aircraft.

(The rest of the article contained facts about Air Force One.)

* * * *

Print and electronic reporters bombarded Greg's office, wanting to know why they had not been informed ahead of time. Radio and television stations interrupted regular programming with the news. Greg said there would be a press conference later in the day.

* * * *

Diane Bana, Capitol Hill correspondent for TV station WNS (Washington News Service), began calling her House and Senate sources for reaction.

CHAPTER 5

Chaos

ONCE THE NEWS WAS OUT, SecDef Bosworth rushed over to Capitol Hill to talk with one of his friends from their days at The Citadel in Charleston, SC – House Speaker Marshall Vance.

"Marsh, what do you think about what's happened to Air Force One?" Boz asked.

The Secretary answered, "I only can tell you what's been going on behind the scenes."

"What are you talking about?" Vance asked.

"Because we've known each other for so many years, I can confide to you about ESRG."

"What's that?" the Speaker responded.

Secretary Bosworth related to him formation of the Group, the way Winston thought he could take it over, and the appearance of National Security Advisor McCormick.

"Whew!" Vance exclaimed.

"Yeah," Bosworth agreed. "Have you seen McCormick?"

"Not in person, but I remember a photo in The Washington Post when she was appointed," the Speaker answered.

"She is something else!" the Secretary commented. "She took over from Winston and ran the meetings with an iron fist! Don't mess with her!"

"I don't think I'll have any opportunity to, as you say, 'mess with her,'" Vance replied. "But, I don't think that's why you're here."

"Have you had a chance to assess the reaction of your colleagues to the news?" he asked.

"Do you mean have my phones been ringing off the hook?" he responded. "Damn straight!"

"What's the general reaction?" Boz asked.

"In a word, chaos!" Vance replied.

"What do you mean by that?" the Secretary asked.

"Well, the general question is this: Who's in charge at the White House?" the Speaker explained. "There's no Vice President."

"And, that puts you first in line to the Oval Office!" Secretary Bosworth asserted.

"Yeah, on paper," Speaker Vance responded.

"Marsh, for Christ sake, wake up and smell the roses!" Boz replied annoyingly.

"Say what?" the Speaker asked.

"Carpe diem, my friend, carpe diem!" Secretary Bosworth insisted.

"What the hell do you mean by 'seize the day?'" Vance replied.

"Jesus," Boz almost shouted, "do I have to spell it out for you? Damn it, rally your troops behind you and have them declare the Office of the President vacant! Then, get Supreme Court Justice Joyce Whittingham-Stern to swear you in! On the way over, I called one of my aides, and he's rushing over a copy of the 25th Amendment. Section 4 spells out what is required to do what I said."

Just then, a secretary knocked on the closed door. Vance shouted, "I said I don't want to be disturbed!" She slid a sheet of paper under the door. The Speaker walked over and picked it up. "Well, your aide didn't waste any time."

As he walked back to his desk, Vance read the sheet. He sat down, looked at his long-time friend, and asked, "Have you read this?"

"My Deputy gave me the gist," Boz responded.

"He should have taken the time to go over each word," the Speaker said sharply. "Let me read it for you: 'Whenever the Vice President and a majority of either the principal officers of the executive departments or of such other body as Congress may by law provide, transmit to the President pro tempore of the Senate and the Speaker of the House of Representatives their written declaration that the President is unable to discharge the powers and duties of his office, the Vice President shall immediately assume the powers and duties of the office as Acting President.'"

The SecDef responded, "So what's your point?"

"Points, Boz. Points; plural!" Vance answered. "You're forgetting one small detail. There is no Vice President. There would have to be a legal ruling as how to implement Section 4 when there's no Vice President. Also, I don't see anything that spells out how, when, and why the President is 'unable to discharge the powers and duties of his office.'"

"That's my point," the SecDef responded. "You can act as Vice President since you're now next in line to the Oval Office."

"Boz," Vance said slowly, "I have a law degree, but you don't. I know enough to guarantee you without a Vice President, Section 4 cannot be used. When did your Group find out about it? I'll bet it wasn't a whole more than 24 hours ago. Christ, Air Force One and the President could turn up any minute. If we tried to grab the Oval Office, and that happened, there could be legal consequences! Boz, you're rushing to judgment."

The Secretary's face turned beet red. "I came here to try to do you a favor," he said, "and this is the thanks I get for it!" With that, he stormed out of Vance's office, and headed for Senator Christopher Cumming's office a short distance away. He needed to speak with the President pro tempore, and now second in line to the Oval Office.

* * * *

Senator Cummings knew Bosworth and the Speaker were long-time friends. He also knew the same could not be said for him and the Secretary of Defense. He did not look forward to the visit, but he greeted Bosworth cordially.

"I believe this is the first time I've had the pleasure of meeting you in person, Mr. Secretary," the President Pro Tempore of the Senate said. "To what do I owe this honor?"

Bosworth came right to the point: "In your position, Senator, I am sure you know about the line of succession to the Oval Office since you are now second in that line." The Senator nodded. "That 1947 law was enacted in case the President could not fulfill the duties of his office, or could or would not take the oath," he continued, and the Senator again nodded. The Secretary continued: "Let me set the stage for my visit by informing you that Air Force One has gone missing on a return trip from Puerto Rico."

Now he had the Senator's attention. "Mr. Secretary," he interrupted, "did I hear you say Air Force One has gone missing?" This time Bosworth nodded. "Good Lord!" the Senator exclaimed. "That's news to me! When did this happen?!"

The SecDef said tersely, "I heard about it a couple of hours ago." He let that sink in before going on: "Such news doesn't travel fast, but the cat's out of the bag."

The Senator expressed consternation, saying, "I'm sorry, Mister Secretary, but you lost me there."

The SecDef went on, "The point is, Senator, it seems we don't have a President. I just discussed this with Speaker Vance, but he does not seem to grasp the importance of this event." The Senator did not either, but he was not going to admit that to the Secretary. "I tried to point out to the Speaker that he is a heartbeat away from becoming President, but he did not seem thrilled with that possibility."

The Senator leaned over to his intercom and announced, "Hold all my calls unless I'm needed on the floor." He turned back to Bosworth and said, "I appreciate your telling me, but . . ."

The Secretary interrupted: "Let me put a fine point on it, Senator. If the Speaker does not want to take the oath, YOU'RE NEXT IN LINE! Get it?!"

Senator Cummings finally "got it." He let out a low whistle, and beads of sweat appeared on his balding head. "I . . . don't . . . know . . . what . . . to . . . say," he sputtered.

Bosworth stood up and asked, "If that scenario works out, are you willing and able to man up and claim your right?"

The Senator now was sweating profusely, and was barely able to mumble, "Of course. Yes. Of course. Mr. Secretary, I don't know how to thank you."

Boz said in a low voice, "When that takes place, I'm sure you would want to have your own people on the White House staff. But, we can talk about that later. Meanwhile, I'll stay in touch." He winked, saluted, spun on his heels, and left as the Senator virtually collapsed into his chair.

As he left the building and got into the rear seat of his vehicle, Boz mumbled, "There's more than one way to skin a cat." The driver turned around and asked, "Sir?" The SecDef answered, "Nothing. Just take me back to the Pentagon." Once there, he called General Francene and said, "I want to apologize to you. I shouldn't have lost my temper. I've been out of the office on some official business and just got back. Anything I should know about the meeting with the Chief of Staff? And, any news about Air Force One?"

The General answered, "No, and no."

The Secretary decided to make another call. "Mr. Fountaineau, this is . . ."

Greg interrupted: "Yes, Secretary Bosworth, I recognize your voice. What can I do for you?"

Boz answered, "Has the press corps found out about Air Force One?"

Greg carefully responded, "Sir, I'm not authorized to say anything at this time about that matter. You should check with Mr. Winston."

The SecDef was about to say "in a pig's eye" when he responded, "Yes, I'll just do that."

Just as he ended that call, another one came in from McCormick.

"Mr. Secretary," she began, "I have received a request from an ESRG member for a meeting, and I would like to reconvene the group as soon as possible."

Bosworth smirked, "How soon?"

She politely answered, "Half an hour."

Bosworth answered, "Fine."

* * * * *

General Francene asked to speak: "On behalf of some of the people here, we feel the Coast Guard search, while well-meaning, is not enough considering the vast area of the Atlantic. We feel, as you apparently do, time is of the essence. Therefore, we propose creating an all-out search effort using whatever means are available, including satellites and even drones. Of course, ships are the primary source. (He nodded to Admiral Ridgely, who had not been part of the discussion group because he was busy on Capitol Hill.) We believe the starting point is correctly identified by the Coast Guard, but then we must widen from there. If we understand correctly, there is no evidence of an explosion. (Winston nodded yes.) As pointed out earlier, that was the case in some past Bermuda Triangle incidents. We are given to understand the depth of the Atlantic Ocean in that region could reach 3 to 5 miles at least. If wreckage or other debris is not found, that is the worst case scenario. With an all-out effort, there certainly will be massive press coverage. (He nodded to Greg, who kept taking notes.) What we say can help, or hurt. We should make every effort to accomplish the former, but be prepared for the latter."

McCormick had briefed Greg and Alicia because she said she might call on them. She called on the Deputy Press Secretary first.

"General, your comment about the news media is spot on," Greg began. "I am getting calls from The White House press corps (no one knew he referred only to Bouchard so far). To be honest, the news deluge is about to break out. It is important – correction –

it is VITAL that all news inquiries be directed to our office for the time being. Events surely will quickly reach a crescendo, and we do not want to escalate that with saying too much, or not saying the facts as we know them. I'm sure your media relations people will not like this approach, but if too many people are telling too many reporters too many things, there could be a calamity. I know that sounds harsh, but the situation calls for control."

McCormick added, "Greg, share with the Group some of the headlines you already have seen."

He read:

"Air Force One Has Become Another Bermuda Triangle Victim"

"President Dies In Air Force One Crash"

"Terrorist Bomb Destroys Air Force One"

"Air Force One Downed By Missile In Atlantic Ocean"

"Skyjackers Divert Air Force One To Middle East"

"Government In Disarray Following Death Of President"

"White House Confused About Which Country Stole Air Force One"

She commented, "Pretty outrageous, right? This is why there needs to be firm control of search efforts. General Francene, what you and others recommend will create a national and international calamity. It is over-reaction. Keep in mind it's been only little more than a day since the disappearance. Headlines like the ones Greg read not only will confuse the public, but could create an unnecessary panic."

General Francene was about to say something, but she ignored him and continued:

"Let me remind all of you that with the disappearance of the President, we do not have a Commander in-Chief of the armed forces. We do not have the head of the Executive Branch of government. I have done some checking, and I find there could be legal ramifications if military ships and aircraft are ordered into the search during the President's absence. I am also concerned about the possibility of an international incident. The use of the Coast

Guard satellite is part of any search and rescue operation.

"There is one other aspect you should be aware of, and that is Capitol Hill reaction. Alicia, give us your report."

SecDef Bosworth squirmed in his chair, wondering if Vance or Cummings had leaked news of his visits.

Alicia began: "Sources on The Hill tell me there is some talk about invoking the 25th Amendment, Section 4, which deals with declaring the Office of the President vacant. However, the procedure requires involving a Vice President, and there isn't one. I'm told that makes this issue moot. I've also learned there is a small but significant group in the House called 'The Young Turks' that could use the disappearance of the President, and the lack of use of the 25th Amendment, as an excuse to pressure the leadership into making deals with them to gain certain votes. There now is a very slim Progressive Party majority in the House, and a virtual split in the Senate, which is why this group seeks to take advantage of the situation."

She paused, because her next few words would explode like a bombshell.

"Just prior to this meeting," she continued, "I received word that a letter from President Merriwether, prepared before he left on the trip, has just been delivered to House Speaker Vance and Senate Majority Leader Winters. In sum, the President has nominated for Vice President . . . . Chief of Staff Jared Winston!"

It was only then that the Group realized Winston was not in the room. Alicia quickly added, "That could change the political picture dramatically as it pertains to the disappearance of Air Force One."

CHAPTER 6

A Political Scarlet Letter

As soon as Speaker Vance received his letter, he wanted to be sure Senate Majority Leader Winters received his. He did.

Vance spoke first. "In all the years I've known Merriwether, I never would have believed he would pull this kind of a trick," he said.

Winters added, "This is like getting a letter from the grave."

"I can't figure out the timing," the Speaker commented.

The Majority Leader paused before responding, "Oh, I can. I'll bet he knew there could be the issue of a Vice President. What better time now, since some of our colleagues are already talking about the 25th Amendment."

"Well, this has to mean Winston had a hand in this," Vance responded. "Very self-serving of him, I would say."

"I'm not so sure about that, Marsh," Winters said. "That's too blatant. Jared does not do anything without Linc's OK. You've got first dibs on the nomination. What's your modus operandi?"

"Since we can't ignore the nomination, we have two choices," the Speaker answered. "We can schedule immediate hearings, or we can delay them. Either way, as far as I'm concerned, it's DOA."

The Majority Leader responded, "The more I think about it, the more I'm convinced there is something more to this than meets the eye, as the saying goes. Does Linc really want Jared to be Vice

President? Or, is he sure it will be rejected after the public will discover there is a big split in both political Parties?"

"If I didn't know better," Vance said, "I'd almost believe this is a signal he doesn't want me to be Vice President."

"So, what are you going to do about it?" Winters asked. "I can't move until you do."

"Well, for starters, I'm going to have Merrill Conway nose around," the Speaker replied. "That's what a Majority Whip is supposed to do. That way, we'll get a feel for how the votes could go."

"That would be my choice," Winters responded. "This letter reminds me of the famous novel by Nathaniel Hawthorne – 'The Scarlet Letter.' The adulteress had to wear an A on her clothing, but it really signified shame. This letter is shameful, as far as I'm concerned."

"You got that right," Vance agreed.

* * * *

It would not be long before Conway would bring Vance some distressing news. "We've got a trouble maker in the ranks, Mr. Bobby Joe Simpson," he explained.

"You can't mean that first termer," the Speaker responded.

"Somehow, he's learned about the letter, and he's spouting off about the 25th Amendment, although I told him that's a blind alley," Conway replied.

"My scarlet letter also is an S, but it stands for shit!" the Speaker said.

Conway did not have the faintest idea what that meant.

CHAPTER 7

Did You Sea That?

The luxury liner Elegante left South Africa on the return voyage to New York after a stop in Bermuda. Captain Enrico Lagano was on the bridge and happened to look skyward through his binoculars. He commented to the watch commander next to him, "There's a high altitude contrail from a large jet heading northeast. The plane must be at least 40,000 feet." The commander responded, "It's probably going to London. Too bad those passengers don't get to enjoy a long trip the way ours do."

The Captain nodded, handed him the binoculars, and left the bridge.

CHAPTER 8

The Plane Facts

"Bouchard here," Greg heard on his phone.

"No, I don't have any exclusives for you at the moment," the Deputy Press Secretary kidded.

"You never know," Bouchard responded. "I wonder if I can ask you to check out something that's not directly connected with the disappearance of Air Force One."

Greg was intrigued. "It's your quarter," he responded.

"I've been lucky to have been a member of the press corps pool traveling with Presidents," Bouchard began. "So, I know that when Air Force One travels somewhere, a C-17 Globemaster also has to go along because it carries the President's limousine and security vehicles for the Secret Service. It can't fly as far without fueling as Air Force One. Its speed is more than 500 miles per hour, while Air Force One can do well over 600. My recollection is this means it generally leaves ahead of Air Force One. I know it can fly 2,400 miles without fueling, only about one-fourth of the distance Air Force One can go without refueling. Although it also has four jet engines, the C-17 has high wings, and a stubby body."

Greg interrupted, "I'm impressed. You've done your homework."

Bouchard ignored the comment, and continued, "Having said that, Greg, it stands to reason it left Ramey ahead of Air Force One. Can I ask to be notified when it lands at Andrews?"

Almost without hesitation, Greg answered, "I don't think I

have to check with anyone on that. There's no indication it, too, is missing. Once it lands, I will let you know there aren't two missing aircraft. By the way, I don't feel an obligation to notify any other reporter unless the question is posed."

Bouchard cracked an unusual smile, which of course Greg could not see, and said, "Thanks."

Greg quickly added, "You know full well I was in the news business for many years, and I appreciate a reporter who looks at the whole picture."

CHAPTER 9

Press-ing On

As Greg had intimated, White House reporters were demanding a briefing. He urged General McCormick to conduct a press conference "because I can't hold off the dogs much longer." He did not mean that as a disparaging reference to the White House press corps, but those reporters could be tenacious in search of official comment. "It's now at a level where you should do the talking," Greg explained. After conferring on what types of questions would be asked, the alert went out to The White House press room.

"Members of the press corps," Greg began, "Chief of Staff Winston has stood in for President Merriwether lately. But, circumstances have changed, as you now know. Today's briefing will be conducted by National Security Advisor Mary Ann McCormick. Her bio is being distributed to you. She has a statement to make before accepting questions. Here is National Security Advisor Mary Ann McCormick.

She towered over the podium, and began speaking without notes:

"I am here as coordinator for what is called the Emergency Situation Room Group, or ESRG. It consists of virtually all the Cabinet members, as well as the Chairman and Deputy Chairman of the Joint Chiefs of Staff. Purpose of this group is to develop the procedure to search for the missing Air Force One. That procedure will remain classified for the time being. Suffice it to say, it will not intrude on normal Atlantic Ocean air and sea traffic.

"The facts as we know them at this point are that Air Force One disappeared from the Miami Air Traffic Control Center (she gave the precise time) on its return flight to Andrews Air Force Base from Ramey Air Force Base in Puerto Rico. You know from the press pool on the plane that he stopped off in Miami before proceeding on to Puerto Rico to express his desire that it become the next U.S. state. The last transmission from Air Force One did not indicate any mechanical trouble. No explosions were heard, and no debris has been found. This is a vast area, so the search is complicated.

"I will take your questions now."

Question: "Is it true the plane was in the Bermuda Triangle when it disappeared?"

Answer: "The area of the last transmission is part of what is called that, but research will show that is not an official designation. If you need the latitude and longitude, we can provide that."

Question: "How many people were aboard Air Force One?"

Answer: "There is a crew of 22, and around 100 other personnel. For reasons of security, I cannot go any further than that."

Question: "Why didn't you alert us sooner?"

Answer: "That is where 'ee-surge' comes in. Our first task was to confirm the disappearance. Second, the group needed to create a procedure to deal with the situation and develop an immediate plan of action."

Question: "Who's in charge of The White House?"

Answer: "The answer is a complicated one. You know there is the Presidential Succession Act of 1947 to clearly define who would succeed a President who cannot perform his duties. First in line would be the Vice President, but President Merriwether had not chosen one. Second would be the Speaker of the House, and third would be the President pro tempore of the Senate. Let me be clear on this. There is no definitive proof President Merriwether is not able to perform his duties. We know Air Force One is missing, and so is President Merriwether. That is all we know. The plane and the President could reappear at any moment. So, succession to the presidency is moot."

Question: "Ma'am, you have not answered the question!"

Answer: "Until we have the proof I have outlined, there still is a President. In his absence, I can assure you the government is conducting business as usual."

Question: "When do you expect to have that proof, or an announcement of the re-appearance of the President?"

Answer: "There is no way of telling. I can say this much. When we know, you will know as quickly as possible. I remain optimistic."

Question: "Was Air Force One inspected before the flight?"

Answer: "There is a standard procedure concerning that, and such a procedure was completed prior to the flight."

Question: "Could the disappearance have anything to do with terrorism which is rampant throughout the world?"

Answer: "Speculation is not in my job description."

Question: "Follow-up. Have there been any recent terrorist threats involving Air Force One?"

Answer: "That question is right up my alley, since I am the National Security Advisor. I wouldn't be surprised there are those who would like to learn all the security measures connected with Air Force One. It is no secret the aircraft is a modified B-747 with the latest safety and security devices. Officially, it is designated as VC-25A. Only when the President is aboard does it become Air Force One for identification. Some of you have ridden in the plane, so you know how to get details about the aircraft. Other aircraft are being looked at for further upgrading."

Question: "How can Air Force One go missing, and you can't find it?"

Answer: "I feel confident the plane will be located."

Question: "Why weren't there fighter escort planes following Air Force One?

Answer: “There was no need to because the flight essentially was a ‘domestic’ one. More importantly, budget constraints do not justify it. I suppose President as Commander in-Chief of the Armed Forces could order it.”

Question: “Why were you selected coordinator of ‘ee-surge?’”

Answer: “I’m glad you asked. (She hesitated for effect.) It is part of Operation Breaking The Glass Ceiling.”

“Thank you, Ma’am.” That signaled the end of the press conference.

Reporters could not remember the last time a briefing ended in laughter. Had they taken the time to look into her background, they would have found she conducted many press conferences as Director of the Women’s Army Corps.

As usual, Bouchard did not ask any questions. If he did, he would not be able to continue his success with scoops. Out of curiosity, and because of something gnawing at him, he would call Greg later to ask, “Did any other passengers get on, or off, in Miami and/or Puerto Rico?”

CHAPTER 10

The Hill Is Alive With The Sound of Gossip

NO SOONER THAN the press conference report hit the airwaves as "breaking news" than The Hill became a hornet's nest of rumor, consternation, and speculation. Most of the initial questions were hurled at Speaker Vance. Television stations jockeyed for an interview, which he avoided for the time being. Shut out there, attention swung to Senate President pro tempore Cummings. "No comment" was the response from his press aide. Truth be known, the two men were in a hasty conference in a private room near the Capitol Rotunda.

"Marsh," Chris began, "what the damn hell is going on?!"

The Speaker answered, "Beats me. But, let me ask you something. By chance, did SecDef Bosworth pay you a recent visit?"

Cummings chuckled as he replied, "I was going to ask you the same thing."

Vance responded, "Then, I take it he saw both of us."

Cummings said, "He sure didn't have nice things to say about you. And I thought you two go back a long way."

Vance replied, "Well, to be honest, that friendship just ended. He was all over me about preparing to replace the President. I agree that we don't know for a fact Merriwether is dead. So, succession is moot."

Cummings began to laugh. "What's so funny, Chris?" Vance asked.

"I guess we're airing dirty laundry," the Senator responded. "He paid me a visit which I now know came right after he saw you. He got pissed when you put him off, and he intimated I should be considering somehow becoming next in line. The son-of-a-bitch even hinted that if I became President I should find a place in The White House for him. I guess being Secretary of Defense is not interesting enough for him. Or, maybe his wife wants to be on the White House invitation list. Who the hell knows?"

Vance's pager rang. It was his legislative aide. "Need to see you ASAP, boss!" he declared.

The Speaker excused himself and rushed back to his office. "What's so important that you had to . . . ?"

The aide interrupted, "There's a rumor that before he left on his trip President Merriwether had indicated he was ready to nominate a Vice President."

Vance laughed, and said, "Oh, you mean Chief of Staff Jared Winston."

The aide looked dumbfounded. "How did . . ."

The Speaker responded, "I got my letter the same time Senator Winters got his. We've already talked about it. But, that's all you need to know for now."

* * * *

Bouchard could not wait to call Jared.

The Chief of Staff was not surprised the letter was now public, and had a standard reply for any inquiry: "Any communication between the President and Members of Congress, or any federal agency for that matter, is considered privileged."

As Bouchard thought as he began to punch his story into his computer, that's more bureaucratically creative than "I cannot confirm nor deny . . ."

* * * *

Members of Congress, especially from the Conservative Party, were eager to speculate. They knew their words would become sound-bites on evening television, and quotes in the morning newspapers. The public was drawing its own conclusions, and they were as partisan as the two Parties.

However, Alicia was caught in the middle of the fracas. She was reminded that Jared cautioned her "the less you know, the more honest you can be." Lawmakers were not as understanding, and her ears took a beating. Jared might have been accused of being heartless as far as she was concerned, but he felt it was important to determine whether she had the professional strength to handle adversity. He and the President had talked on several occasions about her future.

When top lawmakers on The Hill could not get any clarification either from Jared or Alicia, and consulting with Vance and Cummings, Representatives and Senators decided to forget Party politics, and work jointly on their own. It quickly was decided there were two issues: One, be on firm legal ground to determine whether Jared could be approved as Vice President. Two, reject the nomination.

No one remembered who made the suggestion, but Vance was the one to call Solicitor General Christine T. Norman. In the Department of Justice, that person argues cases before the Supreme Court on behalf of the government. She was the first African-American female to hold that position. She formerly was dean of the School of Law at Harvard University, also a first.

"Yes, I've heard the rumors," she responded to Vance. "Why call me?"

Vance answered, "How long can President Merriwether be missing before it can be declared he no longer can fulfill the duties of his office?"

She paused before replying, "I'd have to do the research. I don't recall off the top of my head such an issue ever being raised."

Vance persisted, “I hesitate to pressure you, but time is of the essence. We can’t have a government without a President, or at least a Vice President!”

This time she did not pause before saying, “I can tell you this much without fear of contradiction. There would have to be proof, without any reasonable doubt, that a sitting President no longer is able to conduct the duties of his office. Anticipating your next question, I don’t think there is any precedent concerning how much time has to pass to determine this. I would add just one more thing, Mr. Speaker. Unless you have irrefutable evidence the President is dead, the burden of proof to declare the Office of President officially vacant would be enormous.”

How Bouchard discovered the phone call was made would wait until he published a memoir he had been working on piecemeal for several years. News of the inquiry made the evening television news programs following Bouchard’s story. This fueled even more speculation on The Hill.

Winters was furious once he learned of Vance’s call. His supporters “circled the wagons” to the point that Representatives and Senators were not speaking to one another. The Senator finally sent word to Vance stating tersely, “You go your way, and I’ll go mine!”

The sudden rift came to the attention of Diane Bana, Capitol Hill correspondent for cable network station WCN. She had long resented the presence of Bouchard, who seemed to consider the total seat of government as his beat. Over the years, she had developed sources that rivaled Bouchard’s. One of the few times the two bumped into each other on The Hill, she joked, “Maybe I should start covering the White House.” He did not find it amusing.

Diane determined not to let the presence of Bouchard deter her from following up on the tip she got about Vance and Winters. In mining her sources, she discovered the congressional impact of the missing Air Force One. For one thing, she realized that in the absence of President Merriwether, no measure Congress passed could be enacted into law without first going to The White House.

On occasion, a President would allow a measure to become law without his signature. Other times, he could veto it. She concluded the Chief of Staff could not perform that duty, and smiled at the possibility she might have to also "cover The White House."

Following her usual procedure of following up on tips or rumors, she would find a lawmaker to say what was known or surmised. Since Vance and Winters now were at loggerheads, she decided to play one against the other.

Diane's first request for an interview was with the Speaker. On camera, Diane only would do so when asked by an anchor person. She had a reputation not only of being first many times, but being fair.

"Mr. Speaker," she began, "with the shocking news now having gone public that Air Force One is missing, how do you feel about being the literal heartbeat away from the Oval Office?"

Vance did not hesitate: "All we know for now is that Air Force One disappeared from the Miami Air Traffic Control Center, and that a vast search is on. There is no use in speculating. Meanwhile, I have a full time job in the House."

Diane was about to ask a follow up question when she remembered something about the term Air Force One. She would have to look into that later. "Mr. Speaker," she recovered, "I am led to believe there is a difference of opinion (she deliberately did not mention Winters) over how to determine whether the President right now is able to fulfill the duties of his office. Your comment, sir?"

"There is an old phrase that covers that," he answered. "It is, not to rush to judgment. All we really know is that Air Force One has vanished, and there is no word from President Merriwether. I want to go back to your original question. Ever since I was elected Speaker, I was aware of the line of succession. No Speaker ever ascended directly to the presidency. Subconsciously, it is in the back of your mind. Being President is an awesome responsibility. Is anybody really ever trained to be President?"

Debating with herself whether she should end the interview

there and then, or ask more questions, she decided on the latter. "Mr. Speaker," she continued, "there are rumors that the letter from President Merriwether to you and Senator Winters of his intent to nominate Mr. Winston to be Vice President came after his disappearance. What is your reaction to that?"

Vance never expected that question, and he could not help but pause. "Where did you hear that?" he asked. (Old time politicians had developed of method of deflecting a "hot button" question by – to use a tennis expression – lobbing the ball back into the opponent's court.)

Diane was equal to the task and ignored his question. "Now that you've heard it, what is your opinion?" she persisted politely.

"Mr. Winston is a very loyal aide to the President," he responded. That was it.

Should she pursue the question? Of course. "Mr. Speaker, I respectfully submit that does not answer my question."

He remained quiet. She thanked him, and left.

In her mind, she was developing what she would report on the news program in the evening. First, she needed to interview Winters to create a balance – or, maybe a schism.

She began by asking the same question about the timing of the nomination letter.

"I really don't have an explanation for that," the Senator replied.

"Senator, why didn't he send the letter before he left?" she asked.

"I don't mean to be disrespectful, but you need to ask him that if and when he reappears," he answered.

"So, you do expect him back?" she continued.

"Hope springs eternal, Ms. Bana," he responded.

CHAPTER 11

Winston

As expected, the revelation of the Winston nomination letter went viral. Electronic and print journalists went all out to get comment, often interviewing one another. Jared remained stoic, and refused to make any comment, because everything seemed to be going according to plan.

His background became fair game for inquiring reporters, as well as for anyone using the social media. Virtually everyone zeroed in on the fact he was divorced, but nothing was known about the circumstances surrounding the separation. Yes, they were college sweethearts. Yes, they were married. Her name was Julianne Fromson, and she grew up in a suburb of Pittsburgh. She was an accomplished pianist, as well as valedictorian of her graduating class. No details were found about the marriage, or even where it took place. The marriage lasted only five years, according to available records.

Winston also was a bright student. A feature story in the campus newspaper mentioned he earned scholarships for sports and for academic merit. In sports, he participated vigorously. It was in college that he became interested in politics, volunteering for local elections. He was Merriwether's "campaign" manager when he ran for senior class president.

When Merriwether married Mary Jo Dietrick, Jared was his best man. When Winston married Julianne, Merriwether was his best man.

No matter how hard investigators tried to get more background, there just did not seem to be any, other than Mary Jo died of complications from esophageal cancer. Mrs. Merriwether had been a heavy smoker until her marriage. At her husband's insistence, she quit cold turkey, but that did not stop the cancer from taking its toll. (In future years, a reporter would discover her death came after her first pregnancy was terminated for medical reasons.)

Winston's stature physically and politically made him a force to be reckoned with. He went out of his way not to abuse the trust Merriwether had in him. He was the epitome of the motto "speak softly but carry a big stick." His voice may have elevated a notch or two over the years, but he was known to be firm but fair.

Winston knew what he was supposed to do, and he would not let the President down, even if it meant accepting a position he never wanted – Vice President.

Although Winston's record clearly indicated he majored in political science, very few people gave him credit for being a canny strategist. President Merriwether once said, "Jared, you'd make one hell of a leader!"

Only the President knew the one blemish on Jared's almost impeccable record. In college, Jared tried to break up a fight in the football locker room that stemmed from some unauthorized drinking. Afterwards, one of the participants who had fortified himself with half a bottle of illegal booze confronted Jared in a dark area of the football field. It was evening by the time the practice session had ended, and Jared was headed for his dorm room. Suddenly, the fellow teammate confronted him. He swung at Jared with a large knife, yelling, "I'll cut your mother-fucking gizzard out of you!" Jared adroitly stepped out of the way of the lunging player, and tripped him with his foot. As the would-be assailant reeled awkwardly to the ground, he fell to the sidewalk, and banged his head on the curb. Jared stared at the fallen body before deciding he had two alternatives. He could seek help, or he could run. After picking up the knife, he chose to run. Police arrived on the scene hours later after an evening jogger discovered the dead player. They routinely questioned Jared because witnesses described the locker room incident. Linc signed a sworn affidavit that he and Jared had been studying in their dorm room since well before and after the incident could have taken place. The coroner ruled the fall resulted from a "self-inflicted fatal concussion," noting there was enough alcohol in the youth's system "to kill a team of horses." Jared waited for months before being able to discard the knife, which was never found.

All the campus police report showed was that "a number of students were questioned about the incident. It was determined the victim was alone, and apparently lost his balance; the fall caused his own death." The victim was not well liked. He played on the football team only because his father was head of the alumni association. His father resigned after the incident.

CHAPTER 12

Political Ping Pong

THE WINSTON NOMINATION LETTER sent shock waves throughout the House and the Senate. Hearings were cancelled or rescheduled, either because of President Merriwether's disappearance, or the Vice President's vacancy matter.

Members were either contacting fellow Progressive Party members electronically, or meeting one another in person. That is why Vance and Senate Majority Leader Winters each had difficulty rounding up enough of their fellow lawmakers to caucus on the twin events of the day. The Speaker decided not to share any strategy with Winters.

Vance told his group as much as he knew about President Merriwether and Winston. "While these are separate issues, they are co-mingled," he explained. "I want your views on which has priority over the other." After hearing from half a dozen of the most influential members, he said, "It seems obvious the disappearance should be our Number One concern." Before asking for individual viewpoints, he shared with them the essence of his interview with Diane. "Keep in mind we are between a rock and a hard place," he began. "We need to take some action. Until the President is officially declared unable to fulfill his duties, all we can do is create a plan and be ready to put it into action."

Merrill Conway, the Majority Whip, asserted, "Marsh, you're putting us in an awkward position! If there is a vacancy in the Oval

Office, and absent a Vice President, you are next in line of succession. That's a conflict of interest."

Vance immediately responded, "Merrill, you are right. Take over the meeting."

Seeing no opposition, Conway said, "Thank you, Marsh. Ladies and gentlemen, I think the first order of business should be to block the nomination of Winston. Yes, he's nominally a Progressive Party member, but his fierce loyalty is to President Merriwether. I remind you mid-term elections are not that far off, and there is a possibility we could lose control of the House. I don't have to tell you the consequences of that. We need to protect our majority. If not, the Conservatives will occupy the Oval Office.

"As to whether or not President Merriwether can function, the major question in my mind is who makes that determination. (There was a murmur, as many there looked at one another because no one had mentioned that before.) To repeat a term I've heard used, until then, everything else is moot. Having said that, I respectfully suggest we turn our attention first to the Winston matter."

Vance did not appreciate how Conway had taken control of the situation, and virtually forced him to take a back seat. He was about to say something when Conway continued: "First, I think we will need a legal opinion to determine whether that letter is legal under these circumstances. Second, consideration for a nomination like this normally comes before the House first. If the letter still is in effect, then we certainly can schedule a hearing that will take up some time. Regarding the nomination, as President Lyndon Johnson used to say, 'That dog won't hunt.'"

What went on in that meeting somehow reached Senate leaders. While the Progressive Party majority in the House was substantial, the one in the Senate was razor thin. Winters took a "straw poll," and discovered there was no assurance the Progressive Party could prevail on any type of vote. Some mavericks in his Party had begun to flex their political muscles.

In a private meeting with key Committee chairpersons, Winters pointed out: "I like the President. I admire Winston's loyalty, but he does not have a political track record we can support if indeed his nomination comes before us.

"By the way, this may be of interest to you, and I ask your confidentiality. I have been given to understand that Speaker Vance got his wrist slapped a bit by Mr. Conway who pointed out the Speaker has a conflict of interest in dealing with the proposed nomination. If the President cannot fulfill his duties right now, the Speaker is next in line to the Oval Office. In simple terms, blocking the nomination certainly would benefit the Speaker. That's why Mr. Conway took over the meeting. How about those apples?

"Gentlemen, I suggest we put on our thinking caps for the rest of the day and meet again tomorrow morning at 10." (Senator Constance Pearlstein chafed at the omission of female members in his remark. She chaired a small group of female lawmakers who planned to make a strong effort break up the "good old boy network" on The Hill as a tribute to the late President D. Taylor Fairchild.)

The gist of the Senate meeting soon got back "across the aisle" to House members, especially Representative Conway. Contacting his key colleagues once more, he said, "I'm not about to let the Senate dictate what should be done regarding the nomination. Keeping that in mind, let's meet earlier than they have scheduled."

Word of that maneuver sailed back to the Senate. Winters contacted his top advisors, and asserted, "If Mr. Vance can be overpowered by Mr. Conway, that certainly suggests he might not make a strong President, even though he is a Progressive Party member in good standing. Then, we're faced with the next in line behind him, Senator Cummings. This is getting more complicated by the minute."

CHAPTER 13

You Have To Give To Get

One thing Alicia learned during her time on The Hill was this; if you want a favor from a Member of Congress, you have to give him, or her, something in return. One saying to illustrate this comes from "You scratch my back and I'll scratch yours." Others referred to it as "log-rolling." As a result, once she relocated to the White House, she knew President Merriwether had played that game for years. She decided she did not need his permission to continue that effort.

Alicia had studied the work of Bryce Harlow, head of congressional relations for Presidents Eisenhower and Nixon. In essence, he had as many friends from one Party as the other. As a result, the relationship between those Presidents and Congress got results, albeit sometimes behind the scenes.

Another reported example was the relationship between President Lyndon Johnson and House Speaker Thomas "Tip" O'Neill, who shared some libation "after 6:00 p.m." when things really were decided.

While some Senators and Representatives were angry at Alicia for not giving them advanced notice about Air Force One being missing, most appreciated her predicament of taking orders from Jared. Her good standing helped her hear about dissention among the two factions. Actually, she received a call indicating the liberal "Mounties" and the conservative "Starboards" were meeting secretly. In effect, she realized there could be dissention within dissention.

She reported this to Jared, who surprisingly smiled. That confused Alicia at first; then, it reinforced her gut feeling this all could be part of a secret plan between the President and Jared. "Let the pot stew in the congressional kettle," he said finally. "Just keep your eyes and ears open, and keep me informed. My guess is Members of Congress will concentrate either on delaying the nomination, or blocking it altogether. That's going to get more attention than the search for Air Force One."

Alicia could not contain her curiosity. "Jared," she finally said, "I'm beginning to think I am being manipulated for some spurious reason. I know the job you and the President expect me to do, and I'm more than willing to do everything I can for this administration. It makes me uncomfortable knowing I am being used. Maybe I'm too altruistic after all these years dealing with politicians."

Jared did not immediately respond, as if he were trying to find the right words. "Alicia," he responded in a firm tone of voice, "sometimes the adage of going along to get along applies. You are perceptive in having the feeling I am not telling you everything. That part is right; when you work directly for a boss who gives you directives, you literally obey – except if you feel it will get him or her in trouble. I can tell you this much. The President expects us to warn him in advance of any decision before he makes it. If you don't say anything, and he falls flat on his . . . face, and you tell him at that point that you could have saved that from happening, you will be fired on the spot. Sometimes you don't realize you create jealousy of other staff members because you report directly to him, and not to anyone else. You report to President Merriwether through me, unless he wants it otherwise."

She did not expect such a comprehensive reply, but he was not through yet.

"There are people who want your job," he continued. "They're positive they can do it better than you can. Maybe there is someone out there who fits that description. (She could feel a bit of anger developing.) The President has told me on more than one occasion he hasn't found that person yet. I'm not implying he is looking. (She suddenly realized he had a wry sense of humor.) You faced adversity with Senator Stafford, and held your own. Otherwise, you would not have been hired for this position. The President has complete confidence in you. He knows this situation will put your political feet to the fire. You have an inner resolve that he feels few people see. The only other thing I can tell you is, look at the BIG picture, not flashes. There's more to politics than an event in and of itself. (Isn't he ever going to take a breath, she wondered?) I'm taking time to tell you all of this because, in the face of political chaos, your mettle is being tested. You are passing with flying colors. It won't always be that way, and you may err now and then. Alicia, if you don't have faith in yourself, you will fail. You are not a failure."

Finally he paused. She was about to rise out of her chair when he went on, "The congressional wolves are getting ready to surround the Oval Office. This is not going to be another Alamo, but there will be a lot of ammunition used – especially from Capitol Hill. Hold your ground. You have the power of the Oval Office behind you. Think carefully before you act. We are talking about the President and The White House. Maybe you never played high stakes poker. Part is skill, and part is luck. You can make your luck; you've got the skill."

She felt glued to her chair. (Why this political pep talk? Is Jared preparing her for fast-moving events?)

"Any questions?" he asked. Before she could answer, he said, "You've been away from your desk too long already. I enjoyed what you had to say." (Yes, he did have a sense of humor.)

One thought now occupied her mind, and it reminded her of a quote attributed to President Truman: "If you can't take the heat, get out of the kitchen." (I'm not leaving the kitchen, she determined!)

No sooner had she returned to her office than telephone messages from The Hill, and even some reporters, were piled up on her desk. She returned each one in the order they were received, even though it meant skipping dinner. Most were easy to answer. Others she had to research, and told the caller that. They, too, were returned as quickly as possible.

Two calls got immediate attention. One was from Vance; the other was from Winters. Each wanted to speak with the President "as soon as he returns." She realized the importance of those words. (Apparently they believed the President would be returning, she decided.)

When Alicia was finished with the calls – for now – she thought back to Jared's talk. What is the BIG picture here? The only way she could develop an answer was to have more facts. She decided she would have to be patient. She also decided to take the bull by the horns, and call the leadership of the House and Senate. She had one question for Vance and Winters: "What would it take to support the nomination of Jared Winston?"

She did not like the immediate similar answer from both: "He's got about as much of a chance as a snowball in hell!" She thought about reporting that back to Jared, but he did not authorize her to ask that question.

Out of gut reaction more than political discretion, she then asked, "Is that your opinion, or that of your colleagues?" She had received an inkling of some dissention in the ranks that was more challenging the leadership than shooting down the nomination. So, the questions were not as innocent as the two men believed. All Vance and Winters did was reiterate their responses.

* * * *

Alicia had become fascinated with Bouchard and how he was able to scoop his White House colleagues. One word came to mind – persistence. Then, a second word – politeness. Bouchard never brow-beat anyone he contacted. If he did not get the response he was seeking from one source, he moved on to another. She decided to put that procedure into action herself.

She was able to find direct phone numbers for the leaders of the "Mounties" and the "Starboards." She did not want to text them because those could be too easily compromised. She only asked to meet with them – separately, of course – anywhere they chose. During those sessions, she assured them she had not been directed to meet them, but that they should understand they had direct access to her. Each of them came to the same question: "What's in it for me?" She anticipated that by answering, "This is not the time to talk specifics, but you will have my attention at appropriate times. The only thing I ask is that our contacts remain absolutely confidential." They assured her of that. However, she knew you could not always trust what a politician says. If there is something "in it" for them, they're interested because they're dealing directly with the Oval Office now. She knew she was risking everything in making such contacts. But then, she did not promise anything. She thought of it as political flirting. She also decided if it came to having to play hardball, so be it. She had to protect The President at all costs.

It was not long before Alicia began getting "hidden signals" that all was not honky-dory between the official leadership of the House and Senate, and the "Mounties" and the "Starboards." To her, this meant a potential schism that could be exploited later on. For all her time working with lawmakers, she still was amazed at how politically selfish they could be.

She decided she needed to share her information with Jared. "Good call," he said. (She did not get the pun at first, but then smiled.) "That schism within the schism is something to keep in mind. You just earned your pay – and a good night's rest. This has been quite a full day, and we need to be sharp tomorrow because the political pressure is sure to increase. By the way, Greg told me he is getting more and more media inquiries. Reporters are not happy we can't give them any new information, but that's the way we have to play it."

* * * *

As she was about to leave her office, the phone rang. "Bouchard here," he announced. "What's cooking with the 'Mounties' and the 'Starboards?'"

She almost dropped the phone. "Excuse me?" was all she could answer.

"My sources tell me you might be working out a deal with them," he continued.

Alicia could not quickly decide what to say. "Did your sources tell you what kind of deal I am supposed to be working out with them?" she finally replied.

Bouchard had begun to admire Alicia more and more, so he responded, "Of course you wouldn't tell me what you told them, and I certainly wouldn't tell you what they told me. OK, I think we understand each other. That was a classic maneuver on your part. I won't reveal my source if you tell me what you can, when you can. Naturally, I will have to verify this with sources of my own. Talk it over with Winston. You two make a sharp team. Something's cooking somewhere, and I want to be the first one to find out what it is. Thanks for not hanging up."

Alicia rushed back to Jared's office, and was glad he still was there. After repeating what Bouchard said, he thought for a moment before responding, "He's one persistent reporter, but that's what sets him apart. Very clever of him not wanting something immediately from you. And, very clever of him to think about doing some checking on The Hill. He surely has an amazing array of sources. He's giving us some time, and asking for something in the near future. Alicia, I think Greg still is here. Tell him what you told me. And then, for gosh sakes, GO HOME!"

CHAPTER 14

All The News That Gives You Fits

THE NEXT MORNING, Alicia's first phone message was from Diane. She was running a close second to Bouchard. A quick call to Greg confirmed her guess that he received the same call asking what was going on with the "Mounties" and the "Starboards."

Diane had the advantage of electronic immediacy, but Bouchard had the advantage of depth. Her reports made the 6:00 and 11:00 p.m. television news programs. His made the morning newspapers. Essentially, they relied on "respected sources to confirm" what they speculated – that, as Jared had explained to Alicia – there was a rift developing between the House and the Senate, as well as between the liberal "Mounties" and conservative "Starboards." This, Diane and Bouchard concluded, was a direct result of the disappearance of Air Force One, which has thrown Congress into disarray.

Several television networks expanded on Diane's report by having interviews with "experts" in the politics of government. Newspapers followed up on Bouchard's story with op ed columns by similar "experts." In turn, they produced a flurry of responses by watchers of television and readers of newspapers. Barely more than 24 hours had passed since Air Force One was reported missing.

As if that were not enough, those viewers and readers began deluging the offices of their lawmakers with phone calls, texts, etc. In addition, the Stock Market was edging downward.

CHAPTER 15

The More The Messier

VANCE AND WINTERS SCHEDULED separate meetings with their most influential fellow lawmakers, some of whom belonged to the "Mounties" and the "Starboards." Each essentially told their colleagues that "we are faced with political stagnation because President Merriwether has not been heard from." Vance and Winters both concluded their leadership could be at stake, especially since mid-term elections were looming.

"In a matter of hours," Vance began, "the disappearance of the President has caused us legislative heartburn. This never has happened before, and therefore we could not have been prepared for what could be a catastrophic situation."

Winters took a different tack, saying: "This is a time when differences have to be put aside. Both sides of the aisle in the Senate and House have to step into the breach to assure the public that government can continue to operate smoothly for the time being."

Electronic and print reporters were flooding legislators' offices with demands for comment. Because events were moving so fast, neither Winters nor Vance had an opportunity to coordinate responses. Instead of a "single" voice, there was a cacophony of opinions from whomever reporters could cajole for comment.

Reporters next turned to the agencies they believed were involved in the search. Like Congress, the ESRG had not met that morning to also develop a reasonable response. As a result, even more conflicting reports were creating increasing "News Breaks" on television and radio.

Diane and Bouchard each were mining all their sources to try for new "angles" to what was turning out to be public panic.

* * * *

As Jared expected, Admiral Ridgely contacted McCormick to arrange an immediate meeting of ESRG – sans Winston.

"Things are getting out of hand fast!" the Admiral asserted. "We just can't sit on our asses and not do anything!"

General Francene showed unusual irritation with the Admiral by responding, "Haley, everything that can be done is being done. Visual search had to be suspended because the weather suddenly has turned bad. In cooperation with other agencies, we are using electronic devices of various types, including satellites, to continue. We're committing all the assets possible. It takes time to assemble them."

McCormick decided to calm down the rhetoric and said, "I've received word that several foreign countries have offered assistance. Would you believe Russia is one? We've got to prevent overlap."

CIA Director Sperling asked to speak. "I notice that Deputy Press Secretary Fountaineau is not here to take notes."

McCormick responded, "He told me he is being deluged with press inquiries, and must remain in his office."

"So, who is to assume that role?" the Admiral persisted. "Why do we need someone to take notes anyhow?"

She answered, "It is important that some record be kept."

The Admiral later would regret his next words; "Who is the junior among us?"

CHAPTER 16

Much Ado About Something

After the morning's flurry of meetings on The Hill, Vance called Winters, and asked if they could meet privately. One of the many "secret" rooms in The Capitol was used.

"Let's put our differences aside," Speaker Vance began. "I think we need a united front on the Winston nomination. I've checked with some legal experts, and they agree the letter is valid and must be acted on one way or another."

Senator Winters asked, "What do you have in mind?"

Vance answered, "First, I suggest we officially acknowledge receipt of the letter. Second, I suggest we ask the FBI to do a complete background search on Mr. Winston. I had one of my aides do a rudimentary one, but there is not a whole lot new from what we already know. I don't know about you, but I'm not going to demand the FBI drop everything else and conduct the due diligence on him. The vetting process should take some time. Who knows what might turn up that could disqualify him? Then, there's the matter of hearings before both our Judiciary Committees. That should take even more time."

Winters smiled and said, "I guess time is on our side. Maybe all of that could run into the mid-term elections, and there might be additional delay. Those elections could determine a lot of things."

* * * *

The way things work on Capitol Hill, it was not long before Bouchard and Diane explored the same "territory." They confirmed their suspicions with various sources. They both decided to do their own research on Winston. Like the Speaker and the Majority Leader, Bouchard and Diane were surprised at Jared's lack of urgency. So were many pols in the nation's capital. On television and in the newspapers, there was a lot of speculation about that inaction. All asked the same question: Why? One pundit opined that perhaps Winston really did not want the position, but could not say no to his long time mentor and idol. One of the more openly President Merriwether haters said, "I have it on the best authority that both men are of the same sexual orientation."

* * * *

Diane mulled over all these reports, and did something she never thought she would do. She asked her bosses if she could do a "think" piece for the 6:00 p.m. news show that evening as a follow-up to her regular report. After she explained what she planned to say, there was an executive conference. That took half an hour, after which she was given the OK:

"I normally would not get into the opinion business, but I feel strongly about how the media are treating this situation," she began. "We have substituted fiction for fact. Everyone except The White House has hit the political panic button on the assumption Air Force One has disappeared forever, and its remains never will be found. My news colleagues may never forgive me for this, but until we know for sure what has happened to Air Force One, we should not rush to judgment. Yes, there are repercussions on Capitol Hill, my beat, and some intermediary plans should be developed. But, as of this broadcast, there could be a lot of political egg on some decision makers' faces if there is a logical explanation to what happened to Air Force One. We should wish for the best, but prepare for the worst. As my idol Walter Cronkite used to end his television newscast, 'and that's the way it is.'"

* * * *

Bouchard asked a rare favor from his boss. In a small bold box outline on Page One of his paper the following morning, these words appeared: "Diane Bana, you said a mouthful last night." It was simply signed "Bouchard." (That may have been the only compliment he paid a professional competitor in his entire career.)

CHAPTER 17

Raucous Caucus

AIDES IN THE OFFICES of Senators and Representative generally are "young." Some graduated from interns to full-timers. The pay could be described as insulting, but with a foot in a political door, careers can be made. Most importantly, they gossip about the gossip they have picked up at work. Many socialize with one another, and gossip is traded, albeit carefully. If their bosses found this out, they would be kicked out of the door in a hurry.

A dozen or so aides repaired to a nearby bar. Most focused on the schisms within schisms which were developing. They agreed that literally overnight, civility among lawmakers in both political parties as well as both sides of the Capitol was fracturing. They also agreed many of their bosses suddenly were faced with taking sides, and that was not something they were used to. The aides usually only could tell their bosses what they thought he or she wanted to hear.

Perhaps there was too much libation during the evening. Out of nowhere somebody suggested they form their own "secret" group. They decided to call themselves the "Raucous Caucus" because they represented different Party affiliations, and included separate House/Senate members. As the drinking increased, there were some bets made on what might have happened to Air Force One, and the fate of the Winston nomination.

Neither Bouchard nor Diane knew any of this, but they both learned valuable lessons covering their beats. If you want to know what is going on, make friends with office secretaries and aides.

That is why members of the "Raucous Caucus" received phone calls from the two reporters. Usually such contacts paid off, but for some reason that was not given to Diane and Bouchard, the aides were not forthcoming with tips. That piqued their interest. Rather than alienate these sources, both decided to accept what was equivalent of a code of silence. Bouchard and Diane both believed either their sources knew something vital, or they had agreed to protect their bosses because of the political turmoil.

Bouchard turned his attention to the missing Air Force One, while Diane kept calling every Hill source she had. The last call paid off.

* * * *

The tip enabled Diane to detail the chaos on Capitol Hill. After watching her that evening, Bouchard grudgingly admired her tenacity. A gnawing feeling he had been wrestling with caused him to wake up in the middle of the night.

He never was one to stand on ceremony when it came to being a long time member of The White House press corps. After all, he had been on Air Force One before as part of the press pool. Suddenly, it struck him as odd that he was not selected for the trip because of his years at The Miami News. While there, he befriended fellow reporter Enrico (Rico) Perez. As such, he learned enough Spanish to be able to carry on a basic conversation.

"Como esta usted, Rico?" Bouchard asked without saying hello.

"Muy bien, mi amigo," came the response. "Long time no hear from you, bouche." (That was an unflattering word Rico used to tease him.)

"El telefono still works both ways, pobre," Bouchard replied.

"Smart ass!" Rico said. "You wouldn't call unless you wanted a favor. Right?"

Bouchard countered, "Es verdad. I do have something I want to run by you. I'm sure you know about Air Force One vanishing.

If I remember correctly, you came from Arecibo."

"Your memory is not playing tricks on you, mi amigo," Rico replied.

"I think I recall you saying a cousin of yours is a civilian worker at Ramey Air Force Base," Bouchard continued.

"Si," Rico responded. "So?"

"Very unfunny," Bouchard said sternly. "I'm serious. This could mean something very important to me."

After explaining what he wanted to know, Rico said, "OK, no more kidding. I'll call him right now, and I'll try to get back to you pronto."

Rico was true to his word. The call came back in half an hour. "You really are a smart ass," he said. "You're right. Air Force One did refuel at Ramey. Why do you need to know that?"

Bouchard felt his friendship with Rico was solid enough to confide in him. "You can't use what I'm going to say for a story until I let you know," he began. "Agreed?"

"Sounds sneaky to me, bouche, but if we can't trust one another, too bad," Rico replied.

"The mileage to Miami, Puerto Rico, and back to Andrews would hardly put a dent into how much fuel Air Force One carries," Bouchard responded. "So, why would the plane have to be refueled for a relatively short flight back?"

Rico thought for what seemed like a long time before answering, "If I didn't know any better, I'd say . . . . "

"My thought exactly," Bouchard interjected.

"Jesus Christo!" Rico shouted. "You really are one smart ass! I assume you're looking to have the biggest scoop of your unsavory career, mi amigo. I promised to wait for your OK to run with the story. Could we do it simultaneously?"

Bouchard did not hesitate to respond, "Es un trato. I've got to do some more checking before I go with it. Muchas gracias, mi amigo!"

* * * *

Bouchard called Winston and asked if he could come to his office. "You really should be working with Greg, not me," the Chief of Staff answered.

"Mr. Winston, I believe it would be in both our interests if I could see you alone," Bouchard commented. The quiet insistence of that remark persuaded Winston to agree.

When he arrived at The White House and was escorted to Winston's office, Bouchard asked politely and softly, "I would appreciate it if we spoke behind a closed door." Winston hesitated, but he admired Bouchard's reputation, and agreed.

"What's with this cloak-and-dagger attitude?" Winston asked.

Bouchard replied, "I won't be taking notes, sir, and I ask that you do not share my remarks with anyone for the time being. I realize the sensitivity of the situation, and I feel I can trust you if you trust me."

Winston was not used to being spoken to this way. But, he sensed sincerity in Bouchard's words. Finally he asked, "Do you play poker, Mr. Bouchard?"

He answered, "On occasion, but it's not high stakes poker."

Winston leaned forward and responded tersely, "If I read you correctly, this is a high stakes poker game we're going to be talking about!"

Bouchard managed a tight grin and said, "Deal, sir."

When Winston heard what Bouchard said could be a story of monumental proportions, he did not react. He looked Bouchard in the eyes, and neither man blinked. "That's quite an assumption on your part," Winston finally said.

Bouchard had thought long and hard about what to say next. "Sir," he began, "I am fully aware of the consequences. I also understand national and international security. I have not discussed this with my boss, and that could get me into real trouble. I admit I could be putting my career on line. So, I have a suggestion for your consideration."

He paused purposely to give Winston a chance to understand what he was saying. Finally, the Chief of Staff said, "I'm listening."

Bouchard tried to hide the sudden pounding in his chest, and not to take a deep breath. “Mr. Winston,” he finally said, “I sat on a previous story, and it worked out well. I would be willing to sit on this story until you feel it is proper to make the situation public. In doing so – and you might want to check with Greg on this – I need to be ahead of the television people. I’m sure you’re aware of our deadlines, so I wonder whether you could wait until our papers come out in the morning to confirm the story. I will use whatever you want to say. I would prefer it be on the record.”

Winston did not reply immediately as he mulled several things over in his mind. “You’re asking a lot,” he said, “and we could incur the wrath of the entire news media. I certainly have to . . . (he stopped there lest he tip his hand) . . . study the consequences. Obviously, you have done your homework, but don’t take that as confirming what you have been told and you have surmised from that. Mr. Bouchard, this is the highest stakes poker you ever have encountered. I’m as concerned about the losers as much as the winners. Give me an hour to think about this. I know you understand I now have to involve Greg as well as Alicia.”

Winston got up first, and Bouchard knew there would not be a handshake. “Thank you for seeing me, Mr. Winston.” As he left the office, Bouchard realized his hands were shaking.

* * * *

As soon as Bouchard left his office, Winston again closed the door so he could use a special communication system. Afterward, he asked Greg and Alicia to come to his office. Once again, the door was closed.

* * * *

When Bouchard received Winston’s call exactly one hour later, he heaved a sigh, and then called Rico. “We have a deal.”

Rico responded, “Fantastico!”

* * * *

As Bouchard hung up the phone, a messenger was distributing copies of the Air Force One manifest. He gave it a quick once-over, and tossed it aside. Just as quickly he retrieved the list. One name got his immediate attention – Dr. Inez Rodriguez. Who the hell is she, and why was she on Air Force One?

Bouchard quickly Googled the doctor's name. There was very little about her, except she was doing research on children's diseases that had been labeled incurable. He immediately called Rico again, and asked him to look into the doctor's background. "Sorry, mi amigo, but I need the info like yesterday!" he insisted.

When Rico returned the call, he said, "This has become interesting. You'd better sit down! She has acquired grants from the Mayo Clinic to do massive research into a so-far incurable childhood disease called – and I have to say it slowly – Farnesyltransferase Inhibitors or FTIs. She seems to have made significant progress."

Bouchard thanked his friend and put in a call to The White House physician Dr. Frankhauser, who also was the head of the Bethesda Naval Medical Center. The answer he received almost caused him to drop his phone when he heard: "He's on Air Force One with the President."

* * * *

Now, he turned his attention to the other name. Instead of calling Alicia, he sauntered by her office. She looked up and asked, "Anything I can do for you?" He slowly approached her desk and answered quietly, "Heard from Tim lately?"

Alicia could not control her shocked look. Finally she responded irritatingly, "What makes you interested in my private life?"

He answered her question with one of his own: "Can we talk off the record and behind a closed door?"

At first, she did not accept the fact that suddenly they were on a one-to-one basis. But, she realized he had asked the question respectfully. Still, she answered tersely, "I'm not in the habit of having closed-door conversations with reporters. Perhaps you should be talking with Greg, not me."

He was persistent, responding, "Ms. Rineheart, I respect your position in The White House. Under different circumstances, I would be having this conversation with Greg. Maybe what I have discovered might change your mind." He did not wait for her to respond, and went on, "I know Tim is on Air Force One, and I'm sure you do too. What I don't know is why. He's not in the news business anymore, and the two stops Air Force One made were out-and-out photo ops. To be honest with you, I am getting very suspicious about the vanishing act put on Air Force One. I can't go into why I have doubts, but I can tell you this. I am learning things that are making me believe Air Force One did not succumb to the Bermuda Triangle."

When she arose from her chair and came around the front of her desk, Bouchard felt she literally would kick him out of the office. She stared at him before saying, "Maybe I shouldn't be saying this, but . . . I'm as curious as you are about what is going on, but I can't say anything more because I don't know anything more."

Bouchard responded, "I appreciate your frankness. I have a lot more inquiries to make. I will let you know anything about Tim that comes my way before anyone else. This conversation never took place."

He opened the door just enough to determine whether anyone could see him, and left. She stood there now with more questions than answers than ever – and more angst about Tim.

* * * *

Bouchard could not figure out any connection between Tim and Dr. Rodriguez.

CHAPTER 18

Source(ry)

DIANE'S LAST CALL was to one of the five Joint Committees of Congress. Chairmanship rotates with each Congress between the senior Senator and senior Representative. That person has the most total time on Capitol Hill. When the chairmanship changes, so does the position of Staff Director. The current one was the mother of one of Diane's university classmates.

Long-time staff people get to know one another pretty well, and they often exchange or hear gossip. This helps them "protect" their boss.

That is how Diane was able to learn of the cross-current of dissent on The Hill because of the President's absence which created confusion among law makers. And then, there was the Winston nomination to compound matters.

What shocked Diane the most was the rapidity with which self-preservation spread among lawmakers in a relatively short time. She was told many aides were concerned mid-term elections could affect their jobs. But, Diane had a reporting job to do, and her first order of business was to find others to confirm what she just learned.

She went back to her sources, and told them what she knew, and that if she found out, other reporters would also. That presented a dilemma for her because she would have preferred naming names. But then, either those sources would be fired, or she would have to fall back on some euphemisms like "those close to the situation but not authorized to speak on the record."

In addition, she was concerned about literally "adding fuel to an already roaring fire." Facts were facts, and she was not in the business of judging politics. Because Diane's sources trusted her, they confirmed what she had learned knowing she would protect their names. In turn, Diane was well aware of court cases where reporters were jailed for not revealing their sources when they were called to testify. She recalled that was what happened to Bouchard a number of years previously. He stood steadfast until the contempt citation was quashed. She accepted the fact she too might face jail time because she would never compromise her sources, which no doubt would be labeled disgruntled whistle-blowers. Congressional aides do not have Civil Service protection.

The dilemma widened when she had the confirmation she needed. The question arose about when to go live with the information. If she sat on it too long, another reporter could come up with the same story. She did not like being scooped. Her inclination was to let the political chips fall where they may. She did not make up the story; she just reported it. In the end, she would have to present her story to her news director, who probably would bounce it up the bureaucratic line, eventually to the legal department.

That is just what happened. The head of that department said he would have to review legal precedents on unnamed sources. When Diane heard this, she argued that time was of the essence. The attorney was adamant. The political stakes were so high that her television station took the cautious route.

Diane had never felt so strongly about a story. She hoped her years of experience reporting on Congress would favor her urgency. She was not concerned about winning a prize for her scoop; she had many other awards already. However, her sense was the country at large would suffer the consequences of an absentee President. At one point, as she continued to agonize, she could not help but wonder whether the delay smacked of the fact she was female and the attorney was a male. While women had made strides in political reporting, she long believed there were not enough of them in the top decision-making positions. Could she be so naïve to think that was not a factor, she asked herself? What if it were Bouchard in her job? Would the decision be different?

As it turned out, events would exacerbate the legal quandary.

CHAPTER 19

Aired Out

SECURITY WAS EXTREMELY TIGHT as a four-engine blue and white jet touched down gently on the main runway at Ramenskoye Airport. The some 5,700-mile flight took nearly twelve hours.

CHAPTER 20

Go to Hill, You Say

DIANE ALMOST JUMPED OUT OF HER CHAIR when she received the call giving her the go-ahead for the story. Details of the fracturing Capitol Hill community landed like a bombshell! Everyone was calling everyone else, trying to figure out who spilled the beans, not denying the political pot was boiling.

Jared stifled a smile.

Alicia was inundated with calls from reporters asking for comment. She did not have to check with Jared to know not to say anything.

Although he was scooped, even Bouchard was impressed.

Chief lawmakers conducted witch hunts with their staffs to try to find out who blabbed to Diane. Senior staffers quizzed their underlings. It was like no one cared about Air Force One and President Merriwether.

Junior Senators and Representatives who literally trembled at the sight of their senior counterparts now were forming groups to "get even." As one put it, "There's now strength in numbers." Pet projects that never were considered at the higher level now became bargaining chips.

"Young Turks" felt emboldened. "If the big boys want some legislation passed, they need to sweeten the pot," one put it. The loose "federation" of the "Young Turks" held a hurried meeting, and decided the first test would be the nomination of Winston.

They could not care less whether he was approved or not; they cared more about what they could get in return for their vote.

Winters called a meeting of his senior colleagues. The shock came from Senator Cummings. "Am ah the only one who is appalled – I repeat appalled – at Mistah Win. . . . ston's birth name?" the Senate President pro tempore asked. No one knew what he meant. Cummings continued, "Ladies and gentle . . . men, isn't it enough that a man of color once sat in the Oval Office, and that those of Hispanic persuasion were a heartbeat away from the Oval Office, but now we are faced with someone with Heeee . . . brew heritage who could be our next President?"

It only took a moment for everyone to check out the Birth Certificate attached to the report. They discovered Jared Winston was born Jacob Weinstein to Sam and Fanny Weinstein.

Winters was the first to react. "Mr. Cummings," he began, "this is neither the time, the place, or the reason for such a comment!"

Cummings's jowls swelled as he countered, "Ah jest was pointin' out a fact, Mr. Majority Leader."

Senator Cummings never thought his remark would leave that room in a heartbeat. That's all the "Young Turks" needed as a rallying cry to challenge what they now called "the insensitive leadership of both Houses of Congress." In their haste, the "Young Turks" ignored what Winters said in rebuttal.

Diane could not believe what she heard only minutes later. She was only half an hour from her station's 6:00 p.m. air time. That was all she needed to find one of the "Young Turks" who proudly rebuked what he called "insensitivity of one who is two heartbeats from the Oval Office." He did not object to being quoted by name. By her 11:00 p.m. slot, she had contacted Senator Cummings, who said, "Mah remarks were taken out of context by a very junior Senator, and Ah'll leave it at that, mah dear."

What Cummings did not add, but Diane pointed out, was that he had just been re-elected to yet another six-year term.

CHAPTER 21

The Defecation Strikes The Oscillator

When the ESRG met again, members were surprised to see Jared sitting at the rear of the room. McCormick explained, "I asked him to attend."

"What's the search status?" she asked. When no one responded, she said firmly, "Do all of you think we're playing tiddlywinks?!"

CIA Director Sterling finally spoke up: "Ma'am, we've been picking up electronic chatter from all over the world. All we've gotten so far is an argument among some Middle East terrorist chieftains on whether to take credit for the missing aircraft. Since no one – and especially the Russians – seems to know anything more than we do, this is more puzzling than ever. In discussing the disappearance with my staff, our conclusion is to consider whether Air Force One somehow has not crashed into the Atlantic!"

There was total silence. General Francene finally said, "It appears that was an alternative we did not even consider. I think we may have jumped to the conclusion since Air Force One vanished from the radar, then it must be well under water. With the Bermuda Triangle's reputation of being the graveyard of the Atlantic, we just forgot to look at alternatives."

Just then, there was a knock at the door. It was Greg with half a dozen copies of the morning paper's last edition. He asked McCormick: "Would it be all right to distribute these? I sincerely apologize for the interruption, but I think you need to read a Page One story by Bouchard." He quickly left the room. So did Jared, but no one except McCormick noticed, because they were focusing on the Bouchard story.

The new lead on the story chronicled some of the inquiries Bouchard had made. He included the fact that Air Force One had refueled at Ramey.

General Francene reacted with "SHIT!!!" No one else seemed to understand his outburst. He explained, "The only reason Air Force One would refuel would be that it was going to fly a lot more miles than it would take to return to Andrews Air Force Base!"

"What the hell are you talking about?!" Admiral Ridgely asked testily.

General Francene continued, "If Air Force One has not crashed – remember, all we know is went off the radar – but it has a full tank of gas . . . ."

Admiral Ridgely interrupted: "What the hell are you suggesting?!"

The General suddenly turned around to where Jared had been sitting and was astonished to see the chair was empty. When he pointed that out to the group, Sterling asked, "Are we being played here? Is this some kind of cloak-and-dagger operation?" He wasn't sure who chuckled first, but then realized the irony of what he said. He was too intense to worry about that, and went on: "I think we have been suckered by the President."

General Francene joined the verbal fray: "As I was saying, Air Force One can fly some 7,800 miles on a full tank of gas. And, it can be refueled in mid-air. I'm convinced it never crashed, but is headed somewhere far away. I'll need to check whether any tanker planes have filed a flight plan. If so, maybe we'll have an idea where Air Force One could be going."

Admiral Ridgely said, "If we thought the Bermuda Triangle is too big to be searched thoroughly, I'm thinking of a 7,800-mile circle from where it disappeared from the radar. That means Air Force One could damn near be a helluva lot of places in this world."

It was McCormick's turn: "I think we better be careful about this new approach. We've probably scared not only America, but also a lot of other nations about the possibility Air Force One is at the bottom of the Atlantic. But we still don't know why, or even where."

"Come to think of it," General Francene offered, "Air Force One has the capability literally of disappearing from radar. This cannot leave this room, but that is one of the new security improvements we have come up with." No one was surprised to hear this. He added, "Why this subterfuge? It can't be some whim by the President. We're talking about a multi-million-dollar aircraft with a lot of sophisticated equipment, as well as the lives not only of the President but also about 100 other people."

The CIA Director added: "The political implications of a subterfuge are enormous nationally and internationally!"

Admiral Ridgely was almost at the stroke point: "Merriwether better have one damn helluva reason for . . ."

McCormick interrupted: "Before anyone runs off the rails, are we now agreed that Air Force One is not a Bermuda Triangle victim?!" There was an awkward silence. She continued: "Let me put it another way. Is there anyone who still feels the plane is in Davey Jones Locker?" (She could not resist using a Navy idiom for bottom of the sea as a dig at the Admiral.) No hands were raised to the second question. "Then, we have to figure out where it is!"

CHAPTER 22

It's Getting Manifestingly Clear

BOUCHARD WENT BACK TO LOOKING at the manifest from Andrews. He suddenly realized there were only handful of news people in the press pool – wire service, network and cable television, radio, and the morning Washington Dispatch.

He called Greg and asked, "How come so small a press group?"

The Deputy Press Secretary answered, "Umberto arranged for local coverage in Miami, especially someone from the Telemundo studio there."

Bouchard persisted, "How about Puerto Rico?"

Greg responded, "That was taken care of by El Nuevo Dia, the San Juan daily, and the many TV stations there."

Bouchard decided this was not important enough to pursue, so he went back to the manifest. He stopped at the name of Vice Admiral/Dr. Frankhauser. He recalled that the White House physician, and head of the Bethesda Naval Medical Center, had rushed to the Oval Office when then Speaker Ed B (no period) Ross suffered a massive stroke, and could not take the Oath of Office. Bouchard remembered doing a side-bar story on Dr. Frankhauser, noting that early is his private practice career he had a double specialty as a urological oncologist. He had joined the Navy Reserves because his father had been a career officer in that service. When his father died of a heart attack, he transferred to regular status, and rose steadily until he earned one large band with two stripes on the sleeves of his dress uniform. He preferred to be called Dr. Frankhauser.

When he was promoted to head the Bethesda facility, he also had a White House responsibility. It turned out Dr. Frankhauser had never flown on Air Force One with President Merriwether. Bouchard wondered whether this was an oddity, or that the President had not been in office long enough to make many Air Force Trips. Was there any significance in this trip? Since he began wondering where Air Force One was now – and not in the Atlantic Ocean – Bouchard was more curious than ever why Dr. Frankhauser was on the plane from the get-go. Did that have something to do with the destination Air Force One could be heading for? Does someone on the plane require medical attention? Is there some connection between Dr. Frankhauser and Dr. Rodriquez?

Then, there was Tim. What the hell was he doing on Air Force One anyhow? He no longer was in journalism covering the White House, but now was Executive Director of an organization called the Bardon Foundation. He Googled that name, and found it mainly dealt with reporting on government and ethics in politics. (Boy, he thought, ethics in politics is an oxymoron.) So, why is he suddenly on this flight? He could not see any connection at all there. The more he thought about it, the more his head began to throb.

This presented a dilemma to him. Tim's relationship with Alicia was not a secret.

Bouchard called her. She responded, "I think you have the wrong number. You probably want Greg."

"No, Ms. Rineheart, I need to ask you a question," he responded.

"Mr. Bouchard," she quickly replied, "you know full well I cannot comment on what goes on between my office and The Hill. Maybe you should be talking with the Chief of Staff."

He persisted: "Ms. Rineheart, I just have one question, and it pertains to Tim."

She almost dropped the phone. "I don't understand."

"Ms. Rineheart, please," he said. "Just one question. Why is Tim on Air Force One? His name is on the official manifest."

"I only recently found out from Greg," she responded.

Bouchard hesitated. Was she lying, or did she really not know the answer? He decided to give her the benefit of the doubt and said, "I'm just trying to verify who was on the flight, and why."

She did not want to make any other comment, but could not resist a question of her own. "Mr. Bouchard," she said, "since you seem to know more about the flight than I do, is there anything new about the search?"

He did not expect that seemingly innocent question, and certainly did not want to tip his hand about what he now suspected. As quickly as he could, he answered, "The last I heard, the search still was going on. Honestly, there is nothing new there." In truth, that IS all he knew officially.

"If there is, could I impose on you to let me know?" she asked. "Certainly you know that Tim and I are . . . friends."

"Of course," he replied. "Thank you, Ms. Rineheart. Goodbye."

No sooner had the call ended than she went to Jared's office, and told him about the call. He merely said, "You handled it well. If he calls me, you and I will be on the same page."

* * * *

Bouchard mulled over Alicia's responses, and decided she did not have a clue about the flight.

He called Fountaineau, and asked if there were any new developments regarding the search.

"No news is good news," Greg commented.

"That depends on how you look at the situation," Bouchard snapped back. "I'm sorry, Greg," he said quickly. "That wasn't fair. I'm sure you meant you were hopeful. I am too."

The Deputy Press Secretary said, "I understand. We're all a bit edgy. Thanks. If I hear anything, I'll let you know."

Bouchard was about to add "Me first?" but decided not to. Greg just was doing his job, and could not play favorites. He knew that if he asked a question no one else did, he would get an honest response.

CHAPTER 23

Congressman Who?

CONGRESSMAN ASHER HUDAK was the epitome of a little known movie "The Man Who Wasn't There." You rarely saw his name in the newspapers, and he was averse to television or radio interviews. He was there when it came to representing his constituents, albeit without fanfare. He was re-elected so many times that he actually had more seniority than most of his lawmaker colleagues. As such, he could have had his choice of committee chairmanships; he chose the House Ethics Committee, to some an obscure and almost unpublicized group.

The HEC (some referred to it as "Aw, HECK") is the only committee that has 10 members – five from the majority Progressive Party, and five from the Conservatives. As a result, other Representatives considered it ineffective because most votes could be ties.

Hudak was in his element. He had been a successful labor mediator during his private law practice days. He also believed, much to his being teased about it, that there should be ethics in government. There were those who belittled Hudak, referring to him as "Goody Two Shoes." (In the early 1900s, a Philadelphia newspaper lauded a Senator in an article headlined "A Goody-Goody" as "a paragon of innocence and true goodness.") Hudak was not an innocent, but he believed in the goodness of people. He developed the knack of avoiding tie votes by finding something both sides of his committee could live with.

Diane covered a speech he made to his alma mater in which he urged graduates to consider government service as a calling. After the piece was aired – it did not get much coverage nationally – he sent her a note of thanks. It was the only one she ever received. She framed it and hung it in her cubicle along with part of a headline from some obscure feature story headlined "There's Hope Yet."

As a matter of courtesy, Speaker Vance periodically invited him to lunch. As a matter of personal preference, Vance enjoyed these occasions because he felt it brought him back on an even keel. That was years ago, and Vance had other lunches that transcended those with Hudak. However, Vance now felt he could use Hudak to deal with the virtual rebellions in the House. Most especially, he heard there were rumors to the effect Conservatives and the "Starboards" were talking about a coalition to challenge the Speaker.

That is why Vance called a meeting of the senior House members of the Progressives, Conservatives, "Starboards," "Mounties," and the "Young Turks." Grudgingly, they all attended.

"I understand the diversity among us," he began, "but events dictate we temporarily set aside individual preferences and work together. There is no secret we face two major simultaneous problems. First, we do not have a sitting President, and we have been without a Vice President. Second, before he left on his trip, President Merriwether wrote a letter of intent to nominate Chief of Staff Jared Winston as Vice President. Therefore, we are faced with two decisions. To set the record straight, we cannot find a legal precedent to declare the Office of President vacant. There has not been any communication with Air Force One since it vanished from radar yesterday in the general area of the Bermuda Triangle in the Atlantic Ocean. That raises the issue of the proposed nomination. The House and Senate can go ahead and schedule hearings on the nomination of Mr. Winston. If he were approved, he could be designated Acting President. There have been occasions in our history where that has happened. If Mr. Winston does not gain approval, and the President cannot be found, America could be faced with political stagnation.

"Because I have a conflict of interest as next in line to the Oval Office, I have decided to turn over leadership of this meeting to the Honorable Asher Hudak. As you know, he chairs the House Ethics Committee. More importantly, I respect his ability to listen to all sides before a decision is made. In that regard, he has an enviable record of accomplishment. That is what this meeting is all about. I encourage an open discussion from the groups you represent. I suspect at some point your views will reach the eyes and ears of the news media. You are your own judge in that respect.

"Mr. Hudak, the meeting is yours."

There was a cacophony of voices wishing to be heard. Hudak gently rapped the gavel Vance had turned over to him, and kept doing it until everyone quieted down. He gazed around the room before saying, "Decorum is in order. Please raise your hand when you wish to speak, and I ask silence when that person has the floor." He had a way of gaining immediate respect.

Almost every speaker vented his or her spleen, some more passionately than others. Hudak went from one to another without delay, only interrupting when he felt the speaker was "out of order." Some addressed the problems singly, others simultaneously. All kinds of proposals were offered. After almost an hour, it was obvious the absence of President Merriwether was a political perplexity. Hudak knew from the start there could not be a solution to that problem, so he was willing to let the Members figure that out for themselves. Finally, he said, "I gather this is almost a Gordian knot. We keep coming back to the realization there is no precedent for how to determine the President is not able to function because we cannot prove he might not just pop up tomorrow. Can we agree to hold off for a day or two? Meanwhile, perhaps we can explore the legal ramifications of how to declare the Office of President vacant."

Someone immediately shouted, "No delay!" Hudak did not bother to identify who that person was before saying, "We certainly would have political egg on our faces if we took some action only to have President Merriwether back in our midst. Again, keep in mind those mid-term elections. Some of us could suffer the consequences of haste. If there is no objection, can we meet again tomorrow and assess the situation then? United we stand, divided we fall."

Although there was some grumbling, the meeting ended.

* * * *

After Senate Majority Leader Winters learned about what happened at the meeting, he decided to also wait another day.

CHAPTER 24

No Fuel Like An Old Fuel

ALMOST ALL OF HIS WHITE HOUSE press corps colleagues paid only passing interest to Air Force One manifests except Bouchard. He prided himself on detail, which is why he yet again went over the one issued at the start of President Merriwether's trip.

He almost dropped the sheet when a weird thought crossed his mind. He called Greg and asked, "Are there amended manifests for Miami and Puerto Rico?"

The Deputy Press Secretary smiled and replied, "Only you would pose that question."

Bouchard persisted, "Yes, or no?"

Greg could have fudged a response, but having been a newsman himself he replied, "Yes. Come to the office, and I'll give you copies. No one else has asked for them."

A quick glance proved his suspicion was correct. At Ramey, five new "passengers" were added. Bouchard remembered a featured story he once did on Air Force One, and knew the cockpit crew consisted of a pilot, co-pilot, and navigator, all officers, and a flight engineer, a high ranking noncom. The amended manifest listed the ranks, and Bouchard decided the four new men made for an additional cockpit crew. There could be only one conclusion: Air Force One was going to fly a long way, and for safety purposes a "relief" crew was on hand. He also knew Air Force One had a range of 7,800 miles. While it could be refueled in mid-air, he reasoned that only would take place in an emergency. If there were a threat to The President in the White House, he could board Air Force One, and it could fly indefinitely with mid-air refueling.

The other name, of course, was Dr. Rodriguez.

Bouchard continued to mull. So, this flight had to be within the 7,800-mile range. Consulting a world map, he quickly determined north or south directions were improbable. That left east and west. By realistic elimination, he settled on east. About half the fuel would take Air Force One toward Africa. Northeast would go toward Great Britain. More fuel could be the Middle East. Directly east is China, but that might be beyond the fuel limit. Farther northeast is western Russia. Now that would be a doozy, he thought to himself. Why go there when relations between America and Russia were not exactly warm? Wait! Why not?! That would be a political coup. OK, maybe so. But why such secrecy and subterfuge?

If President Merriwether and Air Force One are not at the bottom of the Atlantic Ocean, but headed for Russia on some secret mission, I have to conclude he'll be back in Washington in a matter of days.

Very interesting!

CHAPTER 25

Congressional Mettle of (dis)Honor

ALICIA WAS BOMBARDED with calls from those irate Members of Congress who complained about the President's absence, as if she could do anything about it. She went into total damage control mode. The good news was she was learning whom President Merriwether could continue to count on once he returned. After Tim's call, she trained her mind to accept the absence for whatever reason as temporary.

Those who remained supportive of the President were confiding in Alicia about what was going on. As one put it, "Many on The Hill are acting like a pack of hyenas feasting on a kill." (She made a note of that to give to the President.) But one call really surprised her.

"Ms. Rineheart, this is Diane Bana from Washington News Service," she began. "I wonder if you can spare me some time to come over and chat with you."

"On the record, or off?" Alicia asked.

"Whichever you want," Diane quickly responded.

"Let me put you on hold for just a minute so I can end another call," she lied.

"Sure," Diane agreed.

Alicia immediately called Jared, who said she should speak to Greg about the appointment. Greg was surprised, because Bouchard was the one who usually asked for interviews. "This could be interesting," he commented. "For future reference, Jorge and I would appreciate it if you checked with us first. But, in this case, with Diane's reputation, you did the right thing. I think she would have been uptight if she realized you had to check with us first. This way, I believe she will treat you fairly. Of course, please let me know the gist of the interview once done."

Alicia asked, "Should it be on the record, or off?"

Greg did not hesitate: "It really should be one or the other. Otherwise, you get confused, and that can put you in hot water. My gut feeling is to make it off the record for the first time."

"Off the record," Alicia told Diane.

* * * *

"Thank you for seeing me on such short notice," Diane began. "Let me describe what appears to be going on, and then I would appreciate any guidance you can give me. If it is all right with you, whatever I decide to use will be as coming from 'an administration source with knowledge of the situation.' Is that ambiguous enough?"

Alicia knew Diane's reputation was as a reporter who never betrayed a source. "Does that make me another 'Deep Throat?'" Alicia asked teasingly.

Diane laughed and answered, "Hardly."

"I'm sure your sources have alerted you to the internal war going on," Diane said. "The core of the infighting is centered on the President's absence. How long do you think The White House can withstand this political onslaught? I imagine your ears must hurt from the criticism."

Alicia thought for a moment before responding: "How much time do we have? That one question opens up a can of political worms. Of course, you realize I cannot control or predict what Members of Congress say or do. In the relatively short time I've been in The White House, we had a majority supporting the President. I've tried to role play – that is, putting me in the shoes of lawmakers.

That way, I can understand some of the frustration on Capitol Hill. Because the President was an influential Member of Congress, he understood the need for cooperation. He also believed in the motto of 'you've got to give to get.' When I was Chief of Staff for Senator Stafford, there was no question his decisions were based on what was in it for him and his constituents. Naturally, that was before his illness took hold. So, President Merriwether has his finger on the pulse of lawmakers. There is no doubt in my mind he believes firmly that the framers of the Constitution were wise in creating three branches of government because that provided the checks and balances necessary for a democracy." She paused a moment, and then continued: "I know that sounds like the party line, but that is the way the President feels the Oval Office should operate when it comes to Congress."

Diane silently was surprised at the response, but calmly asked, "Does the White House feel it has lost that relationship with Congress?"

Alicia had to think about her answer before responding: "Diane, as Chief of Staff Winston has said, until there is proof the President cannot perform the duties of his office, the whole issue of government leadership is moot. I know that's a legal term, but it fits. Personally, I remain optimistic about his return. It's almost like the Titanic situation where some passengers, and even crew, shoved others to get into life boats; many men bravely gave up their places for women and children. I get the impression Capitol Hill is sort of like that now. There are those who already have jumped ship, and it's only been a relatively short time since Air Force One vanished from radar. Should the President and Air Force One reappear – yes, I am an optimist -- those self-serving lawmakers may regret their selfishness. Please don't misunderstand; I'm not implying in any way shape or form there will be political revenge. However, long-time politicians have long-time memories. I'm sorry to see the situation has produced the worst in some lawmakers for whom I have had great respect."

Before Diane could say something, Alicia added, "I apologize for rambling on so long."

Diane smiled and replied, "Although we never met, I knew how loyal you were to Senator Stafford during his declining time when a lot of others tore into him. That rates high in my book." Alicia almost blushed. Diane continued: "From what you have said, loyalty aside, you feel the President will return. Considering some Members of Congress not only have their eyes on The White House, but also are fighting for power among themselves, what effect do you feel this will have on the country?"

"Wow!" Alicia responded. "That is some question! Give me a minute." It took longer than that, but Diane was willing to wait. "I think the answer will be what happens at the mid-term elections. Every member of the House is up for re-election, as are a number of Senators. Power on The Hill could change in an instant. The line of succession to the Oval Office could change drastically when it comes to individuals. For example, the Progressive Party has majorities in the House and Senate – albeit a slim one in the latter. Keeping in mind there is no Vice President, first in line now would be Speaker Vance. Second would be Senate President pro tempore Cummings. I doubt Vance would change, but another Senator could become second in line."

Diane said, "That brings up another issue. What's your take on the nomination of Jared Winston for Vice President?"

Alicia smiled, "I know this will come as a surprise, but I'm biased on that one. I think the world of Jared. I doubt that opinion is shared on The Hill. I feel sure lawmakers by and large will do whatever they can, either to indefinitely delay action or downright kill it. I don't think I would comment any further on this."

"I think I've taken up enough of your time, Alicia." Diane said, looking at her watch. "I really appreciate your comments. To be honest, you've confirmed a lot of my own feelings. I can't let that influence my reporting, though. I'd like to stay in touch, either on or off the record."

When Alicia related the gist of the interview to Greg, he said, "Diane is one clever reporter. But then, you sure held your own. Ever think of teaching political science?"

She responded, "Maybe in my spare time."

* * * *

While Alicia walked over to Jared's office to brief him, Greg made his call. Just then, Bouchard appeared. Some of his questions seemed to overlap those Diane asked of Alicia.

CHAPTER 26

"Druzhba"

As the blue and white modified B-747 taxied to a secluded part of the airport, a number of vehicles rushed there. Once the plane's four jet engines were turned off, a special stairway was pushed to the front cabin door. It opened, and several Secret Service agents hurried down the stairs, followed by the print and electronic pool news people to record the event. At the same time, several armed uniformed Russian guards arrived and stood next to them.

The door of one of the limousines opened and Andrei Borochenkov climbed out. He was the heir apparent to the presidency of Russia after Vladimir Putin did not to seek another term. President Merriwether appeared at the cabin door, and then descended down the stairs with Whiz close behind him. The two Presidents embraced each other.

"How was your trip, Mr. President," Borochenkov asked in surprisingly clear English.

"Well, we were in the neighborhood, so we decided to drop in," President Merriwether retorted, adding slowly in Russian, "Thank you for inviting us."

The Russian President laughed heartily and responded, "There's nothing like traveling nearly 8,000 miles and going through eight time zones."

"By the way, I see that banner over there, but my Russian isn't that good," President Merriwether said.

"That's Russian for 'friendship,'"President Borochenkov replied. "It's pronounced 'druzhba.'"

Just then, another man left one of the other vehicles. "President Merriwether," Preston Vandergriff said, "long time no see." Even the Russian President laughed at the comment from the U.S. Ambassador to Moscow. Vandergriff, a top level State Department diplomat and expert on Russia and its various dialects, was a holdover from the previous administration.

The Russian President said, "Ambassador Vandergriff has been hired as your interpreter," and gave a belly laugh.

President Merriwether countered, "I'll have to check his job description."

Before they were ready to leave, President Merriwether said, "Mr. President, I have a favor to ask."

President Borochenkov asked, "A favor already? We haven't even had a toast."

President Merriwether responded, "As you know, Americans have been told Air Force One vanished from radar after takeoff from Puerto Rico. As usual, we had what we call a press pool on board, but smaller than usual. They expected a return flight to Andrews Air Force Base, and therefore did not bring their passports. Since we will be gone for several hours, I hope you will permit them to leave the plane and go to the terminal – under an 'escort' of course. Also, we would like to refuel our aircraft for the next part of our trip."

President Borochenkov gave an order in Russian. His chief aide saluted and nodded yes.

President Merriwether added, "My chief Secret Service officer brought his passport since he has to accompany me . . ."

The Russian President smiled and responded, "Da. Bring him along. Let us get started. Moscow is less than an hour away, and that will give us a chance to talk, you and me."

"Before we leave, I would like you to meet one other person," President Merriwether said. With that, he sent word to have Tim come to the limousine.

President Merriwether got into the back seat with President Borochenkov and introduced Tim. "Mr. President, I will explain his presence later."

* * * *

The political climate outside of Air Force One may have been balmy, but inside, a storm of protest had formed even before the press pool people were about to deplane.

Gerry Bartlett of the Associated Press was the senior member of the pool. Ever since Air Force One diverted from its pre-designated return flight to Andrews Air Force Base, she had been raising holy hell with Umberto.

"Where are you taking us?!" she demanded of the Press Secretary. "We should have been able to see the U.S. east coast from the left side windows, but not more and more of the Atlantic Ocean! Where I come from, that's called kidnapping!"

Umberto tried to placate Gerry, but it only made her angrier. Finally, she shouted, "I counted on being home last night because it was my 25th wedding anniversary! My husband and I had BIG plans! The worst damn part is that we could not communicate with anyone back home! I don't know how you did it, but I'll sure as hell will find out! And, here we are, sitting at a Russian airport 12 hours later, and you're telling us since we don't have our passports that we'll be 'held' in what passes for a terminal."

"Gerry, I truly am sorry," Umberto apologized, "but all will be made clear. I'll give you all a briefing once we're settled in the terminal."

"That's just dandy!" she continued. "I see we'll be escorted by friendly Ruskie armed guards!

"Gerry," Umberto said calmly, "I've worked out an arrangement where all of you will be able to file your stories once we're airborne, along with any photos."

"I know what my lead will be!" she insisted. "White House reporters kidnapped; Being held in Russia."

* * * *

While this was going on, Dr. Rodriguez and Dr. Frankhauser left the plane unseen, and were hurried into a waiting limousine. Her luggage also had been taken off.

* * * *

Gerry and her fellow press pool members were led to a dining area. Hot meals prepared on Air Force one were brought in. Rest rooms were made available.

"I'll do the briefing in half an hour," Umberto promised.

* * * *

"First of all, on behalf of the President, we apologize for the diversion," Jorge began.

"Make that deception!" Gerry declared.

"As I was saying," he continued, "before you ask questions, please let me give you the full picture. Afterwards, once we're airborne, you can file whatever you have.

"The purpose of this mission is for Presidents Merriwether and Borochenkov to discuss matters of mutual concern in private. I'll define those matters later when I get permission from President Merriwether. Why the secrecy? Relations between the U.S. and Russia almost reverted to the Cold War during the Obama administration. Since then, with a new Russian President, there became a window of opportunity to find areas of mutual concern. Our Ambassador to Moscow, Preston Vandergriff, played a vital role in easing tension to make this meeting possible. He is with the two Presidents as I speak.

"President Merriwether felt an unpublicized meeting would be palatable to the Russians, and it has turned out that is what happened. The scheduled trip to Miami and Puerto Rico provided the opportunity.

"The question of press coverage, naturally, became a vital issue. The decision was made to do what was done as the only alternative, knowing there would be risks. Gerry has enumerated the main one. The President feels that when all the facts are known, the action taken will be clearly understood."

"Maybe that's what you think, Jorge!" she persisted. "We were held incommunicado like prisoners at Gitmo in Cuba."

"Given that the flight to Moscow would take almost 12 hours, we did not feel there was any alternative," Umberto tried to explain."

"Well, how long is our on-land imprisonment going to continue?!" she demanded.

"To the best of my understanding, somewhere around six hours at the most," he replied almost sheepishly.

"What?!!!!!" almost every reporter shouted at once.

"I said, no more than that amount of time," he continued. "I will caution you about this. If it is a lot less than that, you may have major second stories."

"In other words, Jorge, less time means less agreement," Gerry countered.

"You said it, I didn't," he responded. "OK, let the questioning begin – with you, Gerry."

"Gee, thanks a bunch!" she snarled. "Here goes. How could Air Force One have diverted and not been missed?"

"Oh, it was missed the moment the Miami Air Traffic Control Center lost radar contact with Air Force One," he answered.

"Christ!" she reacted. "You mean -- strike that. How was that accomplished?"

"Another good question," he responded. "I cannot breach security, but suffice it to say Air Force One has that capability."

"So, for the last 12 hours, by my watch, we have been considered missing," she went on. "That means everyone in the world thinks we've vanished off the face of the earth, right?"

"That's one way of putting it," Umberto answered.

"Well, that sure must be comforting to our families, friends, etc.," she continued. "Americans must be scared shitless, and politicians must be going nuts because the President ain't around at the present time! I assume there's one helluva search going on, right?! So, for the next six hours more or less, we're still prisoners here."

Ignoring the sarcasm, Umberto added, "The debriefing with President Merriwether about the topics he and President Borochenkov discussed might just make quite a story for all of you, and justify some of your concerns."

Gerry and the others realized they were not going to receive any more useful information from the Press Secretary. She finally said, "I saw that big banner in front of the terminal, but it's in Russian. What does it mean in English?"

Umberto was hoping no one would ask, but he had to answer, "Friendship. I'm sure the President asked the same question."

* * * *

"Before we go to my office in the Kremlin, I want to make a stop first," the Russian President said. "I believe you have never been to Russia, let alone Red Square."

"No, I haven't," President Merriwether replied.

"We will make time for a short visit, because you must see it," he explained.

"Yes, I would be delighted," he replied.

"Mr. President," Borochenkov continued, "there is a reason for this. In 2009, President Obama and his family visited here. He was supposed to return in 2013 for talks with Mr. Putin, but for reasons we shall not discuss in the spirit of friendship, the trip was canceled."

"I'm flattered by your invitation," Merriwether responded.

"We will enter Red Square through the Resurrection Gate arch," the Russian President said. "We will do a short bit of walking while I explain some of the famous places there. You may have seen newsreels of parades in the Square, but there is much, much more."

As the left the limousine, Tim remained behind with Vandergriff while the two presidents (plus Whiz and a small plain clothes Russian security detail) strolled.

"My 'office' is just behind us," he began. "The colorful onion-shaped domes of the Cathedral of St. Basil the Blessed are off to the far right. That's where all the tourists snap their pictures. (He stopped.) In front of it is the famous Lenin Mausoleum."

"Wait!" President Merriwether said. "Am I seeing things, or is that the famed GUM state department store I've heard so much about?"

"Da!" Borochenkov answered. "We also have a very large underground shopping mall called Okhotay Ryad. Would you like to stop there and perhaps buy one of the famous Matroshka nesting dolls as a souvenir? I can get you a good price!" He laughed.

"I'll save that for my next trip here," Merriwether joshed.

The Russian President beamed, and continued his tour guide role: "Many tourists do not realize the Bolshoi Ballet Theater is close by. There is so much more, but as you say, we will leave that for your return trip here."

They returned to the limousine, and continued on to the Kremlin. President Borochenkov could not resist one last comment. "Mr. President, don't you find it strange that the White House is painted white, but Red Square is not painted red?" They laughed.

* * * *

When Gerry noticed the limousine carrying the two Presidents returning to where Air Force One had been parked and refueled, she looked at her watch and realized that indeed almost six hours had passed. That was a good sign, she mused.

The pool photographers were encouraged to take many shots, unhindered by the Russian security detail. The two Presidents shook hands warmly before Merriwether, Whiz, and Tim climbed the stairs. Just before entering the cabin, the President turned around and waved one last time. Borochenkov returned the gesture. No sooner had the cabin door been secured than Air Force One's four engines whined. Minutes later, it taxied to the runway, and took off – headed westerly. Only then were Gerry and the others told the next stop would be Ramstein Air Force Base in Germany. They did not notice Dr. Rodriguez was not on the plane. But, there was another surprise in the offing.

* * * *

Once Air Force One reached cruising altitude, and the pool reporters and photographers were getting ready to file, Umberto summoned them to President Merriwether's quarters, explaining the President would conduct a briefing.

"I know you are anxious to file your stories and photos," he began, "so I won't delay you much. Ordinarily, I would have shared with you the details of the topics Russian President Borochenkov and I covered. Instead, I'm going to give you the generic titles, but I will discuss the details in a special press conference I have decided to give tomorrow afternoon at 1:00. Obviously, that will mean the early and late evening television news programs will have sound bites, and the morning papers the next day will have fuller coverage. That may not sit well with some of you, but I want the American public to hear it directly from me. In return for the inconvenience I may have caused you in the way this trip was taken, I will provide you with an advanced copy of my remarks. On the advice of Press Secretary Umberto, who has weathered the anger some of you have rightly exhibited, advanced copies of my remarks are embargoed until the press conference. However, this will enable you to form questions based on facts you will have ahead of time, but your colleagues will not. Is this arrangement acceptable to you?"

Gerry for one was caught completely off guard. She looked at her colleagues, who looked back at her. "Any objections?" she finally asked. There were none. "Mr. President, I guess we have a deal."

"Thank you," he responded. "I assume you will lead off with the announcement that Air Force One is no longer missing. Of course, the way you want to handle the details is up to you. I should tell you there has been chaos on Capitol Hill during my absence, and you might want to check that out.

"Now, to my meeting with President Borochenkov:

"First of all, I cannot say enough about the efforts of Ambassador Preston Vandergriff, We consider it a thaw in a version of the 'Cold War' that has existed between our two nations.

"Second, President Borochenkov and I discussed two main issues. One was global warming. The other was the potential of arming drones with nuclear-tipped missiles. They are two separate subjects, but ones which affect our nations as well as others around the world.

"Incidentally, President Borochenkov has tentatively accepted an invitation to visit the United States in the very near future. Speaking of him, I will share with you something he said on the ride back to Air Force One: "It will shock a lot of people to learn that there are some subjects our two countries can agree on, and they are of great importance. I wish you a safe journey home because I understand there are some angry people on Capitol Hill who will have some very harsh words on your return. I believe the expression is 'want your scalp.' I told him 'that is the understatement of the century!'

"I won't delay you any longer, except to say our next stop will be Ramstein Force Base in Germany."

As the pool reporters returned to their section, Umberto provided the following background on Ramstein: "It is located in southwest Germany 80 miles from Frankfurt. The base is headquarters for the 86th Airlift Wing, and is the main facility for evacuations of military personnel. In addition to being the headquarters for U.S. Air Forces in Europe, it also is a NATO installation. If you need more data, I can arrange to get it for you."

* * * *

The President contacted Jared to tell Alicia to make the Ramstein stop known to Vance and Winters. He told Greg to alert the rest of the White House Press Corps. The commanding general at Ramstein was notified to have a large group of military personnel there, and that the President would like to speak with some of them briefly. Greg also was told that the President would have a press conference the following day at The White House.

* * * *

It did not take long for television and radio stations throughout the United States to break into their evening programs with the announcement: "BREAKING NEWS! AIR FORCE ONE HAS NOT VANISHED! PRESIDENT MERRIWETHER AND ALL THOSE ABOARD ARE SAFE AND RETURNING TO THE UNITED STATES FROM RUSSIA! STAY TUNED FOR MORE DETAILS!"

Newspapers had to recall printers and reporters in the early morning hours to revamp Page One of their publications for early morning distribution.

CHAPTER 27

A Lot of Explaining to Do

THE VERBAL EXPLOSION ON CAPITOL HILL echoed far beyond Washington, DC. Diane was bombarded with phone calls from many Members of Congress from both the Progressive and Conservative Parties. She quickly learned from Vance that he and Winters had met with various colleagues.

"We have decided on two courses of action," Vance announced. (That alone would be worth news breaks, she concluded.) "First, when the President gets settled back in the Oval Office, he will need to explain the outlandish disappearance and reappearance of Air Force One and its occupants to determine whether recourse is appropriate. Second, Mr. Winters and I will be responding to his nomination for Vice President (she noticed Jared was not cited by name) by asking that it be withdrawn. If not, the nomination will be given due consideration, which by our calculations may take an extended period of time."

In her report, Diane made a clear note that this response was agreed to by top members of both the President's own Progressive Party as well as the Conservative Party. What she did not elaborate on was what she felt was meant by "whether recourse is appropriate." When she aired her scoop, Bouchard, remarked, "If I didn't know any better, I would say Congress might just want to impeach him."

* * * *

After they filed their stories, Jorge met with the pool news people and said, "The President realizes this trip caused anguish not only for your bosses but also your families. He will personally speak with your loved ones and your families if you wish. On the plus side, you have exclusives on the meeting of the two Presidents. Because they wanted to talk freely in private, we could not alert you to bring along your passports. The President will hold a news conference tomorrow to discuss the subject of their get-together, and that may help understand why and how the meeting took place. I'm sorry I cannot go into more detail, but I know you will alert your editors to the press conference."

Gerry Bartlett, as an old saying goes, "laid Jorge out with flowers." "The apology just doesn't cut it for me!" she began. "I agreed to go on this junket because I was led to believe I would be home that evening. My husband and I had made special plans for our anniversary. Not only was that shot to hell, but I'm sure my husband went nuts when he could not contact me! I really don't give a damn what grand design the President accomplished with Borochenkov, but I'll never forget the adverse impact it had on my family life!"

Jorge was painfully silent. He would have liked to have said "we'll make it up to you," but that would only added salt to the emotional wound. He did manage "perhaps the President . . ." but she interrupted, "What's done is done! I never thought I would have to assess my professional life against my personal one. I've been through a lot since I've been with the AP, and I've been treated damn well! But this . . . . . ."

She could not continue. He was about to say "I'm sorry" when she turned away. Suddenly, she wheeled around and asserted sternly: "Here's a news break for you! My reporting days are over! My husband – who by the way is scheduled for heart bypass surgery – and my children mean more to me than what I always thought was the greatest job in the world! Put that on your news conference agenda!"

When he finally had a chance to speak with the President, Jorge quietly related the incident. President Merriwether responded,

"That's collateral damage I never anticipated. I certainly respect her priorities. Maybe under other circumstances we could have worked things out. This is something I won't easily forget."

* * * *

Instead of appearing in the press briefing room, President Merriwether decided it would be held in the Oval Office. That turned out to be a nightmare because the room could not accommodate all the reporters who wanted to attend. Jorge had the unenviable task of arranging seats by seniority. As a result, many stood in the outer office. But the President had an ulterior motive for the location. He would be addressing not only the White House press corps, but also the American public at the same time.

"I have some prepared remarks, after which I will accept questions from the reporters," he began. "To begin with, I owe you, the Congress, and the American people an apology for the events that have taken place. My absence aboard Air Force One caused consternation and concern. However, the meeting in Russia with President Borochenkov had to be secret.

"President Borochenkov invited me to discuss a matter of importance to both of us – the climate. Former Vice President Al Gore was ridiculed some years ago for his focus on climate change, yet he received a Nobel Prize for that effort. This matter is not to be dismissed, and is more serious than believed. President Borochenkov pointed out that climate change is having an adverse effect on Siberia in northern Russia. The Russians are greatly concerned because despite the brutal climate there, Siberia is rich in natural resources such as coal, oil, and metal ores. They contribute greatly to the Russian economy. The greatest concern – and here is where the United States could be affected – is that global warming eventually could release vast amounts of methane and carbon monoxide into the atmosphere. That could accelerate global warming, and could develop into an atmospheric Catch 22.

"In addition, we both agreed there is great concern some rogue nation may have some drones that they could arm with nuclear-tipped missiles. That puts a new meaning on nuclear war.

"So, why the secrecy of our meeting to discuss a matter that impacts on our civilization as we know it? Simply put, in recent times, relations between our two nations have been – shall we say – strained. But here come problems we both can address. I am proposing we take whatever steps possible to accelerate the work of people like the former Vice President on global warming, irrespective of other disagreements Russia and the United States might have. We may have to change some laws, do away with some, or make new ones to make every effort we can – to use a catch phrase – to save the planet.

"I hope Members of Congress will understand these are not partisan problems. These are global problems. In that regard, President Borochenkov and I agreed to merge our resources to seek ways to deal with them.

"For the reasons I have presented, I felt the best interests of both nations would be served if the two of us met without prior publicity.

"Admittedly, in using subterfuge, there was some personal collateral damage, and I am deeply concerned about that.

"In closing, I do have an announcement that may please some but puzzle others. President Borochenkov has agreed to visit the U.S. in the near future. Hopefully this will be at a time when both of our countries will have begun to address the effects of climate change. One of his stops will be at an organization that shuns publicity but has an interesting charter. It is called the Bardon Foundation. (Bouchard and Alicia would agree, that explains why Tim was on Air Force One.) It has created a center for future journalists who want to cover government. An adjunct of that will focus on the need for ethics in politics. (A number of Members of Congress literally fell off their chairs at this point.) I respectfully submit the latter should not be an oxymoron.

"Thank you. And, now it is time for reporters to take over."

Question: "Mr. President, why did you bother with the side show in Miami and Puerto Rico?"

Answer: "I'm glad we start off with an easy one. It was not a side show. I have not shied away from the pledge former President Fairchild made – making Puerto Rico and the District of Columbia the next states. But, since we had the plane handy, it made sense to take a bit of a side trip."

Question: "Mr. President, were there any other subjects you and the Russian President discussed?"

Answer: "I believe a Vodka toast entered the conversation. We focused on global warming and nuclear-armed drones. Keep in mind we were not able to spend a great deal of time together. I hope when he comes to the U.S. we can extend our conversation perhaps to other topics."

Question: "Mr. President, how was Air Force One able to vanish from radar – and in the middle of the Bermuda Triangle?"

Answer: "As to the first part, that is a security secret. I can't say any more about it than that. As to the second part, from what I'm told, there is no such thing as the Bermuda Triangle. It is an area that is subject to unusual weather conditions. At no time were we in any danger. Air Force One is quite an aircraft. Boeing should be very proud of it. Actually, that area of the Atlantic is much vaster than most people realize."

Question: "Mr. President, you have submitted to Congress the name of your Chief of Staff Jared Winston to be Vice President. News reports indicate it is literally DOA – Dead On Arrival, to use a police phrase. What is your reaction to that?"

Answer: "Mr. Winston and I go back many, many years. If I were not convinced he has the qualities to be Vice President, I would not have forwarded his name. We have three branches of government for a very good reason – checks and balances. There is a well-worn phrase around the nation's capital – the President proposes, Congress disposes. I only can submit a name, and lend whatever support I can. In the end, lawmakers on Capitol Hill have the final say. Jared has filled every expectation I ever had of him. He may be too firm for some, but he is fair."

Question: "Mr. President, a follow up, please. Why not consider, say, a Member of Congress?"

Answer: "Who says I did not?" (You could hear Capitol Hill shake.)

Question: "Who, Mr. President?"

Answer: "In the song 'The Gambler,' singer Kenny Rodgers's lyrics about poker went something like this – 'Know when to hold 'em, know when to fold 'em.' I'm holding my cards on that one."

Question: "Mr. President, were you aware some Members of Congress were planning to declare you unable to perform the duties of your office?"

Answer: "I certainly am now. I know some lawmakers were upset because I had not nominated a Vice President until now. A quick study of history shows this is not unique. Previous Presidents have gone short and even long times without one. President Truman did not have one for his entire first term. Let me explain this. At no point was I not in communication with the White House."

Question: "Mr. President, back to the Vice President. Do you have a Plan B if Congress does not approve your nomination?"

Answer: "That presumes the nomination will fail. Let's see how that turns out."

Question: "Mr. President, assuming what you did was bold, did you consider what you described as 'personal collateral damage?'"

Answer: "I believe I answered that earlier. Virtually any major decision a President makes is not going to go off perfectly. Sometimes you can anticipate possibilities and prepare alternatives. Sometimes you are surprised, and not prepared. I will leave it at that."

"Thank you, Mr. President."

* * * *

Jorge and Alicia rushed from the Oval Office as soon as they could because reporters were shouting more questions at them. At his urging, they took temporary refuge in Jared's office, since he remained at The President's side.

"What did you think?" she asked.

"Would you believe he did not want to be prepped about potential questions?" he answered.

"I wish I could be a fly on the wall in The Capitol," she commented.

"I think your ears would be burning," he responded. "He cut them off at the pass, as the old Hollywood cowboy movie actors used to say."

"There was something for everyone," she added.

* * * *

As soon as the press conference ended, Bouchard called Alicia.

"Did Congress call the fire department?" he asked.

At first, she did not get the joke. Then she answered, "For sure, a lot of ears are burning. And, I'll bet some of the language is singeing the wall paper. From what I hear, you were right on target figuring out where Air Force One really was headed."

"Just a lucky guess," he responded. "Off the record, I'm certain the President carefully avoided being trapped by some other questions that did not get asked. I still want to know why Dr. Frankhauser went along, and even more-so why Dr. Rodriguez. While the President made sense about the topic he and President Borochenkov focused on, I want to know what else went on. Jorge probably was in the loop, as was Secret Service Agent Whiz. Neither of them will talk. What do you think will be reaction on The Hill?"

"I knew you were going to ask me that," she answered. "Off the record, I'll have to check my sources. Vance and Winters may have jumped the gun on the Winston nomination. Truth be told, I'm not convinced the President does NOT have a Plan B. Winston always has been on the sidelines, or behind the scenes. He's been the traffic cop and bouncer for the President. My gut feeling is this: Vance and Winters still will try to undercut the President to ridicule the nomination. I wouldn't be surprised if their planning is tied in with the mid-term elections. Lawmakers will spend at least six months prior to that raising money for re-election – especially the House. They won't want to be concerned with making decisions like the Winston nomination then."

"It's been interesting talking with you," he said.

"Same here," she replied.

* * * *

Alicia was told the President wanted to see her in the Oval Office. "We need all the votes we can get for Jared," he said. "Call in all our favors, and invent a few if you have to. Ask them what they want in return, and check with Jared, and or me, before you promise anything."

CHAPTER 28

Unexpected Collateral Damage

STORY FROM THE ASSOCIATED PRESS:

Frank Bartlett, retired publisher of the Montgomery County News, suffered a massive stroke yesterday, two days after his 25th wedding anniversary, and died at Suburban Hospital in Bethesda, MD. He was 60 years old.

Bartlett was the husband of Geraldine Bartlett, long time reporter for the AP. She was part of the press pool on Air Force One that vanished for 48 hours this past week with President Lincoln Merriwether on board.

In addition to her, he is survived by two children, a brother, and two sisters.

* * * *

After the funeral, Gerry wrote a letter to President Merriwether, and enclosed a copy of the story. The envelope read "For the President." Her name was where the return address normally would be. She gave it to Jorge, and asked him to deliver it personally to the Oval Office. Without asking any questions, he did so.

As Jorge handed him the letter, President Merriwether read it aloud: "Mr. President, this is why I was so upset at being held hostage on Air Force One. I never realized that once I returned home, he only would live two more days. I cannot face you anymore, and so I am resigning from the AP."

He slumped in his chair, dismissed Jorge, and then summoned Jared. After he read the note, Jared did not make any comment. The President swiveled his chair around, stared out the window at the Rose Garden, and then sighed.

* * * *

At the next press conference, the chair where Gerry normally sat was empty.

CHAPTER 29

Political Fireworks

To SAY VANCE AND WINTERS were furious is an understatement. They vented their spleens when Diane contacted them. "If the President thinks he has sweet-talked the American public into accepting one of the dirtiest tricks in political history, he is in for a rude awakening!" the Speaker bellowed.

"He put a lot of people at risk with that stunt, and caused a lot of unnecessary anguish to ones who didn't deserve it!" Winters added.

Diane asked, "Since you both are fellow Progressive Party members of the President, isn't this sort of political mutiny?"

Both answered simultaneously, "You bet your bottom dollar!"

She persisted: "So, what does that mean?"

The Speaker answered, "There are ways we can convey our disillusionment."

Diane followed that up: "Such as . . ."

The Majority Leader replied, "We'll spell out the specifics at the appropriate time."

She continued: "Have you conveyed your displeasure to the President?"

Vance answered, "Once you air this interview, he will know."

* * * *

Diane's next calls were to Martha Schoenfeld, Minority Leader in the House, and Victor Amaroso, Minority Leader in the Senate.

Schoenfeld: "This is a problem for the Progressives. It's for them to work it out. They don't need any help from us."

Amaroso: "The President seems to need some training in time management. The mid-term elections are not that far off, and we feel the public will indicate whether the President's trip, and the way it was done, was justified."

* * * *

Umberto asked to see the President in the Oval Office to determine whether he wanted to be interviewed by Diane about the turmoil on Capitol Hill. Jared and Alicia were there. "Bouchard is one savvy reporter," Jorge said. "He sure has some interesting sources." The President did not seem stressed over the request.

"Mr. President," Jared said, "you've got to meet this head-on."

"Alicia, does this jibe with what you've heard?" the President asked.

"I tried to reach Speaker Vance and Senator Winters, but they avoided my calls," she answered. "I was about to go to The Hill to see them in person."

The President thought for a moment and said, "Alicia, call their offices and say I would like them to come to the Oval Office at their earliest convenience. No, change that. Say I want them. You don't have to give a reason. They'll know the reason."

"Mr. President," Jorge said as Alicia left, "may I be permitted an observation based on a hunch?"

"Speak up," he answered.

Jorge responded, "When I was in Journalism School, one of my professors had been a reporter years ago. His paper was part of a major chain that had just begun to buy television stations. In his city, the paper was the largest afternoon daily, and the TV station also was the largest. The editor would not accept television as a news outlet and forbid any of the staff to cooperate with co-owned property. Before long, the station began to expand its news coverage at the same time afternoon dailies were beginning to lose readership. Eventually, the paper ceased publication, and readers only had a morning paper."

"What's your point?" Jared asked.

"Mr. President," Greg began, "I feel we need to accept the reality of electronic and print journalism and understand their strengths. That way, we can use both to our advantage."

"I'm not sure I follow you," the President responded.

"Sir, when you consent to an interview, we need to keep in mind electronic journalism now is a 24/7 business," he replied. "They go for what we call sound-bites. Each story gets only so many minutes, so responses need to be short. On the other hand, if you want to convey perspective, newspapers will give you a lot of space. That old professor once said he used to get calls from readers who would say, 'I saw part of a story on TV last night, but I wonder if you could tell me more detail.' TV has talking heads, some of whom never, as the old saying goes, let facts interfere with emotion. Op ed pieces in papers can be rewritten to get the right words. All I'm saying, sir, is that in giving an interview, keep in mind when the public will hear or read what you have to say, and how you say it."

"OK, Greg, invite her to the Oval Office," the President said. "I would prefer to speak with her alone. Afterwards, we can discuss what transpired."

Before she arrived, President Merriwether switched on his secret recording device.

* * * *

"Mr. President, thank you for seeing me," Diane began. "I am sure you are aware of a virtual revolt on Capitol Hill by your own Party leadership. What is your reaction to that?"

The President smiled and answered, "As I have said many times, I believe strongly in the separation of powers in government. Yes, we are members of the same political Party, but that does not mean there cannot be disagreements. I have not been back in The White House long enough for me to confer with Congressman Vance and Senator Winters. Alicia Rineheart has been trying to reach them on my behalf, but has not been successful. The three of us need to talk because I need to know the specifics of their concerns so I can address them. I would prefer doing that in private, not in the media. In my television talk, I tried to explain the focus of my trip. In view of reaction on The Hill, I suppose I did not accomplish that."

"Mr. President," Diane continued, "it would seem the point of contention is what appears to be the subterfuge used. Specifically, it is alleged the mysterious disappearance of Air Force One created unnecessary chaos and consternation on Capitol Hill, and for the country at large. You did explain your reason why you took that step, but now it would appear there is even more anger."

"Ms. Bana, I chose my words carefully hoping that would be a clear explanation," the President responded. "I assumed lawmakers on The Hill would understand this involved the future of society, not the future of politics. Even in previous administrations this subject was broached, but little was accomplished to take the necessary steps to address what can be done. We cannot control the atmosphere, but we can control what we pump into it. The fact that Russian President Borochenkov and I are of the same mind should have been a clear signal of how we both see the big picture."

"Mr. President, leaders in Congress do not appear to share that view. They feel you tricked them with your trip," she said.

"I do not feel I broke any laws in doing what I did," the President began.

Dana interrupted: "Sir, I am hearing rumors that there are those who think you did."

President Merriwether continued, "I'm not in the rumor business. I prefer working together to resolve differences. If we all agreed with one another all the time, we would be nothing but robots. The term 'democracy' implies differences. We should respect other's viewpoints even when they do not agree with ours. I do not want to fight political battles in the media. I realize you want a story, and I am willing to be as open as I can with you."

Diane could not contain a smile when she asked, "Mr. President, is there anything that is not open?"

The President answered, "There are matters I cannot discuss, but I am trying to respond to your questions as best I can. We pride ourselves on being an open society, but in truth we apply our own definition to that term."

"Mr. President, thank you for taking the time for this interview," Diane said. "I hope there will be other similar occasions."

Rising from behind his desk, President Merriwether replied, "You don't have to wait until some lawmakers say things that you want me to defend. I respect the work you do, and how you do it, Ms. Bana. Speaking of that, how do you feel about the animosity on The Hill?"

She never expected that, but answered: "I report what I'm told, Mr. President."

After she left, Diane wondered who interviewed whom. She felt he did have some good quotes, even though she was convinced the President adroitly got around succinct answers to her questions. Little did she realize she should have followed up on her question, "Is there anything that is not open?"

CHAPTER 30

Word Play

DIANE DID NOT HAVE A LOT OF TIME before she had to prepare her piece for the 6:00 p.m. news. Winters was not available.

"Mr. Vance," she began, "I have it on good authority President Merriwether is willing to work out any differences with you and Senator Winters. Your comment?"

"Ms. Bana, he should have considered that before he pulled the stunt with Air Force One!" he asserted. "It gives me a great deal of pain to say that since we both are members of the Progressive Party, and he was my mentor. I cannot imagine how the Conservatives are reacting. (She would get around to that soon.) I hope the President understands how this will play around the country when Members like me are up for re-election."

"Are you implying the President's trip could adversely affect those elections?" she asked.

"I can't speak for others," he began his answer, "but in my District, the voters say that while the trip may have been worthwhile, the way it was done does not speak well for the openness of government the President keeps talking about." (Diane doubted that, but did not want to press that point any further.)

"Mr. Speaker, I hear rumors that unless the President recants such opinions, there might be support for impeachment proceedings in the House," Diane bluffed.

"You did not hear that from me, Ms. Bana," Vance insisted. "I serve at the pleasure my fellow House members. It may be premature for such drastic action."

"But, sir," she jumped in, "are you ruling that out?"

"I do not make such decisions," he answered evenly. "If that is the will of the House, so be it. Can we move on to something else?"

"Mr. Speaker, on another subject," she said, "do you feel the same way as President Merriwether and Russian President Borochenkov that climate change was worth the trip?" (She knew he could answer yes or no, but hoped for an elaboration.)

"I can't speak for my fellow lawmakers, but personally I feel we have not paid enough attention to such an important problem," he said. "Thank you for asking."

"And, what about the nuclear-armed drones subject?" she asked.

"That is scary," the Speaker responded. "Yes, that is a major concern."

Diane felt she had more than enough for her next report, and thanked Speaker Vance.

After the interview ended, she called Alicia and told her in essence what Vance had said.

Both the President and the Speaker felt Diane had been fair. Winters was fuming that he was not quoted at all. He vowed he would find a way to make up for that oversight. But then, he was not up for re-election as Vance was.

CHAPTER 31

The Call of Calls

"REMEMBER ME?" the voice asked.

Alicia almost dropped the phone as she almost yelled "Tim!! Oh my God!! Tim!! I feel like an ass not calling you!"

Tim replied, "To be honest, you wouldn't have been able to reach me."

"Why not?!!" she replied.

"Well, the long flights did a number on me. Dr. Frankhauser – he was on board the flight – ordered me into George Washington University Hospital for some tests. I just need to get accustomed to not being 40,000 feet in the air for 12 hours."

"It's been crazy around here!" she declared.

"I can just imagine," he responded.

She asked excitedly. "When can I see you?"

"The doctor at GW gave me the all clear, so any time you're not putting out fires over at Capitol Hill," he answered.

"Tim, I can't promise, but unless the President orders me to spend the night here, I think I can get away around 8:00 this evening," she responded. "My niece left for graduate work at an out-of-town college. After this, I'll make sure you have my spare door key."

* * * *

Much of the evening was spent in small talk. Just before Alicia made it clear he was to spend the night with her, Tim said, "There are some things about the trip I just can't talk about. I hope you understand."

She almost cooed: "I can live with that. Now, get undressed already!"

CHAPTER 32

Hindsight Is 20/20

THE SUNDAY MAGAZINE article headline read: "We Were Prisoners Aboard Air Force One". (The authors were the White House "pool" reporters, minus Gerry Bartlett.)

"What started out to be a routine goodwill trip by President Lincoln Merriwether to Miami and Puerto Rico turned out to be a 48-hour nightmare for us. The first two stops were easy ones, which we were told focused on his pledge of statehood for both. We filed our reports and relaxed for the return flight to Andrews.

"When two hours had passed, the plane should have been descending. We looked out the windows and could not see the ground. Later, we would find out we were at 40,000 feet at that time. We asked Press Secretary Jorge Umberto what was going on. He said 'there had been a change in plans.' We asked him for an explanation, and he told us we would be briefed later. We were shocked when he added that we were not to make any calls while we were in the air 'for security reasons.' We were supposed to be home that night. What would our friends and families think happened to us?

"While we were trying to figure out where a flight that long would take us, we discussed two passengers. One was Tim Anderson, a former White House correspondent whom we knew. He now is head of a non-profit organization called the Bardon Foundation. The other was a woman, who boarded at Ramey Air Force

Base in Puerto Rico, but whose name and background never were made known to us. We still do not know who she is, or why she was on Air Force One.

"During the flight, we repeatedly badgered Umberto for more information. He was not forthcoming. When we asked to speak with the President, the Press Secretary explained 'all will be made clear later.'

"So, here we were, imprisoned in Air Force One, going somewhere that would take half a day, and not being able to communicate with anyone. By accident, we discovered another cockpit crew also had boarded the plane at Ramey. There was no explanation for that. Secret Service personnel restricted us from roaming around Air Force One. Everyone was polite, but tight-lipped.

"Those of us who had been on previous Air Force One flights never had been treated like that before. It was unnerving. We never knew about vanishing from radar.

"Finally, an announcement came over the public address system to prepare for landing. But, where? It was not until we were taxiing toward a terminal that we noticed the words were in Russian, a language none of us knew. Well, we thought, finally we will get the explanation for this cloak-and-dagger operation.

"Then came the big shocker! Since we obviously were on Russian soil, we realized none of us had brought our passports. Because of that, we could not leave the airport. Instead, we were escorted off the plane and into a secure area of the terminal by armed Russian guards. Yes, we all were scared half out of our wits. This was bizarre! Once we were in a small room, Umberto finally showed up. He apologized, on behalf of the President, for the secrecy of the flight. He told us President Merriwether would be meeting with Russian President Andrei Borochenkov, and that later we would be briefed on the gist of their talk. He explained the two men would be driven to Moscow, about an hour away.

"We tried to complain, but to no avail. We were brought food – actually a delicious meal from Air Force One, but we were not allowed to leave the room except for bathroom breaks. We always were accompanied by the unsmiling Russian guards.

"About six hours later, we were told the two Presidents had returned, and we were escorted back to the plane before President Merriwether boarded. Umberto held a mini-briefing with us; only he could be quoted on this: 'American President Lincoln Merriwether met with Russian President Andrei Borochenkov at the Kremlin. The meeting was extremely cordial, and several matters were discussed. President Merriwether will disclose the details in a press conference to be held tomorrow in the Oval Office. President Borochenkov stated he has accepted an invitation from President Merriwether to visit the United States in the near future.'

"Air Force One is a very comfortable aircraft, but there was a distinct chill in the air between where we were seated and where the President and Umberto were located.

"Then came the second surprise – we were going to make a stop after two hours. As the plane touched down on the runway, we could see a host of military aircraft. As we passed the control tower, we could see that we were at Ramstein Air Force Base, Germany. When we asked Umberto why we weren't told about this in advance, he said, 'That's a security matter.' We thought that was an insult because that huge military installation has very high security all the time. At the last minute, Umberto cautioned us that 'this is strictly a meet-and-greet stop. The President wants to press the flesh with the military. We'll be on the ground a relatively short time, which will include refueling the aircraft.'

"That last remark became a matter of noir humor for us because we asked the Press Secretary, 'What country are we going to next?' He did reply, 'the U.S., non-stop.'

"White House correspondents have covered presidential trips for years, but we doubt they ever have been subjected to such treatment, other than during war time.

"Perhaps President Merriwether has a grand design. The question in our minds is this: Was it worth the subterfuge and the angst it caused? We would like to give the President the benefit of the doubt, but we can only speak for ourselves in cautioning him that we will take a more critical look at how his administration deals with the news media. We are reminded of the famous quote by attorney Brendan Sullivan who said to Senator Daniel Inouye during the Iran-Contra hearings, 'Well, sir, I'm not a potted plant.' Then there is this version: 'What are we, chopped liver?'

"We have a role to play; we just want to play by the same set of rules as those we report on. Don't take us for granted, Mr. President. Trust is a two-way street."

* * * *

After Gerry Bartlett's letter, Umberto hesitated about showing the Sunday Magazine article to the President. He decided if he did not, Merriwether might be blind-sided not only from the media but also from Capitol Hill. He also made sure Jared and Alicia also read it. (Jorge noticed Alicia looked as if she had a fitful night's sleep.)

The President called Jared into the Oval Office and told the aide who screened his calls, "I don't want to be disturbed." Jared waited for him to start the conversation.

"We knew the trip, and the procedure, would be calculated risks," the President began. "I feel bad for Jorge not knowing the full schedule of Air Force One, but then he could not mislead the pool reporters. Yet, they blame him. At this level of government, that has to come with the territory. Sometimes we have to use people. Jared, I can't look back. I know there is a price to pay, but you are the only one who knew why it had to be done the way it was done."

"Mr. President," Jared responded, "one thing I've learned about politics is that you must consider all the repercussions of your decisions. Once that's done, and you have committed to your decision, you can't second-guess whether you did the right thing or not. Anyone who does that is doomed to failure. You've done the best you could, all circumstances considered. As President, you can't dictate how history will treat your decisions. Historians will make their own judgments. Was it worth it? Time will tell."

President Merriwether always valued Jared's opinions, even though he disagreed with some of them.

"In hindsight, there is one thing I truly regret," the President said. "I should have trusted the pool reporters. Jorge urged me not to keep them in the dark. I ignored his advice, and now I see that was a huge mistake. My God, I did not have any idea Mrs. Bartlett's anniversary was that night. If I did, I would have had Jorge pick someone else from the AP."

"Mr. President, what's done is done," Jared commented. "I once heard of a university commencement address in which the speaker – who was a widely known business executive – told the graduates to 'learn to fail.' Sir, if you've learned something from the trip to help you make better decisions later, that transcends second thoughts."

The President digested those words before continuing, "Jared, you know I do not subscribe to using people for my personal gain. I've learned to how to play politics. I'm not a Pollyanna, but the incident with Mrs. Bartlett hurts."

"Mr. President," Jared responded, "someday the whole story will be revealed. You do not have to justify what you've done, or how you've done it. I know you've thought long and hard about this trip, and what it will mean not just for America but the world. That's noble, but it comes with a price in more ways than one. The presidency is larger than the person who sits in the Oval Office."

"Jared," the President replied, "you always know how to push the right buttons. I know you too are going to pay a price, and you're willing to do it. That's pretty noble. There's one decision I've made, and don't talk me out of it. I'm going to the mat to fight for your nomination. Maybe you and I are the only ones who know how I've come to that decision, and why. Yes, we both are going to pay a price for that effort. And, Alicia is too. I never had second thoughts about giving her such an important but thankless job. The mid-term elections are going to be more important than many realize."

"Mr. President," Jared responded, "you know how I felt, and still feel, about the nomination. If it does go through – and that's a huge IF – you know I will give it the best effort. I'm humbled that you even considered me. You know I am very comfortable being Chief of Staff. I know why you did it, and I needn't say more. However, I certainly will not be disappointed if Congress successfully challenges the nomination."

"I will," President Merriwether quickly replied. "Having said that, do you have any second thoughts about our overall game plan?"

"No, sir!" Jared said emphatically.

* * * *

Even during their evening in bed, Tim was having second thoughts. And it was giving him another round of headaches, which he kept from Alicia.

During the trip, Tim sat in the cabin not far from the President's private area. He saw things that perhaps he should not have seen. He overheard conversations he was not supposed to hear.

The only person he could trust was Alicia, but there was no way he could confide his qualms to her. After all, she works for the President, and represents him on The Hill. That is an awesome responsibility. One of the many things he admired about Alicia was her integrity. She showed a lot of mettle standing by Senator Stafford when others avoided him. The President could not confide in her, and then assert she had to keep that to herself. Maybe he should have turned down the trip, but when the President wants you there, you go.

Tim knew he had a problem with pressure. That is why he was so pleased with his new position. Then came the trip. It would be worth it when Russian President Borochenkov would give a major speech at the Foundation's annual dinner.

* * * *

Ones who were not having second thoughts were on The Hill. And, neither was Whiz Wiscznewski, head of the Secret Service detail on Air Force One. He, too, could not say anything about the trip to his fiancé, Frankie Green, former high ranking official of the Capitol Police Force.

CHAPTER 33

Jabberwocky

MANY IN THE HOUSE OF REPRESENTATIVES still could not understand how Bobby Joe Simpson ever got elected. "He must have talked his opponents to death with his constant running off at the mouth," Speaker Vance once told a colleague. "He keeps bugging me to put him on this Committee or that without any regard for seniority."

Why this came to Vance's attention was Bobby Joe's reaction to the President's explanation of his mysterious trip. The freshman called a White House correspondent he somehow knew and announced: "There's a conspiracy of evil goin' on at 16 hundert Penn Avenoo, and we – I mean us on Thah Hill – ought to do somethin' 'bout it! The Prez got lot of nerve sendin' us thah name of that Chief Staff to be Veep, and that guy ain't nothin' but his bud."

The reporter called Vance for reaction. "The Gentleman represents a District within his state, and he has to answer to them, not the Speaker," Vance parried.

The Speaker would have let it go at that, except the reporter continued, "Congressman Simpson said he is going to ask you to hold hearings."

Vance responded, "Since he has talked with you, but not me, what hearings is he referring to?"

The reporter said, "Please hold while I turn this into a conference call with him."

The Speaker was about to hang up when Simpson came on line and the reporter asked, "Congressman Simpson, what type of meetings do you have in mind? I have the Speaker on the other line."

"Well, uh, say, ahem, well Ah's tryin' to decide," he answered. "Ah'll get back to you on that."

Vance did not say anything, and the reporter said, "I guess I'll get back to you when he gets back to me."

"That won't be necessary," the Speaker explained. "He doesn't call meetings! I do! If he wants one, he knows how to request it, and that's to come and talk to me."

Vance thought that put the lid on it, only to find out Simpson declared he would hold a news conference in his office "with a special announcement." He immediately had his Chief of Staff contact Simpson's office and assert, "Tell the Congressman to be in the Speaker's office in five minutes!"

In addition to being referred to as Simple Simpson behind his back, he also was called Mr. Jabberwocky for his inane tirades. He arrived at the Speaker's office two minutes early.

"Let's get right to it!" Vance began. "There are certain rules in the House, which you apparently have not had the time to read and comprehend! My colleagues have elected me Speaker, which means they have respect for leadership! You do not go off half-cocked with calls for hearings! If you have something more than ego to offer, as Archie Bunker used to say, 'stifle it!' Now, suppose you justify the need for a hearing, or hearings! You do not chair even a subcommittee, so it better be solid! That remark about 'a conspiracy of evil' is pretty harsh!"

Simpson's face turned beet red. No one ever had spoken to him like that before. Usually, it's the other way around. Finally he stammered, "Uh, Mr. Speaker, no disrespect intended. No sir. But, mah constituents are outraged – outraged, sir! – at what they read in thet article 'bout Air Force One!"

The Speaker wanted to nail him to the wall, as the expression goes, but instead responded, "We all read the article. We may do something about it, but at the right time. And, to anticipate your next remark, no, you will not be part of any hearing on the matter. Oh, by the way, on your way out, think about sending me a list of those calls of outrage you mentioned."

Irritated as he was with Simpson, Vance was mad at Mr. Jabberwocky for having the same idea he and Senator Winters had discussed. "At the right time," they both agreed. The Speaker spread the word to his lower echelon leaders in the House to keep track of Simpson and what he says and does. "He's a loose cannon. When he shoots off his mouth, he does us harm," he explained.

Simpson sulked back to his office, and made up a lie that the Speaker needed advice from him "on a very private matter." Although he was reprimanded, he vowed his turn would come "at the right time."

* * * *

Despite the encounter with Simpson, Vance needed to speak with Winters. "Maybe we'll have to move up our time table," the Speaker explained. "This might just work for me and my colleagues' advantage during the upcoming mid-term campaigning."

Winters responded, "It also could help those in the Senate who are running for re-election. I'm told some of the races could go either way. You know we can't lose control of the Senate. You don't have that concern in the House."

"Maybe not," Vance replied, "but, if the Conservatives win over enough seats, my influence will be diminished. I think the question is this, Ansel. Do we act before the elections? If so, how much before? Or, do we wait until the final year of President Merriwether's term?

Winters paused before answering, "I say before, while we know how many votes we can count on. Also, I think the *Sunday Magazine* article forces our hand. I'm already hearing rumbles about it. I just wish the President had stayed away longer."

Now Vance had another problem. He had to act carefully lest Simpson get the credit for any hearings.

* * * *

Diane heard rumors about the Simpson/Vance dust-up. She called Alicia partly to alert her and partly to get any comment. "Thanks for the heads-up," Alicia said. "You know I can't comment about rumors, but if anything develops from this end, you'll be the first to know."

No sooner had the call ended than Alicia notified the President and Jorge. "If Diane knows, chances are the other media won't be far behind," the Press Secretary commented. Sure enough, Bouchard called Jorge and said, "Bad news travels fast."

* * * *

Simpson never learned to control his mouth. In his office, he complained loudly that "I've been taken to the Speaker's woodshed and spanked!" He couldn't let go of that, and started things in motion that would quickly reach the Oval Office.

During his original campaign for the House of Representatives, he gathered around him a group of rabid supporters. He owed them a lot because he literally came out of nowhere to be elected. He was lucky that Congressman Charles Doerner actually decided to do as little as possible to seek re-election. He had been in the House for a dozen terms, and felt all that was needed was his name on the ballot. Even before that happened, Doerner made the mistake of doing what he considered a "minor" favor for an old friend who had income tax problems. All he did was contact the Internal Revenue Service. Somehow, Simpson heard about it. He couldn't personally blow the whistle on Doerner, so he sent an anonymous letter to the local newspaper with just enough information for a reporter to do some digging. Even Simpson was surprised to learn it was not the first time Doerner had "made a friendly call to the IRS." When the story broke, Doerner at first denied any wrong doing, saying all he did was make a phone call. But, the hint of impropriety small as it seemed, was enough for the veteran Representative to announce he would not seek re-election.

In a heartbeat, a raft of politicians announced their candidacies. As much as Simpson wanted to make it to Washington, he did not think he had a prayer because some of the candidates were well known. He really did not have the credentials to use to his advantage; the highest "office" he ever held was that of a councilman. His full time job was as a men's clothing store salesman. But, in meeting with some close friends, he realized the fact that there would be a packed race would work to his advantage. He and his cronies did the math and figured out that if they could concentrate his meager campaign on a few neighborhoods, he could get just enough votes to win. The others could ony hope for their share of the rest. His campaign was quiet but effective. Even the local paper barely mentioned him. His slogan was, "I'll never forget who elected me!"

His strategy paid off. The local paper described him as the "out-of-nowhere" winner. Where before he was not a publicity seeker, once he got to Capitol Hill, his persona changed. His close clan of cronies convinced him he would be unbeatable because he had the "energy." To him, that meant making himself heard. No sooner was he sworn in than he made the customary rounds of the House leadership. But he could not stop making suggestions on how Congress could/should operate. He hired only those who had helped him, and refused to keep any of Doerner's experienced staff.

Fellow Representatives tolerated him, thinking he literally was a political flash-in-the-pan. He did learn to keep close touch with those who put him in office, but also reached out to others. Getting re-elected the first time was surprisingly easy. He eagerly looked forward to the second re-election campaign.

However, he never learned the seniority system that is Capitol Hill. He felt he knew all he needed to know. One thing that eluded him so far was serving on a subcommittee or even a committee. He could not understand why.

CHAPTER 34

The Follow Up, And A Surprise

Bouchard asked Umberto for another interview with the President. "Honestly, it will take only a couple of minutes," he explained. "I don't mind if you sit in. And, if you want, the Chief of Staff is welcome, too."

The Press Secretary felt that was an easy sell, but President Merriwether asked, "I can understand you being there. But, why also Jared? OK. Set it up."

Bouchard apologized for the short notice.

"Mr. President," he began, "based on what I have been hearing (he was not about to mention Simpson's name), coupled with the Sunday Magazine article, what effect will all of this will have on the mid-term elections?"

President Merriwether had not expected such a complicated but thought-provoking question. "Mr. Bouchard," he began slowly, "you are assuming there will be some effect. That gets into the predicting business, which is something I studiously avoid."

"Sir," he persisted, "what if that situation becomes an issue at that time?"

"If it does, and I'm not admitting it will be, that would be a more proper time for you to ask me for a comment," the President answered, dodging the question.

"Mr. President," Bouchard continued, "will you campaign for Progressive Party members in both the House and Senate who are running for re-election?"

The President smiled and replied, "If asked, certainly I will. It's much too early for anyone to approach me on that." Bouchard would have loved to follow that up with, "What if you are not asked?" But, he decided against it.

"One final question, Mr. President," Bouchard said. "With all due respect, sir, I have to ask this. How would you describe your relationship with the House and the Senate, not just with your fellow Progressive Party members, but also the Conservative Party?"

Bouchard saw a tautness in the President's face. "I respect your right to ask such a question," he began. "I may feel one way about that relationship, but those on The Hill may feel differently. To get to the point I think you are making, I have heard about some unhappiness with my trip. I knew there would be a risk on the way it was to be handled, and I already have apologized for certain aspects of it. I still defend the purpose of it, and I hope the public withholds final judgment for the time being. Events are taking place that have a direct bearing on the White House, but I cannot elaborate more at this time. There are those on The Hill who support me, while there are others even in my own Party who do not. A President must expect to face diversity of opinion from time to time. I refer you to a book written by Doris Kearns Goodwin titled 'Team of Rivals." It's the story of President Lincoln and his Cabinet, some of whom hated his guts. His genius was in utilizing the best from everyone, even though he did not agree with them from time to time. And, in case you were going to ask, my first name was given to me in honor of that President. Don't jump the gun on what Congress might or might not do. If the House and/or the Senate want to take some action regarding the trip, that's their right. I am confident the truth will prevail, and it may surprise many."

The President clearly indicated the interview was over by standing up and offering to shake hands. Bouchard thanked him and left.

* * * *

Umberto was shocked when he came to the podium for his daily briefing with White House correspondents. Sitting in the front row in her former usual seat was none other than Gerry Bartlett.

"Welcome back," Umberto said. "I don't understand . . ." She stood up to applause. "My executives convinced me to return to work," she began. "It's what Frank would have wanted me to do. Despite my outburst to the President, I know my role as a reporter, and I will do my best to be as objective as possible. I'm not in the opinion business."

She sat down to more applause.

CHAPTER 35

Reaction

As Diane and Bouchard expected, their "breaking news" stories were analyzed on Sunday morning.

The President met with Jared, Jorge, and Alicia to go over what they read and heard. There was a lively discussion on "damage control." President Merriwether finally said, "We have to take the bad news with the good news. That means no reaction from us when the other reporters want follow-ups. We have to concentrate on our political agenda."

Alicia was the first to respond. "Mr. President," she began, "it's ironic that Congressman Simpson accuses the White House of having what he called 'a conspiracy of evil.' From what my sources tell me, there is a 'conspiracy of evil' brewing on Capitol Hill. Mr. Simpson apparently has touched some political nerves with his ranting, and there could be a challenge to the House and Senate leadership. On the one hand, Mr. President, you've got the leadership of Congress literally out for your scalp. On the other hand, there seems to be the makings of an internal revolt."

Jared added, "Mr. President, that could be a break for us."

President Merriwether responded, "Alicia, just how serious do you think it is for the House to take some action about my trip?"

She answered, "Hard to say at this point. The public is not convinced you successfully justified your trip. The Senate has to wait for the House to act, and only some of those lawmakers are up for re-election as you know."

The President continued, "From what Alicia has been telling me, some of those I considered friends in the House are not so friendly these days. I guess I cannot blame them because I know the pressure of constant campaigning. No sooner are you re-elected than you have to think about the next term's race."

"Sir," Alicia said, "it will be interesting to see if Simpson creates a problem for Vance, and how the Speaker reacts to it."

No one spoke because there seemed to be unity of thought. Finally, Jared broke the silence by saying, "We have to be prepared for the worst."

The President responded, "Are you implying impeachment?"

Jared nodded.

President Merriwether looked at Umberto and asked, "How would that play in the media, Jorge?"

The Press Secretary had to think a moment before answering, "It depends on timing. Right now, we're getting hammered. Your approval numbers are dropping. Bouchard and Bana have struck a news nerve, to put it bluntly, sir. I don't think the media are ready to support a call for impeachment because that is heavy. We have to be careful never to give the impression we are in a panic mode. Mr. President, although there is rough going at the moment, you have positives. For one thing, I would suggest looking into a definite commitment from Russian President Borochenkov to visit the U.S. and give a major speech at the Bardon Foundation."

"Jared? Alicia?" the President asked, "anything to add or subtract from what Jorge said?"

The Chief of Staff responded first: "Absolutely continue to act presidential. As I heard Jorge once say, 'don't let events control you; you control events.'" The Press Secretary smiled.

"Mr. President," Alicia replied, "let's see whether the House implodes politically. If all they do is attack you, it could backfire. Besides, sir, some of the criticism is coming from your own Party. I'm not sure they understand the implication of a political revolt.

That could help the Conservatives. I wouldn't be surprised to find Bana picking up on that. And, Bouchard would not be far behind."

"Amen to that," Jorge added.

Jared noticed the President looked a bit tired and quickly said, "I think we have pooled our thinking properly. Let's leave it at that for the time being." Alicia and Jorge took their cue and left the Oval Office.

They saw Dr. Frankauser sitting in the waiting area.

CHAPTER 36

Maneuvering

THERE WAS AN "UNEASY TRUCE" for the next few months up to the mid-term elections.

Congressman Simpson used that time to begin drumming up support for his coming "crusade." He held numerous meetings with members of "The Young Turks" as well as "The Starboard" and "The Mounties," plus members of the Conservative Party. They agreed on a common theme – "level the playing field for a democratic Congress." Their aim was to narrow the majority in the House and hopefully take over leadership of the Senate. The latter almost worked – actually, voters created a tie with 48 Progressives, 48 Conservatives, and 1 Independent for each Party. In the House, the tally ended up with 220 Progressives and 217 Conservatives – a shocker, to say the least!

No Progressive Representative or Senator asked President Merriwether to campaign for them. Numerous pundits concluded this diminished the Party's control in Congress. Furthermore, there was the issue of a tie vote in the Senate.

No sooner had the election ended than President Merriwether held a strategy meeting again with Jared and Alicia. "Now is the time to push for your nomination," he said, looking at his Chief of Staff.

"Mr. President," Alicia commented, "I think the importance of that probably won't sink in until Congress reconvenes in January. I've done some checking on The Hill, and the Simpson 'bandwagon' seems to have gained traction."

The President responded, "I was hoping just the opposite. Maybe we underestimated Mr. Simpson."

"Mr. President," she continued, "my feeling is if Mr. Vance wants to deep-six the nomination, he will do it by calling a lame duck session. My research indicates there were three such sessions for a specific matter in 1954, 1994, . . ."

He interrupted, "and the one I called in 1998 when I was still Speaker. Members don't like them because once elections are over, they want to get out of town during the hiatus between the elections and the convening of the next Congress."

Jared said, "We should count on what Alicia – and you, Mr. President – just said. He'll call the session, make sure there's a quorum, have someone make a motion to reject, and it will pass. The session will end, and that will be that."

Alicia had a thought that so excited her she stood up and remarked, "Mr. President, you may have an ace in the hole."

"I didn't know you played poker, Alicia," he responded.

Quickly she replied, "Tim is teaching me. And, no, Mr. President, it is not strip poker." That broke the tension as the two men laughed while she blushed.

"Sorry, Alicia," he continued. "You were saying . . ."

"Sir, should there be a tie in the Senate – and that seems to be a clear indication from the polls – we will need a Vice President to vote – the only time he does. I cannot believe Mr. Winters is not aware of that. I too believe Mr. Vance will insist on the lame duck session. In fact, despite Mr. Simpson and his Conservative colleagues, I feel certain the two leaders will understand the need for hearings on the nomination before the new Congress is sworn in." Jared's face remained stoic.

"Interesting conclusion, Alicia," the President commented. "It makes sense. Maybe we can help that along by some strategic 'pork' being handed out to recalcitrant Members. I like the idea." Only Jared knew what the President really meant.

* * * *

Before Vance called for the lame duck session, he phoned the President. "Sir," he began, "you have one last chance to withdraw the nomination."

"Absolutely, not!" he asserted.

"Don't say I did not give you the opportunity to save yourself from embarrassment!" he responded.

A quorum was declared, and a voice vote was taken so lawmakers would not have to be held accountable. The nomination was defeated. The lawmakers never would know Jared had agreed to serve only as long as President Merriwether was in office.

One person had his hopes revived by the defeat – SecDef Bosworth. Boz felt it's time he threw his hat into the ring and begin to campaign for Vice President. Little did he know President Merriwether had a Plan B.

* * * *

Senator Cummings, the anti-Semite, hated Jared, but he was more concerned with who would be President pro tempore. He recalled the only time the Senate had rotating President pro tempores was between 1911 and 1913. The Senate was split between progressive Republicans and conservative Democrats. Each Party put forth a candidate, and the ballots were deadlocked until a compromise was reached. Democratic candidate Augustus Bacon served as pro tempore for one day; thereafter, he and four Republicans rotated holding the seat for the remainder of the 62nd Congress.

CHAPTER 37

All Is Not Hunky Dory

PRESS BRIEFINGS AT THE WHITE HOUSE were less than cordial. Umberto tried to remain calm, but questions were getting testier, especially about the rejection of Jared for Vice President. Jorge deflected that by stating, "I will not take that question."

For the time being, Gerry refrained from getting involved. She worked her sources and produced solid stories. She realized it was taking her longer than she thought to get back into the routine to which she had become accustomed.

Some of the others were beginning to show their annoyance with Bouchard, his seeming unlimited access to the President. Umberto tried to point out if they wanted an interview with the President, all they had to do was ask. He was careful not to get to the point where he would be accused of favoritism, or trying to control access to other White House staff members.

One day, he explained the situation to the President, and asked, "Sir, would you be amenable to an informal off-the-record chat with groups of correspondents?"

He thought for a moment and answered, "OK, but space them out. I think perhaps six at a time would be the limit."

When Jorge announced this at the next briefing, there was applause. "You divide yourselves into those groups of six and let me know the availability, and I will run it by the President to set a mutually agreeable date."

* * * *

While Simpson had been compromised for the time being, Senator Cummings fumed, not always silently. He was about to lose the title of President pro tempore. Although mostly ceremonial, it was an affirmation of respect for the longest serving member of the Senate. What stuck in his craw the most, however, is that he would be losing his security protection provided by the Capitol Police. He enjoyed the notoriety of having plain clothes officers hovering around him 24/7. He rode to and from his office not only with guards in the limo, but trailed by an SUV with more guards. They even provided protection at his residence. He would be just another Senator now.

CHAPTER 38

The Blood Hound Sniffs Around

BOUCHARD CONTINUED TO GO BACK OVER the manifests of the flight to determine whether he had overlooked something. He had the nagging feeling there was something behind the scenes regarding Dr. Frankhauser being on the flight. On a hunch, he began checking the daily visitors list for the Oval Office. Yes, he was the White Physician, but still he seemed to be making an unusual number of visits. And, the President's annual checkup at Bethesda Naval Medical Center was not due for some time. One of the staff aides outside of the Oval Office made note of Bouchard's interest, and reported it to the Press Secretary. From then on, there were not any notations of his visits.

Also, he felt it was time to turn his attention to the "mysterious" Dr. Rodriguez. Where did she fit in? And, why was she on board anyhow? Was there some connection with Dr. Frankhauser? Since her specialty was rare children's diseases, was someone's child ill at the U.S. Embassy in Moscow?

Wait a second, he mumbled. The Air Force One manifests only list those who get on the plane, but not those who get off. Therefore, he could not determine whether she got off at Andrews. She got a free ride to Moscow, but how would she get back to Puerto Rico? Is she back in Puerto Rico? If not, why not?

He had a Plan A and a Plan B. His first effort was to ask Umberto whether there were any manifests listing those who left Air

Force One flights in general. Jorge immediately knew what Bouchard was after and responded, "I don't think anyone ever has asked that question. I can check, but I doubt it." When the expected answer came back, Bouchard went to Plan B. It would involve a major bluff.

"State Department press office," the voice said.

"This is Bouchard, a White House correspondent," he announced. "I'm doing a feature story about American doctors with specific specialties they share with doctors in other countries around the world. Sometimes they do it through professional publications. Other times, they are invited to go to another country to lecture."

"Is this a general question, or do you have a specific doctor and a specific country?" the voice asked.

"As a matter of fact I do," Bouchard answered. "I understand a Dr. Inez Rodriguez recently flew to Russia. She is an expert in rare children's diseases in her native Puerto Rico. Could I assume correctly that she would have to check in with our Embassy in Moscow?"

"Yes, that's normal procedure," the voice replied. "Do you have specific dates?"

Bouchard responded, "I only have the date she arrived. I want to get in touch with her, but I don't know whether she still is in Moscow or has returned." (Thankfully the voice did not suggest he could get that information from Puerto Rico.)

"Give me your phone number and I'll get back to you," the voice said. Bouchard was happy to do so because that would confirm he was a White House correspondent.

An hour later, Bouchard was told, "She still is there working with some Russian doctors. I'm not sure what they're doing, but it's something high level."

He took one more chance. "Any way I can reach her there?" he asked. "I'm on a deadline, and I have to verify some medical information only she can give."

There was a pause, and the voice said, "Here's the direct number to the Embassy. Try the press officer there."

"You have been extremely helpful, and I really appreciate it!" Bouchard effused. He could not dial the number quickly enough.

"U.S. Embassy," the new voice said.

Bouchard went through the song-and-dance once more with the same questions about Dr. Rodriguez. He added one more vital query. "I know she arrived on Air Force One with President Merriwether on (he gave the date)."

He was surprised at the pause before being asked, "May I call you back?"

Bouchard tried a different ploy, and gave the White House switchboard number with his extension. He knew that would verify he was who he said he was.

The call was returned an hour later. He decided the press officer had to get clearance for any response. When it came, Bouchard was stunned: "Whether a Dr. Rodriguez is or is not in Moscow is not a matter for us to discuss." He was about to hang up in defeat when the caller added, "You should check on her with the White House Press Secretary for any further information."

"Maybe I bit off more than I can chew," he mused. "I know she flew to Moscow, and I'll bet she's still there. If it was important enough for her to fly on Air Force One, that was no pleasure trip. What the hell is going on?"

Although things had become quiet in the White House – President Merriwether had gone to Camp David along with Jared – Bouchard felt compelled to solve the mystery of Dr. Rodriguez. He spent a lot of time on his computer researching the Russian hierarchy. Then, he had a thought. He typed in the name of President Borochenkov, and scrolled down to his biography. Not much here – wife, three married children, grandfather of five. Oh, hell, he decided. Enough is enough. Maybe I should go up to Camp David for a rest.

He logged off, and was about to leave when he plopped down in his chair. No other reporters were there, so he could think out loud: "Wait a damn minute! Dr. Rodriguez – rare disease expert for children. President Borochenkov has grandchildren! Could that be the connection? But, why?" He logged back on and spent half an hour searching and searching. But, nothing! He had hit a dead end. He did not think he could pull off another bluff with the U.S. Embassy in Moscow. If he persisted, the Russians might report him to the State Department. He finally decided to leave well enough alone. Maybe something will develop on its own later on. However, he would not forget this.

* * * *

Bouchard's "spy" in the Camp David area called him to say he noticed a government sedan approaching the compound. As usual, the "spy" would jot down the license plate numbers. Bouchard was able to narrow down such plates as to which government agency had them. This vehicle came from the Bethesda Naval Medical Center.

* * * *

While he was showering the next morning after a fitful night's sleep of frustration, another idea came to him. He quickly dried himself off, and put on jeans and a sweat shirt. Sitting down at his laptop, he typed in "Air Force One Pilots." The most recent name was Colonel Martin MacAfee. He then searched for any stories on him – there were none. He typed in the name, and it gave his background. Next, he called the Air Force public affairs office and asked permission to interview Colonel MacAfee for a feature story. Arrangements were made for Bouchard to meet him in the public affairs office in the Pentagon the following day. An officer explained he would sit in on the interview.

After some innocuous questions, Bouchard asked him, "Were there any unusual circumstances on your last flight, the one to Moscow?"

The Colonel answered, "Not really, except it was long."

"Long enough to require a relief cockpit crew?" he followed up.

"That was more a precaution than a necessity," MacAfee responded.

"Colonel, I don't want to get into security matters, so if you cannot answer my questions, I'll understand," Bouchard explained.

"Sure, no problem," the Colonel replied.

"I assume you get a list of the crew and passengers," he continued.

"Standard procedure," was the response.

"I understand there were some doctors aboard," Bouchard said blandly.

"That's not classified. Sure. Dr. Frankhauser and Dr. Rodriguez," he explained.

"Who?" Bouchard asked, feigning surprise. "I know who Dr. Frankhauser is, but Dr. Rodriguez is new to me."

"Oh, she's an expert is children's diseases," MacAfee replied. "I was kind of surprised she was on board. Nice woman, though. I got to talk with her because I get teased since I never had my tonsils removed. She laughed about that, but said her specialty was working with children."

"Pardon my curiosity, but I don't get it why someone like that would be on a flight like yours," Bouchard said. "Dr. Frankhauser is the White House physician, so that's understandable."

"I wondered too," the Colonel said. "But, I don't ask about things like that. I'm kind of busy driving the bus." Both of them laughed at that, but not the public affairs officer.

"I understand none of my fellow White House correspondents were allowed off the plane," Bouchard continued. "Did that go for the two doctors?"

"Correction," MacAfee said. "The reporters were taken to an area in the airport, but I heard they did not have their passports, so they had to remain there. Funny you should ask, but I don't remember Dr. Rodriquez coming back on. You understand I had a lot of other things on my mind, like making sure we had plenty of gas for the return flight. I had to laugh about who was going to take her back. Oh, by the way, I remember now that one of my crewmen said he had to take off her luggage and medical bag. He said he remembered her explaining she had to see a patient. Honestly, what passengers do or don't do isn't in my job description."

"Colonel," Bouchard said matter of factly, "I was just curious, but that's not something I would include in my article. I am just focusing on you."

"Thank you for saying that," MacAfee responded. "I know people wonder about my full time job here. I've looked up the other Air Force One pilots, and we're just a bunch of jet jockeys." Again, the two of them laughed.

Bouchard went into some more questions about his background, and whether flying Air Force One was different from other aircraft he had flown.

"The chow on board sure is better," the Colonel chuckled. "Some Presidents like to sit up in the cockpit for the heck of it, but Mr. Merriwether did not. It's no big deal."

When his questions were exhausted, Bouchard thanked Colonel MacAfee "for spending time with me."

"Next time you're part of the pool, be sure to come up and visit the cockpit," he said. "It's not a stick-shift, so you ought to be able to drive it."

"That's a deal," Bouchard said, offering one of his few smiles.

Back home in front of his laptop, he did type out a feature story. Now he was certain Dr. Rodriguez was in Moscow to examine or treat a child of an important person, and not to give a lecture. How to go beyond that? He was frustrated because he had hit another dead end.

CHAPTER 39

The "Chat"

CONGRESS WAS BACK IN SESSION a few days after New Year's Day, and things looked much different because there were many new faces in the House and Senate. There now was only a slender Progressive majority in the House, and an equal number in the Senate. But, there was no Vice President serving as the Senate President. Nor, was there a clear-cut President pro tempore to preside in his absence.

Meanwhile, President Merriwether was back at work in the Oval Office. He scheduled a prime time television version of a "fireside chat" made famous by President Franklin D. Roosevelt, who used radio to outline his agenda for the year. Reporters, lawmakers, and the public would remark how rested the President looked.

He cited global warming as one of his main concerns, and stressed the importance of the upcoming visit of Russian President Borochenkov.

"I also want to explain why we will hold discussions at the Bardon Foundation's conference center in Northern Virginia," he said to open his "chat." "One of that organization's functions is as a center for young reporters interested in covering government as a career. These will be men and women on scholarships similar to the Neiman Foundation Fellowships at Harvard University. Their work will be critiqued by reporters who cover the White House, Capitol Hill, and the various agencies of the federal government.

"As to statehood for the District of Columbia and Puerto Rico, this is not a new effort, but one that should reach resolution. As you recall, this was a priority of former President Fairchild.

"The economy still is unsteady. I will work with the Congress to develop a strategy that benefits the majority of Americans, not just a few.

"There is another matter I want to bring to your attention. My visit to Russia apparently caused some consternation. In hindsight, perhaps the procedure we used at my direction might not have been the best one. I apologize again for any anguish it may have caused. Yes, it involved a risk. However, I sincerely believe in the final analysis you will understand why it was worth that risk.

"With the new structure of Congress, there will be much to do in this session. I am ready to work with lawmakers to achieve a solid society. We all need to do better, and we can.

"Thank you, and good night."

CHAPTER 40

Congress Has Its Own Headache

Speaker Vance told Alicia the President's agenda was not the House's. She received the same assessment from Majority Leader Winters in the Senate. "Neither of them could specify just what the agenda should be," she explained.

This infuriated the Conservatives, and Simpson figured out a way to take advantage of that even though he was a Representative, not a Senator. He had his "in" through Senator Cummings. He arranged to have a private lunch with Cummings to lay out his strategy to create a political headache for President Merriwether." Cummings almost choked on his sandwich.

"Senator, I've heard that some of the new Progressive congressmen are not real happy with the direction the leadership is going," Simpson began. "They call themselves 'The Young Turks.' They think there is too much liberalism from Mr. Vance. They're either sorta middle-of-the-road to conservative. They're kinda keepin' quiet about that, but there's enough of them to give Mr. Vance fits with the slim majority."

"Mah boy," the Senator interrupted, "you're talkin' 'bout our own Party!"

Simpson did not flinch. "Sir, our Party didn't do right 'bout you," he responded, "and they ain't done right 'bout me."

"Mah boy," Cummings replied, "it's not so much about the Party as it is about thet tricky Mr. President Merriwether, and thet you-know-what Wein somethin' who calls hisself Winston like those cig'rets."

"Whatever," Simpson commented. "Senator, what I have in mind is that when it comes to a close vote, we can bargain with the Speaker to get something in return for our votes – like getting on some committees or even sub-committees."

"Mah boy, where do Ah come in?" the Senator asked.

"Haven't you done a lot of favors over the years?" Simpson asked in return.

"Sure have, but Ah never asked anythin' in return 'cause thet's agin mah nature," Cummings answered. "Ah jest did my job and kept mah constituents happy."

"Sir, that's why you're so respected, even though they screwed you out of being President pro tempore," Simpson asserted. "The voters expressed their uneasiness with the President by creating the tie in the Senate.

"Okay, mah boy," the Senator said. "Let's see how this plays out." Cummings never realized Simpson was planning a future run for the Senate, and could use his help there. That was a long shot, but his egotism dismissed the thought of not succeeding. And, he had an even larger ploy in mind.

* * * *

Secrets do not stay that way very long on Capitol Hill, so a tip about the Cummings-Simpson tete-a-tete reached Diane. She had to check that out thoroughly because the Congressman was slowly getting a reputation as a self-delusional king maker. Because Simpson could not help insinuating he had become a power-behind-the-throne – which he was only in his own eyes – Diane did not have to look too far to confirm the tip.

She called Alicia, and asked if she could come to the White House "on a delicate matter."

"On the record, or off?" Alicia asked.

"Off, for the time being," Diane answered.

Alicia replied, "I don't feel confident about that. Not that many years ago, a reporter was termed a 'co-conspirator' by the government in an alleged spy secrets leak case."

Diane quickly responded, "This is nothing at all like that."

Alicia hesitated before saying, "OK, but only if you do not even say 'the information came from a high level source in the White House.'"

Diane said, "I won't even use such language. I'll come up with something we both can agree on before I run with the story. Fair enough?"

Alicia responded, "It could mean my career if you screw me."

Diane promised, "I have my own integrity. I couldn't live with myself professionally if, as you say, 'I screwed you. I'll be right over."

When Diane arrived, Alicia asked her, "What's so 'delicate' that we have have to meet in person?"

Diane then detailed what she had heard and confirmed.

"Are you asking me for a comment?" Alicia asked. "If so, the answer is no."

Diane responded, "In all honesty, I can go with what I have. I'm really looking for some guidance on this. Any reaction the President might have will be helpful. And, I would not quote the President, or you."

"I've been told I know the game of poker, so this sounds like pretty high stakes," Alicia explained.

"Yes, I certainly understand that," Diane agreed, "but this could have some serious implications politically. Frankly, the President sounded almost altruistic in his 'chat' the other day. With a slim margin in the House, a tie in the Senate, and Simpson trying to shake things up behind the scenes, there could be utter chaos on The Hill which could sap the President's political strength."

"You've given me a lot to think about," Alicia said."

Diane got up from her chair and said, "I think you and I work well together without compromising our professional integrity.'

They shook hands. No sooner had Diane left than Alicia went over to Jared's office, and asked if they could have a closed door talk. After she presented the gist of her meeting with Diane, Jared said, "I'll speak to the President about this, but I need to tell him you got this information from Ms. Bana. There have been times when disturbing news has been kept from a President. I've known him too long to fall into that trap. I appreciate your alerting me. By the way, I share the President's admiration for how you are bearing up under the pressure."

She thanked him, and promised herself the pressure would not take a toll on her relationship with Tim.

CHAPTER 41

He Won't Give Up; Neither Will She

BOUCHARD WAS CALLING his friend Rico once again.

"You want me to do what, mi amigo?" Rico asked.

"I think I'm onto something hot, and you've got to help me out," Bouchard pleaded. "I'll owe you BIG time!"

"Si, I get it!" Rico responded. "Tell me again what you need."

"I need as much information as possible on Dr. Rodriguez, especially the major research work she's doing, or has done," Bouchard replied. "Just saying she's into rare children's diseases is not enough. If I know something more specific than that, it could unlock a BIG TIME exclusive for me."

Rico hesitated, "Mi amigo, that could take some time."

Bouchard tried to hold back his anxiety and asserted, "What if I told you this could explain the mystery trip of Air Force One and President Merriwether?!"

"Now, that's a different story!" Rico responded, laughing at his own pun. "I'm sorry, but I could not resist that. I will get right on it and be back to you ASAP, as you people say."

* * * *

The return call came four hours later. Even Bouchard would be impressed.

"You are one crazy man, mi amigo!" Rico laughed. "You really are on to something."

"All right, quit stalling," Bouchard said now annoyed.

"As my cousin in London used to say, hold on to your knickers!" Rico roared.

"I'm going to hang up now, hijo de puto!" Bouchard threatened.

"Who you calling a bastard?" Rico finally said. "Can't a guy have a little fun?"

"Spit it out, and now!" Bouchard asserted.

"Dr. Rodriguez has been doing general research on rare ninos's diseases for some time now," he began, "but recently she made some kind of discovery that could make her world famous. It's something called – I'll have to spell it out – P R O G E R I A. You'll have to look that up yourself. She's been experimenting with some medications made from herbs whose plants are native to her area."

Bouchard interrupted: "Why didn't you get that information the first time I asked to check on Dr. Rodriguez?"

"Hey," he responded, "you didn't say how deep I should go. I thought you only wanted some general stuff."

"I'm sorry, I'm sorry," Bouchard apologized. "I still have my notes from what you told me last time. Muchas gracias, mi amigo. You've really been a life savior."

"De nada," Rico responded.

Bouchard could not hang up fast enough so he could start his Google search. He found a report from the Mayo Clinic which described progeria as "rapid aging." He found a link to a book titled "When Bad Things Happen To Good People" written by Rabbi Harold S. Kushner. His son had this disease, and by age 13 he died as if he were an old man. The Mayo Clinic report stated succinctly: "There's no cure for progeria."

"Holy shit!" Bouchard exhaled. "Some high official in Russia has a grandson who has progeria," he reasoned out loud. As he read further, these words caught his eye: "Drugs known as farnesyltransferase inhibitors (FTIs), which were developed for treating cancer, have shown promise in laboratory studies in correcting the cell mutation that causes progeria." He also found another link identifying a Progeria Research Foundation, located in the North Shore region of Massachusetts. Further research revealed that it had awarded Dr. Rodriguez a sizeable grant.

On a hunch, he called the Foundation. He explained he was doing a story on Dr. Rodriguez and knew she had recently flown to Russia (he neglected to add it was on Air Force One). He was referred to what passed for the press office, and the trip was confirmed. "She called us to say how excited she was to have been asked by President Merriwether to make the trip to check out the grandson of an important government official," the voice on the phone explained.

Bouchard almost was too anxious to ask the obvious next question: "By any chance did she mention the name of that official?"

The voice answered, "I'm not sure I should reveal that."

"I promise I will not reveal my source," he began. "Believe me when I say this story will put the Foundation in a great light." (He almost gagged at using such a trite phrase.)

"Well, since you work in the White House (he had identified himself), and you won't quote me . . ."

"You have my word," he replied.

In a hushed voice, she said . . . . .

He thanked her profusely, and rocked back in his chair.

* * * *

Diane had a dilemma. As she warned Alicia, she could go with what she had. But, she began to feel there was a lot more going on than she originally thought. Could Congress be on the verge of imploding politically for personal reasons? And then, she caught an unbelievable break.

Her oldest sister, Melanie Chapman, was the top administrative aide in the Office of the Director of the Bethesda Naval Medical Center. They would have a monthly Sunday brunch together at a chic French restaurant in the heart of Bethesda called Mon Ami Gabi. In good weather, they would sit outside along Woodmont Avenue. It was one of those days as they the met.

"Those lawmakers sure got you hopping," Melanie said, after they ordered. "I enjoy your reports."

Diane thanked her, and continued, "I think I'm hot on the trail of some big stuff!"

"Like what?" Melanie persisted.

"I really can't say at this point," Diane answered, "but, I think there will be some fireworks on Capitol Hill, and I don't mean the July 4th ones."

"Diane," Melanie said hesitatingly, "I probably shouldn't tell you this because the White House is not your beat, but, there is something that has been nagging me. I could use your opinion."

"I don't have a clue what you're driving at," Diane responded.

Melanie looked around and lowered her voice. "Dr. Frankhauser, my boss, has been spending what seems to me to be a lot of time with the President."

"What do you mean by that?" Diane asked.

"Do you know he was on Air Force One when it ended up in Moscow?" Melanie asked in return.

"What does that have anything to do with anything?," she answered. "He's the White House physician."

"In all the years I've been in my job, I don't remember the boss doing that unless the President has had a medical problem that's been noted in the press," Melanie continued. "When President Reagan was shot, that was a different story."

"What are you getting at?" Diane asked.

"I have a feeling President Merriwether has a medical problem," Melanie replied almost in a whisper.

"He looked pretty healthy in his television appearance the other night," she commented.

"Yes, I agree," Melanie replied, "but, some of Dr. Frankhauser's visits have not been officially recorded. For example, I found out he slipped up to Camp David not long ago. And, he's made more than the usual visits to the Oval Office recently. Maybe my imagination is running away with me, but I have an uneasy feeling about this."

Diane stopped eating, taking in every word. Finally she said quietly, "This could have a tremendous impact on his relationship with Congress. I'll do some poking around, but, so far I haven't heard anything on The Hill about the President's physical health. I've been hearing a lot about his political health, though."

After their brunch ended, and they went their separate ways, Diane went back to her apartment to do some serious thinking. One of the decisions she had to make was how to follow up on what Melanie had intimated without arousing suspicion. She doubted she could go back to Alicia with this approach because either Alicia would know but would not comment, or Alicia did not know but would wonder why she would bring up the subject of the President's health.

While Diane was pondering the implication of this, her mind went back to rumors she was hearing about Simpson. Does this very junior congressman know something about the President? The more she thought about that, the more she concluded he was not that smart, or he would have made something of it already.

She decided, as discreetly as possible, to ask her sources in the House and the Senate about any change in strategy. If any of the leadership knew or believed the President had a medical problem, they would be bolder in their dealings with the White House.

Ironically, Alicia had her own network of sources, and some of them crossed paths with Diane's. That is how Alicia learned Diane was making an unusual number of inquiries around The Capitol about the President's health.

Diane really did not have enough to go with on the air, but the potential impact of this could not be ignored. She just would have to make discreet contact with her sources, although . . .

At first, the idea seemed preposterous. Like Bouchard, she had majored in Journalism. She remembered what one professor – who had been a reporter – observed: "When you least expect it, a big story will plop into your lap. Sometimes you have to go with your professional gut, and make things happen. You just have to keep good contact with your sources." Her gut "told" her to pursue the idea.

* * * *

Congressman Simpson was totally surprised when he received the call from Diane.

"I hear you are an up and coming member of the House," she lied. "I thought we ought to meet some time. I'm not working on any particular story (she continued to lie), but I like to meet the people on my beat."

Simpson fell for the ruse, and responded with his own lie: "I've been a fan of yours for some time. A face-to-face would be great any time you want."

She replied, "Well, there's no time like the present. How's your calendar for this afternoon?"

His calendar did not have any appointments for that time, but he did not want to seem too anxious, so he said, "How's about 4 o'clock this afternoon in my office?"

She answered, matching his bluff: "Hold on while I check." She waited about 30 seconds, and replied again lying, "I have a 5 o'clock, but I can fit in the 4. See you then."

* * * *

Diane arrived 10 minutes late, lying that she had a last minute phone call. After the small talk, she asked: "Congressman Simpson, what do you see as your role in this session?" She had carefully prepared that question he could not answer with a yes or no. She also had heard about his verbosity.

The Congressman grinned broadly and answered, "Well now, for one thing, I see a change in the relationship between Congress and the White House."

"In what way?" she posed.

"Well now, I see the House as being more pro-active, not waiting for the President to pass off to us whatever is on his mind," Simpson explained, not demonstrating any accent. "We can take matters into our own hands."

Diane asked, "Can you give a specific example?"

"Well now, one comes to mind," he offered. "The President seems to push for statehood for the District and Puerto Rico. That's not anywhere strong on the radar here on The Hill. Then there's the global warning business. Ms. Dana – "It's Bana, with a B," she interrupted – excuse me, Ms. Bana, not everyone believes the climate needs to be changed."

She interrupted again: "Excuse me, Mr. Simpson, but I don't recall anyone talking about us changing the climate. I believe the President merely said he is convening a conference of world leaders to discuss the matter. Are you saying the climate is not changing?"

"I'm talking about the political climate on The Hill!" he asserted, proud of the pun. "As you know, there's only a slim margin in the House for our Progressive Party, and an even split in the Senate. The President has to understand that in the past the Progressives had their way in both chambers. Times have changed. Why, just the other day I was talking with Senator Cummings about this very matter."

Whoa, she said to herself. Since when is this young House whippersnapper chatting up the Senator, who for all intents and purposes only had a ceremonial title but no power? She let that go for the moment.

"Let's talk about President Merriwether," she introduced a new subject. "You're in your second term, right?"

"Yes," he answered, not knowing where this was going now.

"Is it safe to say you really have not had too much of a chance to work with him so you can know him?" she asked.

"Well now, not yet," he almost mumbled. "As I said, times are changing."

"Would you like to be more specific?" she persisted.

"Well now, I think we're getting a bit off the track," he responded. "I think the President is a fine man, and I wish him well. But, since you brought this up, Ms. Dana (this time, she let it go), I don't think he exercised good judgment running off to Moscow with that mysterious maneuver of his with Air Force One. What was that all about? We really don't know. (There was no stopping Simpson now, Diane said whimsically to herself). And then, he's invited that Russian."

Diane decided she did not have any choice now and bore in. "Mr. Merriwether has not been in the Oval Office all that long, and you seem to be making a harsh judgment. Do your colleagues feel the same way?"

"Well now, I can't give you figures, but a lot of them tell me they feel the same way I do," Simpson boasted. She knew he was full of hot air, but that was not the purpose of the interview – although she had some juicy quotes to use.

"Congressman," she continued, "are you implying there is a revolt brewing in the House?"

Simpson almost jumped out of his chair because he did not expect her to give him what he considered the opening of his career. "I'm pleased you asked me that question!" he began. "You used that word 'revolt,' not I. You have to be careful about definitions. I would say there are questions my colleagues are raising that could – and I emphasize could – challenge not only the President but maybe even the leadership. You might want to check with Senator Cummings to see if there is a similar feeling over there."

At this point, Diane decided to drop the bombshell question: "Congressman, what scenario can you envision if, for example, President Merriwether did not serve out his full term?" (She knew he did not speak for the House, but she might smoke out whether he knew anything about the President's health.)

"Well now, whew!" he stumbled. "That's a mouthful of a question." (She stifled a giggle. Talk about the pot calling the kettle black . . .) Contrary to his usual way of responding, he hesitated before continuing, "As I recall, there was talk when Mr. Winston was first nominated that the House never would approve that. He did not get my vote. I would have preferred Speaker Vance. But, it is what it is. I'd say President Merriwether better stay healthy."

Diane saw her chance and asked, "Is there any reason to believe the President has a medical problem?"

"Well now, I really couldn't say," he started to answer. "Now that you bring it up, I did hear some talk about why that Dr. What's-his-name from Bethesda Hospital was on that weird flight if the President was healthy. Maybe you know whether he's been on other flights with the President."

"No, he hasn't," she offered. "Would it make any difference on The Hill if the President did have health problems?"

"Well now, oh yeah!" he responded before thinking. "If he's weak, we're strong!" (He later would regret spouting off like that, but for now Diane had all she needed.)

* * * *

Before she went on the air, Diane called Alicia and said she would be using other sources. "I'll let you know in advance if there are questions beginning to surface about the President's health," Diane explained.

Alicia immediately told Jared, who told the President.

* * * *

Usually Diane just went with straight news. This night, she received permission to editorialize. "Does the President have a health problem?" was her theme.

* * * *

Bouchard decided Diane did not have a clue about Dr. Rodriquez.

CHAPTER 42

Ever The Twain Shall Meet

Alicia called Tim and invited him to her townhouse in Old Town Alexandria. "I haven't cooked a meal in ages," she explained.

"Can I bring something?" he asked.

"Just yourself," she replied.

She had enough time to go to the beauty shop, do some shopping, start preparing dinner, and pick out a dress for the evening. At work, she almost always wore a pants suit.

When Tim arrived, he had flowers and two bottles of very good wine – one red, one white.

If all went well, she expected Tim to stay all night. She was surprised when he kept looking at his watch. Finally she asked, "Got a date? Is this a two-fer evening?" She meant to tease, but he was serious.

The minute he said "Alicia," she knew something was wrong. "Look, we need to talk."

She half-meant to be flippant in responding, "Is this going to be a Dear Joan announcement?" (She was referring to the World War II letters servicemen overseas received from their sweethearts at home which began, 'Dear John.' It usually meant a break-up.)

He was serious. "I don't know how you're able to manage your time with all the responsibilities of being congressional liaison. A relationship would interfere, and I can't do that to you."

Alicia could not remember the last time she shed even one tear. "Tim, what are you saying? This relationship is exactly what I need.

I never said this before, but to use a trite phrase, it's lonely at the top. I don't want a life that's all work and no romance!"

He took a deep breath and answered, "Alicia, I love you very much, and that never will change. Right now, we both are under a lot of professional pressure. Trying to grab a few minutes now and then is not fair to both of us. On that flight to Moscow, I spent a lot of time thinking about us. I actually asked the President to let me make that brief phone call. The big meeting on global warming is going to take all my energy. From what I'm hearing and reading, your plate is over-flowing as it is. Alicia, it's me that's having a tough time. You're stronger than I am."

As he paused, she said, "I don't know why this can't work, Tim. When I heard your words from Air Force One, I realized how much I love you. Yes, we're both under pressure, but that can work itself out. Tim, darling, don't . . ." For the first time in many, many years, Alicia began crying.

Tim started to move toward her, but backed off. "I've hurt you, I know," he said. "I feel lousy about that. You're the best thing that's ever happened to me. I know how trite that sounds, but I'm not great with words. I've never been in love before, and to have someone like you share that feeling is more than I ever dreamed of."

"Why, Tim? Why?" she kept repeating. "Is there something you're not telling me?"

"I guess what I want to say – and you'll think I'm nuts – is that . . . . . one day I want to marry you. And I hope you'll still want to marry me. It's just the timing right now is wrong. You've got important work to do, and big decisions to make. I know your reputation is growing by the day. I don't want you to have to worry about having to make time for me."

"But . . ." He leaned over and kissed her wet cheek. "I can't stand in your way right now," he said.

"You're not!" she insisted.

He stood up and said, "When the time is right, I know we'll be back together –unless you get a better offer."

She could not stifle a laugh. "There'll never be a better offer," she said."I'll always be only a phone call away," he responded.

She buried her head in her hands after he left and could not stop the tears. "I've got everything, and I've got nothing," she sobbed. As she dried her eyes, she noticed something on the end table. It was a small box. When she opened it, she gasped. The engagement ring sparkled. No note, just the ring. She could not put it on fast enough – a perfect fit.

Alicia promised herself she never would wear it to the office, but the minute she got home she would put it on. It was to be a symbol of his eventual return. Suddenly, she realized there had to be something he held back, and it had to be very important. She did not have any way of knowing how right she was.

What Tim could not tell her was that on the flight, he overheard certain conversations that upset him because they could affect the woman he deeply loved. Someday he could share them with her – but not now. He hoped he was doing her a favor so she could focus all her inner political strength for the days to come.

CHAPTER 43

"Young Turk(ish)" Delight

PRIOR TO THE MID-TERM ELECTION, Simpson did not notice the change at first. Little by little, his phone calls to fellow Representatives did not get returned. Appointments he tried to get with Speaker Vance were not made. A call he put in to Senator Cummings was put on hold and never answered.

When constituents would call asking for favors, it would take what seemed like forever to get them fulfilled.

However, the seeds of discontent he had sewn were blossoming. Both Vance and Winters became aware of how some of the younger lawmakers now were exhibiting a boldness not normally tolerated. No "threats" ever were made, but it was clear they were dissatisfied with the leadership. It was not that they were threatening a revolt, but rather they would not stay in lock-step with the leadership. And much of this was occurring in the Progressive Party. As a result, the outcome of the mid-term elections could be a harbinger of things to come for the presidential campaign two years down the road.

The "Young Turks" turned to a fellow lawmaker, Merrill Conway. He was from the Midwest, and had challenged Vance earlier. Conway said he would accept the leadership of the group "but only if Congresswoman Pearlstein will be my deputy." She had long complained about the silent snubbing of women for leadership positions. The "Young Turks" unanimously approved both Conway and Pearlstein.

* * * *

It was not long before Alicia got wind of the "Young Turks" action and quickly alerted President Merriwether and Jared. "I haven't heard from Diane Bana on this, so that is a lucky break for us," she explained.

The three met in the Oval Office to discuss the situation and plan a strategy.

"We need to get the 'Young Turks' on our side," the President said.

"Mr. President," Alicia responded, "may I suggest you invite Conway and Pearlstein into the Oval Office for an off-the-record 'chat?'"

Jared responded, "Mr. President, I would suggest you consider first having such informal meetings with Speaker Vance and Senate Majority Leader Winters, followed by House Minority Leader Schoenfeld and Senate Minority Leader Amaroso. That will then justify Conway and Pearlstein."

"I second that motion, Mr. President," Alicia quickly added.

"All those in favor?" the President joked. "Seeing none, the motion is passed unanimously."

The meetings would not have any agenda, so informality would be the order of the day. Jorge was told in advance to mention the meetings at the next press briefing. Both Bouchard and Diane duly reported this, and the media opinionators generally gave the President high marks for "reaching out" to lawmaker leadership. They also concluded it was a shrewd move by the President to include the "Young Turks."

That only irritated Vance and Winters.

"Maybe two years from now, we won't have Merriwether around to make trouble for us," Vance commented after leaving the visit, not realizing how prophetic that was.

"Amen to that," Winters chimed in.

CHAPTER 44

A New Strategy

AFTER THE CONGRESS WAS SWORN IN, President Merriwether summoned Jared and Alicia to begin planning for his State of the Union message in January.

"I think we have to be realistic about statehood for the District and Puerto Rico," he began.

"Are you implying it would cost too much political capital to pursue it?" Jared asked.

"Alicia, what do you think?" President Merriwether asked.

"Mr. President, I think the mood of the Congress is such that statehood is not even on their radar," she answered. "At the same time, the inner turmoil on Capitol Hill may work to our advantage."

"How so?" the President asked.

"Sir, my sources tell me that those visits you had were received with benign political politeness," she began. "There is, if you permit the term, an ugliness I have not seen since I joined Senator Stafford's office. Some of that, to be sure, is internal. Some of that, sir, is vented toward you."

"Interesting," the President remarked.

"Sir," she continued, "if I may be blunt . . ."

"By all means, Alicia," he agreed.

"Mr. President," she went on, "there's something in the air that suggests to me some of the congressional leadership perceives you as weaker than when you succeeded President Fairchild. Some of those very lawmakers were your colleagues in the House. They thought enough of you to elect you Speaker. As I understand it, they even felt you should have become President before she did."

"That's water over the dam," he responded. "That was then, this is now. That's politics. I accept that. Their motto seems to be: 'What have you done for me lately?'"

"Sir, I understand that," Alicia defended, "it galls me just the same."

Jared finally spoke up: "We just have to be smarter than they are."

"And, how do we do that?" she asked too quickly.

"Alicia," the President answered, "I think it's time Jared and I shared some things with you that may make you understand some strategies we have worked out."

She was taken by surprise, and showed it. She was even more aghast when the President said, "Let's take a walk in the Rose Garden."

Although President Merriwether and Jared stood up, Alicia remained literally glued to her chair. "I don't understand," she finally said.

"We'll talk, and you listen," the President said, almost fatherly.

With several Secret Service men hovering behind, the three sauntered around the Rose Garden just outside of the Oval Office.

Two things occurred to Alicia. One, the President did not want to take any chance of being overheard. Two, a clever political tactic was being outlined. Ironically, a third thing crossed her mind. She now understood Tim was right to do what he did, and the way he did it. She would need all of her inner strength to deal with the days to come, and her personal life would have to be on hold.

When the walk ended, Alicia agreed to work with Jared and literally draw up a "battle plan."

CHAPTER 45

The Bluff Works

BOUCHARD STILL WAS SEETHING over Diane. He rarely showed such emotion because frankly, he rarely got scooped. OK, she got the advantage with the President's health angle. But, that left me with Dr. Rodriguez. It was time to play my ace in the hole. However, there was a risk involved.

He called Ambassador Vandergriff at the Moscow Embassy. It took some doing to get him on the line, but Bouchard was patient.

"Mr. Ambassador, thank you for taking my call," he began. "I know you're busy, so I will take as little time as possible."

"No problem, Mr. Bouchard," he replied.

"Mr. Ambassador," he began, "I'm doing a story on the President's visit to Moscow."

"Mr. Bouchard," the Ambassador interrupted, "that's been done already – you know about the return visit President Borochenkov will make."

"No, Mr. Ambassador, I'm talking about Dr. Rodriguez treating the Russian President's grandson," Bouchard said boldly, playing his own ace.

There was quite a pause as the Ambassador pondered what to say. Finally, he asked, "May I inquire where you came up with that supposition?"

Bouchard had role-played before the call, trying to anticipate such a question. "Sir, it is not a supposition," he began, not admitting it was only a conclusion of his analysis of the facts he acquired.

"I know for a fact Dr. Rodriguez is an expert in a disease called progeria, in which a child grows old so quickly that he or she literally is an old person even in their teens."

He decided to let the Ambassador mull that over and wait for a response. Since the Ambassador had not expected this type of call, he had to pause. "Mr. Bouchard," he finally replied, "you assume I have personal knowledge of this, and then, hopefully for you I can confirm it. I ask you not jump to any conclusion when I say I will have to look into this. In return, I assure you I will return your call. By the way, are you on a deadline with this?"

Bouchard would have loved to say "yes," but decided a wait would be worth it – up to a point. "Mr. Ambassador," he responded, "not an immediate one. I'll be honest with you. If I have made this call, there is the possibility other reporters will be doing the same."

The Ambassador thought for a moment before responding, "It seems we are trusting one another. I will return your call no later than 48 hours from now."

Bouchard did not have a choice at this point. He was taking a huge chance no one else would be on this angle for the next two days. "That is acceptable, Mr. Ambassador," he said.

"Thank you, Mr. Bouchard," he replied, ending the call.

Bouchard took not one but two deep breaths before saying, "Bingo!"

* * * *

Ambassador Vandergriff immediately called President Meriwether and recounted Bouchard's phone call. The President said he would call back, and summoned Jared to the Oval Office, along with Jorge.

"Bouchard is a very reputable reporter," the Press Secretary commented.

Jared said, "I think what we have is a question of timing. Sooner or later the story was bound to surface."

Jorge added, "Unless we give him a definite yes or no, he will have yet another bombshell to drop. Sir, would you consider having Ambassador Vandergriff asking Bouchard if he would agree to an embargo until the weekend when there is a news lull?"

Before the President could answer, Jared asked, "Why would he be willing to do that? And, what would we gain by the delay?"

President Merriwether pondered the dilemma and then said, "There might be one other alternative. Instead of putting Ambassador Vandergriff on the spot, he can tell Bouchard that I will give him an exclusive interview on the matter. I don't think we should pussy-foot around this. Jorge, I agree with you that stalling only would give him a second and more potent story. I have a further concern. Release of the story only would serve to further irritate Congress. In fact . . . just a second."

He reached for his phone and summoned Alicia. "She needs to be part of this now."

When Alicia arrived at the Oval Office, the President summarized what had been said, adding the reason for Dr. Rodriguez's mission, and then asked, "What is your estimate of the reaction on The Hill to publication of Bouchard's story?"

She paused, not having even considered such a question, and not knowing Bouchard was on the verge of a major scoop. Finally she said, "Mr. President, the issue would be the secrecy of the trip." She hesitated, thoughts cascading around in her mind, and continued, "Sir, you're crucified if you do, or crucified if you don't. Carried to the extreme, and considering the inner turmoil on Capitol Hill, there could be a call for impeachment in the House. If I may be blunt, you don't have the support in the House you used to have, so there could be a media circus." Jorge nodded in agreement.

The President asked Jared for any further comments. "Mr. President," Jared responded, "I think Alicia nailed it. This would become a case of damage control. Would you be ready to face action on The Hill if it comes to that?"

He knew what Jared really meant, and said, "If that's what it takes, so be it. If there are no further comments, I have a call to make to Moscow." They thought he meant to Ambassador Vandergriff. Instead, his call went to President Borochenkov first. After a long conversation, the President made his second call to the Ambassador, who phoned Bouchard and said, "President Merriwether wants to see you on this matter."

* * * *

As Bouchard was ushered into the Oval Office, he was surprised the two of them would be the only ones there.

"First of all, Mr. Bouchard, our conversation is totally on the record," President Merriwether began. "Let me start by asking you how much you know?" As Bouchard hesitated, the President added, "It will help me to fill in the blanks as best I can."

Bouchard detailed what he knew so far.

The President smiled and commented, "You are quite an investigator. If we had room in our press office, I would offer you a job. I compliment you on what you have learned. Let me start at the beginning, and stop me at any point if you need clarification or have a question."

Bouchard nodded in agreement.

"Some time ago – I can't remember the exact date – it became known to me that President Borochenkov had a grandson who was gravely ill from progeria. By pure coincidence, Dr. Frankhauser mentioned to me that he read an article by Dr. Rodriguez on experiments she was conducting on progeria. I contacted President Borochenkov with this information. Through a series of negotiations, we agreed on the Air Force One vanishing act as a cover up for getting Dr. Rodriguez to Moscow to examine the boy, and determine whether anything could be done for him.

"To justify the trip to Moscow, President Borochenkov suggested we discuss his true concern over the effect global warming is having on northern Siberia. I felt if the talk went as I hoped it would, I could invite Mr. Borochenkov to the Bardon Foundation, which is why Tim Anderson also was on board Air Force One.

"I hope you understand why I could not reveal Tim's presence ahead of time, and why I could not reveal Dr. Rodriguez's presence at all. The only way all of this could work was to have Air Force One vanish from radar over the Bermuda Triangle."

The President paused to give Bouchard a chance to ask questions. He had one ready. "Mr. President, had you considered the effect of Air Force One disappearing?"

"Yes," he responded. "I expected the backlash. In the larger scheme of things, I felt it was the only way to accomplish two actions in one."

"But, sir," Bouchard persisted, "you not only deceived the American public, but the Congress as well!"

The President did not hesitate in responding, "It was a calculated risk, I admit. But I did not see any other way to do it."

"Sir," he continued, "did you anticipate the anger and anguish you caused to the pool reporters?"

"The honest answer is no," President Merriwether answered. "I was truly sorry about that, especially the situation concerning Gerry Bartlett. That was the most unfortunate coincidence one can imagine. Press Secretary Umberto told me she has returned, and I am pleased with that."

"Mr. President," Bouchard went on, "let me get back to the effect on Congress. I understand in your absence there was a meeting of high ranking officials called the 'Emergency Situation Room Group' who were considering some drastic measures in connection with the disappearance of Air Force One. Can you comment on that?"

"Jared Winston attended those sessions, and kept me informed at all times while we were on our way to Moscow," the President explained.

Bouchard followed up immediately with, "Do you think they were planning a coup?"

President Merriwether smiled and answered, "I don't think it would have gone that far. Jared and I had discussed what could, and what would not, result."

"May I be blunt, Mr. President?" Bouchard asked.

The President smiled again, and responded, "You seem to have a reputation for that. But, yes, go ahead."

"Sir," Bouchard continued, "I'm wondering whether Congress might want to hold your feet to the fire, and call for impeachment."

"That has not happened yet, so I won't speculate," he responded.

"If that did happen . . .?" Bouchard persisted.

"While I have regrets on some aspects of the Air Force One episode, I would ask Congress and the public to look at the overall intent of my action," he began. "I could not stand by and not do anything when a grandson of President Borochenkov was terminally ill. Actually, he was the one who asked if we could bring Dr. Rodriguez to Moscow. Congress and the public should understand how global politics works. Russia and the United States have their differences, but when it comes to humanitarian – especially health – issues, that overrides other concerns."

"Are you suggesting this opens the door to détente with Russia?" he asked.

President Merriwether answered, "I am not suggesting that at all. I am trying to explain a singular situation. Of course it will not hurt Russian-American relations. By the way, I would be remiss in not acknowledging the behind-the-scenes work of Ambassador Vandergriff."

"In hindsight, sir, would you have done anything different?" Bouchard posed.

"There's an old saying that hindsight is 20/20," he responded.

Bouchard waited for more than that, but it was not forthcoming.

"Mr. President, I admit I am going to take advantage of this opportunity to interview you by turning to a totally different matter," he began. "How will all of this affect your seeking a full four-year term?"

He smiled a third time before answering: "You weren't kidding by turning to a totally different matter. I have certain plans for the near future, but if I revealed them now, that would not be fair to the rest of the White House press corps. Wouldn't you agree you have enough of an exclusive as it is?"

This time Bouchard smiled, and countered, "Well, sir, I thought I would give it a try. A second exclusive would have been nice."

At this point, he wondered whether he was overstaying his welcome, but the President wasn't indicating that. So, he thought of a question he had not considered asking.

"Mr. President," he finally said, "I wonder if you have any predictions about the next election.

Again, a smile came from the President. "Clever one, Mr. Bouchard," he replied. "After all my years in the House, I learned not to predict anything when it came to politics or the weather. Frankly, this past election almost was a disaster for our Progressive Party. That will make it so much harder for my former colleagues to pass legislation on proposals I've made. I would be lying if I did not admit I would hope for a larger majority in both the House and Senate. I am firmly committed to having checks and balances in government, and also to accepting differences of opinion. However, I would hope our country could return to some semblance of calmness. In the more than half a century, we only have had a brief time when there was not military involvement somewhere in the world. There is a price to pay for peace, but it seems not everyone is ready to pay that price."

"Sir, I just have to ask you this," Bouchard apologized. "What legacy do you feel you will leave?"

"Mr. Bouchard, you just don't give up," he replied. "The legacy I would hope for might not be what historians end up assigning to me. Let's put the shoe on the other foot. What legacy do you hope to leave?"

Never had Bouchard even considered that. He was dumbfounded. It took at least a minute for him to recover enough and respond, "Sir, I think I would like to be known for this interview."

President Merriwether burst out laughing. "Touche, Mr. Bouchard. Touche!"

Rarely has an interview ended on such a high note, Bouchard thought. He and the President shook hands, but he could not help notice it was not a firm grip. He wondered whether that meant he had indeed overstayed his welcome.

After he left the Oval Office, the President summoned Jared, Alicia, and Jorge to listen to the tape of the interview he had recorded.

Alicia was the first to respond. "Mr. President, I think you just guaranteed an impeachment procedure."

Jorge followed with, "It will be interesting to read, and hear, the press reaction to an amazing interview. Reporters will be as jealous of hell that he got it."

Jared had the last word, which puzzled the other two: "Mission accomplished, sir."

The President quietly added, "Part of it, anyhow. I think the time for Plan C may be sooner than we expected."

* * * *

Alicia and Jorge were right in their assessments of the interview.

CHAPTER 46

Repercussions And Opportunities

Bouchard's Saturday story was headlined "President Merriwether Justifies Disappearance of Air Force One." The sub-head read: "There Was A Second Reason For The Episode."

The repercussions came from two sides – the media, and The Hill.

Jorge deflected complaints from not only the White House correspondents, but also from reporters covering The Hill – although not Diane. He promised to explain at a special Sunday briefing. But, this would be after the editorial writers of print, and talking heads of television, expressed their negative views.

The Sunday briefing was acrimonious, to say the least. Jorge was pounded with angry questions, and even some statements. One that stood out was this: "What does it say about your operation, and the President, when one reporter gains a rare and exclusive interview when we have been trying to do that for some time?"

Jorge responded, "Mr. Bouchard (who sat quietly in the back of the room) had specific questions. My recollection is that almost all of you merely asked for an interview. To me, that is a big difference."

"Well, can we interview him now?" one reporter asked.

"About what?" Jorge answered politely. "About Mr. Bouchard's article? The President is not going to discuss what was printed or aired as long as it was factual. His story was factual."

Alicia fielded the anger from Members of the House and Senate, even though it was a weekend and most were home. All she could answer was, "The President stands by the accuracy of the interview."

* * * *

Bouchard was puzzled that Diane did not call to complain he scooped her. He did not know she considered it a bonus, because now she could easily get on-the-record reactions from lawmakers. When she contacted Vance and Winters, both said the same thing: "We need time to digest what was in the article." She said she would call them back on Monday.

In her usual round of checking with sources, Alicia learned that Vance and Winters held a secret meeting that day with key members of their respective bodies, which explained the delay. What she heard next had her rushing to Jared's office.

"The 'Young Turks' are so pissed off – I can't think of a better term – with the President's candor that they want some serious action," she explained. "I don't know if you heard, but apparently the 'Young Turks' movement that began in the House now has a counterpart in the Senate, but not as large."

Jared still maintained his previous sources in the House, so he became privy to what was going on there. This came usually from those seeking to curry some favor with him. After sharing that with her, he asked, "Any idea what they meant by 'serious action?'"

She hesitated before answering, "Right now, I don't have anything I can put my finger on, but I get the impression they are willing to go as far as . . . ."

"Impeachment?" he interrupted.

Alicia could not hold back her surprise. "Yes," she finally replied. "How did . . ."

"I can tell you now that we did what they call a 'risk analysis,' and that was one of the aspects we considered," Jared explained.

"We hoped it would not go this far, but maybe we've underestimated the 'Young Turks.'"

Had Jared and Alicia known it, yet another threat was taking shape.

* * * *

SecDef Bosworth could not wait to call fellow members of the ESRG to a private meeting. His first question went to Admiral Ridgely, the most outspoken member.

"Haley," Boz began, "what's your take on the President's mea culpa?"

"In a word, Mr. Secretary, political weakness," the Admiral answered.

"I'll overlook the fact you gave me two words, but they hit the nail on the head," Boz responded. "I'd like the Group to get together; however, only General McCormick can usually do that. Can we be sure no one will leak this?"

"In a word, Mr. Secretary, no," Ridgely replied.

"Well, tell me the ones you think we can trust, and I'll make the calls," Boz advised.

"One I won't call is General Francene," the Admiral responded. "We never have gotten along."

The Group would later assemble in the SecDef's private office in the E Ring of the Pentagon. McCormick was not invited. Only those with top security clearance could enter that area unless they were approved visitors. News people rarely were admitted, and only if invited to do so.

Prior to the meeting, Boz called Senator Cummings. He did not waste any time, nor mince any words: "Chris, how would you finally like to become President of the United States?"

"Boz, have you lost your marbles?" the Senator snorted.

"I'm dead serious," the SecDef replied.

"Well, let me see," he began with no trace of the exaggerated

Southern accent. "There's a fella named Merriwether who currently owns the Oval Office. Then there's Speaker Vance. So, tell me, Boz, how to do you plan to get rid of those two so I can ascend to the throne, pull a double Jimmy Hoffa?"

"Chris, stop slopping up the bourbon, and listen to me," the SecDef replied curtly. "I'm sure by now you know about the Bouchard interview with the President. This man has become as limp as a wet rag. Read what he said and how he said it. He's a one-termer. When he goes, Winston goes."

"And that leaves old Vance," Cummings interrupted.

"I'm not talking about the current situation," Boz responded. "I'm talking about the election. There's two ways of dealing with this. One, with Merriwether out of the picture, the Progressive Party will be looking for a replacement."

"And who would that be?" the Senator asked.

"I couldn't think of a better one than you!" Boz asserted.

Senator Cummings's jaw dropped. He could not speak.

"Are you still there, Chris?" Boz asked.

"I'm trying to see whether my hearing has left me," he replied. "Did you just say you want me to run for President? Who would be my running mate?"

"You don't pick one until the convention," he reminded the Senator.

"I think you're nuts, Boz," Chris commented, "but I'm still listening. Just how do you think the Party would select me as its candidate?"

"You've got the experience and the reputation," the SecDef offered. "Lawmakers know they can work with you. With you as 'Mr. Outside' and me as 'Mr. Inside,' we got a winning combination."

The Senator did not get it at first. When he did, he responded, "You as 'Mr. Inside? Are you saying you want to be my running mate?"`

Boz smiled. Cummings frowned.

The Senator paused literally with "sugar plums dancing in his head" until he added, "You know that Vance will have a hissy fit, because he probably would want the presidency for himself."

"You just got elected for another six years," Boz explained, "but Vance has to run again. Suppose we see to it that he doesn't win."

Cummings had not considered that. "But, he's the Speaker!" the Senator remarked. "That carries weight."

"Try this on for size," the SecDef continued. "Suppose those 'Young Turks' in the House decide to pressure Vance into calling for impeachment hearings against the President, and he can't control them. That puts the Speaker in a bind. After all, President Merriwether got him that position when he moved to the Oval Office. Vance owes him his loyalty, but he also has an obligation as Speaker. See what I mean?"

"And are you so sure those 'Young Turks' can accomplish that?!" the Senator smirked.

"A smart military man never reveals all of his resources," Boz snarled. "Chris, either turn me down right now, or at least tell me you could be interested!"

The Senator paused, and said, "Well, at least I have to think about it."

"That's all I need to know," Boz replied.

* * * *

He made one more call before the meeting: "Bobby Joe, I need to know who you were friendly with before you shot your mouth off."

* * * *

When McCormick learned of the rump meeting, she called the Secretary. "I did not have any alternative but to tell the President about the meeting, and my not being included," was all she said.

* * * *

"Mr. Secretary," the caller said, "the President would like to see you in the Oval Office within half an hour."

Boz was certain McCormick had told the President about the meeting. When he arrived, President Merriwether did not invite him to sit down. "I expect your letter of resignation to be on my desk by 5:00 today," he said tersely. "If not, an armed guard will escort you from the Pentagon. You only have the time left to get your personal items together."

With that, he turned on the intercom and announced, "Please have Jared come to the Oval Office."

Boz left hurriedly.

CHAPTER 47

Impeach, Or Not Impeach, That is The Question

DIANE WAS HAVING A FIELD DAY getting quotes from House lawmakers by phone. House Minority Leader Schoenfeld commented, "Most Conservative Party members I surveyed feel a sense of uneasiness with the whole tone of the interview."

"How is that?" Diane pressed.

"We feel he exhibited a lack of sound judgment in using such a wild ruse to cozy up to Russian President Borochenkov," she answered. "We should try to maximize on the fact Russia seems to have a more moderate leader than Mr. Putin, but not the way he did it."

"Well, Congresswoman Schoenfeld, how would you have done it differently?" Diane persisted.

"I am not in a position to have spoken with Ambassador Vandergriff, who knew of the ruse, or I would be able to give you an answer. The end did not justify the method."

"How would you explain the last remark in view of the fact one of the objects of the trip was to offer medical help to President Borochenkov's gravely ill grandson?" Diane asked.

"Of course we pray for the child's recovery," Schoenfeld responded, "but what does that say about the Russian medical community?"

"If I may, I want to pursue that further," Diane bore in. "Dr. Rodriguez apparently is the only one in the world experimenting with a drug that apparently could be the child's last hope. The

Mayo Clinic seems to think enough of her work to have granted her a large grant."

The Congresswoman retorted, "I think we've explored this far enough. Is there any other topic you want to raise?"

"Yes," Diane replied. "There is talk that some members of the House would like to hold impeachment hearings on the matter of the trip. What is your view on that?"

"Yes, by all means," she answered. "The judgment of a President is paramount, and should be challenged when appropriate."

"Is this the appropriate time?" Diane continued

"My colleagues seem to think it is," Schoenfeld answered.

"How far would your colleagues want to take such hearings?" she persisted.

"I'm not sure I understand your question," the Congresswoman replied.

"Would you go so far as impeachment?" Diane challenged.

There was more than just a minor pause. Finally, Schoenfeld responded, "Wherever the hearings take us."

* * * *

When Diane caught up with Speaker Vance, she recounted the answers the Minority Leader had given. "Is the mood of the Progressive Party the same as the Conservative the way the Minority Leader has expressed it?" she asked.

"Of course I'm biased, being a fellow Progressive Party member as is President Merriwether," Vance began, "but I feel we must give him the benefit of the doubt. He is the leader of our country, after all. We might have some disagreements with him from time to time, just as a parent often has disagreements with a son or daughter. His dual aims of reaching out to President Borochenkov on such a vital concern as global warming, and facilitating the expertise of a doctor who just might be able to save his grandchild, are commendable without doubt."

"But, Mr. Speaker, the larger question is the method he used, isn't it?" she asked.

"You called it the 'larger question,' Ms. Bana, I didn't," he responded testily. "If enough Members of the House decide to pursue hearings, that will be the way it will be done."

"Sir, I have to follow that up with this question," she continued. "If a strong minority of Members want to start impeachment proceedings, would you hold them?"

"Ms. Bana, that's hypothetical," he retorted. "I don't deal in the hypothetical. Anything else?"

"No, Mr. Speaker, thank you," she replied.

* * * *

It took only minutes after Diane did what she felt was an unbiased broadcast that represented both sides than the phone lines to the station lit up like a Christmas tree. In addition, there were electronic messages galore. The one that intrigued her most came from Congressman Simpson: "If you think your report was fair, interview members of the 'Young Turks.'"

She was embarrassed that she had not considered that, even though she knew they existed. "Give me a name," she finally responded. He did. She called, and what she heard she decided would be a bombshell.

First, she called Alicia, and asked for her assessment of the broadcast. "Off the record, of course," Alicia began, "I thought you did a balanced job."

Diane hesitated and asked, "What if I told you the 'Young Turks' might be thinking about calling for impeaching the President?"

Alicia did not hesitate to answer, "You know darn well I never would address such a question. If you can back that up, then go with it. Everyone is entitled to his or her opinion, but impeachment of a President is a monumental issue!"

As soon as the call ended, Alicia reported Diane's question to President Merriwether, Jared, and Jorge.

The President said, "You said the right thing, Alicia. You're beginning to earn your pay." As soon as he hung up, he summoned Jared to the Oval Office for a private conversation that was not recorded.

* * * *

Chip Bascomb's father, Charles Sr., was a Representative for 12 terms. He only retired when his son was old enough to replace him in a sure-thing election. Chip (a nickname as in 'a chip off the old block') was Charles Jr. Charles Sr. believed his son would continue to carry on under the Progressive Party banner. But Chip was Conservative and campaigned on a platform of small government and "clean" officials. His father died literally of a broken heart.

It was not long before Chip became the new leader of the "Young Turks" succeeding Simpson. He was appalled at the rationale President Merriwether used to explain the Air Force One disappearance. "He took advantage of his office for a mysterious and questionable personal mission that caused chaos and anguish," Chip told Diane when she interviewed him."

When she pressed him further about what action might result, he said, "He must be held accountable for his actions. A defense through an interview just does not cut it in my mind."

"As the leader of the 'Young Turks,' define 'held accountable,'" Diane posed.

"My fellow 'Young Turks' – and I am proud to be identified with that group – and I are discussing this as we speak," he responded.

Diane countered, "Let me put a fine point on it. Do you believe there should be action in the House that could lead to impeachment?"

Chip did not hesitate in answering, "If the House believes the crime fits the punishment, impeachment should be considered."

Diane did not want to correct his misuse of a famous theory of justice, and continued, "Will you then ask the Speaker to hold such a hearing? And if you do, what charge would or could be brought?

"We'll cross that bridge when we come to it," he answered (getting that aphorism correct). "I have asked for an appointment with Speaker Vance."

* * * *

Vance had been trying to avoid Chip, but Diane's report of the interview forced his hand.

* * * *

The Speaker quickly discerned Chip felt he was a co-equal with him. This was something new and uncomfortable for him.

"Mr. Bascomb, you and your 'Young Turks' might be pre-judging the President," he began. "It's like putting the cart before the horse, or better still, pre-judging a man guilty and then holding a trial. That is not the American way of justice."

Chip replied, "Mr. Speaker, we feel the President's actions were so egregious that he must be held accountable, irrespective of his justification."

"Do you not have respect for the presidency, Mr. Bascomb?" Vance asked.

"Respect does not have anything to do with it," Chip responded. "The law is the law, and the law says if a President is found guilty of . . ."

"Of what?!" the Speaker interrupted testily.

"Well, Mr. Speaker, of abuse of power," Chip continued. "If I recollect correctly, a the House Judiciary Committee in 1974 voted to charge President Nixon with three articles of impeachment – obstruction of justice, contempt of Congress, and . . . abuse of power. Before the House could officially approve those charges, he resigned. Had he not left office, the matter would have been forwarded to the Senate."

"If I recollect correctly, Mr. Bascomb, that involved the Watergate matter," Vance countered. "President Merriwether never could be charged with obstruction of justice, or contempt of Congress! To charge him with abuse of power would be a stretch, to say the least! Might as well charge Jared Winston as a co-conspirator!"

Chip tried hard to withhold his rising temper and calmly said just before leaving, "Mr. Speaker, let the House decide that. Unless you act on your own, I will take the floor and ask the matter be brought before the House Judiciary Committee." The Speaker was angry that respect for his position had been ignored, and that he had been given an ultimatum by a very junior Representative.

The more he thought about the audacity Chip exhibited, the more the overall implication concerned him. To refresh his memory, he rechecked the copy of the Constitution he kept in a top drawer of his desk. Under Article II, Section 4, a President could be "removed from Office on Impeachment for, and Conviction of, Treason, Bribery, or other High Crimes and Misdemeanors." Abuse of power fell under "misdemeanors."

Under Section 3, a presidential Senate impeachment 'trial' must be presided over by the Chief Justice of the Supreme Court, the Honorable Joyce Whittingham-Stern, the President's appointee and friend. What a legal conundrum that would be!

The more he thought about the reference to Winston, he smiled. "Chip let his temper get the best of his understanding of the law, and that is a weakness I intend to explore," he mused. "Winston was, and continues to be, Chief of Staff when the trip to Moscow took place. The Constitution states the Vice President as President of the Senate presides over an impeachment trial there. There is no Vice President. Chip was lax in doing his homework."

* * * *

Word of Chip's meeting with Vance, but not its contents, reached Bouchard. The fact that the leader of the "Young Turks" had a meeting with the Speaker was news in and of itself.

By happenstance, an old Army buddy of Bouchard's, who is a civilian Army employee, told him he recognized Senator Cummings coming out of the Pentagon.

"In all the years I've been working there, I don't think I ever saw the Senator in the building," his friend told Bouchard. "It may have been a courtesy call, or something unrelated to the fact you just cover the White House, but I thought I'd let you know."

* * * *

Since Bouchard followed Diane's broadcasts with interest because of his belief there was a connection between the White House and Congress, he had to pursue this even if it meant invading her territory.

He called Alicia, and asked if he could stop by. When he revealed what his Pentagon friend had told him, she said, "It could be nothing, but it could be something. I'll check it out when I get a chance. Thanks for the tip."

She immediately walked to Jared's office, and repeated the tip. He, too, said what she said. "By the way," she remarked, "what do you think about the meeting in the Speaker's office?"

"I'd loved to have been a fly on the wall listening to what is going on," he answered. "I've spoken to the President about it, and he feels there's most definitely something brewing. He did say the 'Young Turks' leader really had nerve facing up to the Speaker. That is something we need to watch carefully, so keep in close contact with your sources on a daily basis. This could explode at any minute."

"Jared, can I ask you something in the strictest confidence?" she asked.

"That's an interesting way of putting it," he answered. "Of course."

"What is there about the President's health I should know?" she asked.

"It's complicated, Alicia," he replied. "I've asked him several times if I can share that subject with you. It's his decision. On the plus side, if anyone asks you, you honestly can say you do not know of any problems."

"Which means there is," she countered. "OK, I understand. I would rather know, but I understand."

"That's why the President and I think so highly of you, Alicia," he remarked. "You have such a rare quality of loyalty that it is impressive. I know you speak your mind when you have to, but, you do that before a decision is made. The President hates it when someone does not warn him in advance; after he falls on his face, that person says in essence 'I could have told you so.' If he believed you needed to know at this point, he would have called you into the Oval Office to tell you himself."

"Thanks for the compliment," she responded. "It's just I want all the information at hand so I can do the best job for him."

"You're already at that point, especially with the added responsibility you took on," he replied. "I'll bet you've already been offered some tempting lobbying jobs with the K Street firms."

She smiled and responded, "And, here I thought they just wanted a date."

For one of the few times, Jared actually laughed out loud. "I think I'll check with Tim on that," he said reaching for the phone.

She feigned shock, and said, "Oh, no! Don't do that! He'll be jealous!"

"With good reason," Jared remarked, as she left before he could notice a slight blush on her high cheeks.

* * * *

"I was just going to call you," President Merriwether said to Jared. "There's an interesting development brewing, and I need your reaction."

CHAPTER 48

Make Room For Another Guest

AMBASSADOR VANDERGRIFF'S CALL to Tim was unexpected.

"Mr. Ambassador, what a pleasant surprise," Tim said. "How are things going in Moscow these days, sir?"

Ambassador Vandergriff replied, "Not as hectic as when you guys showed up."

They both laughed.

"Tim," the Ambassador began, "I had a thought I'd like to run by you and the President."

"Sure," Tim replied.

"It's about President Borochenkov's visit . . ." he began.

"Oh, no!" Tim almost shouted. "Don't tell me . . ."

"No, no, it's still on," the Ambassador assured him. "But I wonder if you guys could agree to another guest."

"There's always room at the inn," Tim joked nervously. "Who?"

"I think the President should invite another President," he answered.

"Who?" Tim repeated.

"How about China's President Jiang Ying-han Situ?" the Ambassador asked.

Tim blurted, "Why?" He recovered quickly and added, "Of course."

Ambassador Vandergriff continued, "China has been having as big a problem with air pollution as Russia. And, it could be complicated by what is happening in the north of Russia, although China's problem is more concentrated."

"That sounds fascinating!" Tim exclaimed.

"I've taken the liberty of broaching this subject with my counterpart in Beijing," the Ambassador explained. "He told me air pollution there and in eastern China is quite high, especially during the winter months. I learned also that President Jiang has been trying to deal with the increased pollution caused by China's industrial growth, but not with much cooperation. That is why I'm wondering whether the President would extend an invitation to President Jiang to join President Borochenkov at your conference."

Tim responded, "I'm flattered you asked me, Mr. Ambassador, but I think you should talk directly with the President."

"The reason I mentioned it to you first, Tim, is on the basis of your having been a newsman," he began to explain. "I think it would be a news coup for the President, who I understand has been suffering the slings and arrows of outrageous politics."

Tim had to laugh at the reference to Shakespeare, but replied, "And how! Come to think of it, that would not hurt relations among the three nations."

"I sort of had that in mind," the Ambassador teased.

"Sir, it sounds golden to me," Tim remarked. "Go for it!"

* * * *

President Merriwether had the same reaction as Tim. "What a super idea!" he asserted to Ambassador Vandergriff.

"Mr. President, I suggest you allow me to have my counterpart in Beijing approach President Jiang with the idea," the Ambassador offered. "If it is acceptable, then you could make it formal with a phone call to the President."

"That's the diplomatic way!" he responded enthusiastically. "Do it!"

"Sir," the Ambassador added, "I believe it would be received extremely well not only in the American press but in Russia as well as in China. And, I'm sure it would be reflected throughout the world."

"I'll mention that to Jorge," the President quipped.

Ambassador Vandergriff made the contact with his Beijing counterpart, who enthusiastically agreed. Usually, Chinese officials do not respond immediately to involving their President. This time, the reply came the following day. When he received the go-ahead, Ambassador Vanergriff called President Merriwether, who in turn called President Jiang.

As predicted, the announcement made jointly in Beijing and Washington, and followed in Moscow, went viral around the world. President Merriwether beamed and seemed to be peppier than he had been lately.

* * * *

Alicia took the time to call Tim and congratulate him. "Aw, it was nothing," he teased.

"I'm jealous that the press will be paying more attention to you than to me," she teased back. "It just makes me love you more."

"That's the most important thing," Tim responded seriously.

"Well, Mr. Big Shot, there's one more important thing," she said.

"And, that is?" he asked.

"I had been wearing your ring only at home, but that's come to a stop," she responded. "Before you think we're not engaged, be advised, my love, that the ring is going to be on my finger all day at the office as well!"

Tim replied almost sheepishly, "I suppose it's only because I'm a big shot now."

They both laughed.

And, Alicia did shock everyone, especially Jared and the President, when she showed it off the next day.

CHAPTER 49

Strange Bedfellows

As soon as Chip left the meeting with the Speaker, he called Simpson, who called the SecDef. He was shocked to learn Bosworth had been sacked. He asked for, and was given, Boz's home phone number. Chip filled him in.

"Congressman Bascomb, I think we should meet very soon," Boz offered.

"Sir, at your convenience," Chip responded, his heart rate increasing. "It would be an honor."

"Son, are you a meat eater?" the SecDef asked.

"Sure am, Mr. Secretary," Chip answered hungrily.

"I'm not the Secretary anymore, but let's meet at the Prime Rib on K Street," Boz posed. "How's 7:00 this evening?"

Chip did not even bother checking his calendar. "Fine with me, sir" he answered. He would make sure he arrived at least by 6:45.

* * * *

As they sat down at an especially reserved table toward the back, Boz said, "I knew your father by reputation. Fine man. Fine man."

"Thank you, sir" Chip beamed. "I'll be sure to let him know." (Boz did not know the two were no longer on speaking terms.)

"Chip – May I call you Chip?" he began. He did not wait for a response, and continued, "We seem to have mutual views as pertains to the President. I've heard some good things about you, son. And, your standing up to the Speaker was impressive. (Chip was surprised Boz knew such things so quickly.) Do I understand you and your 'Young Turks' really are pushing for an impeachment hearing?"

"Mr. Bosworth," Chip replied, "I guess it's no secret now. Yes, we feel strongly about it. The Speaker does not."

"So I've heard, son," Boz replied. "But, don't let that deter you. (He leaned forward now because the noise level was rising.) Even though I got kicked out of the Pentagon, I've still got a group that feels the President overstepped his authority with that Air Force One business. I think there might be an opportunity for us to help each other in this matter."

Chip leaned in and responded, "That would be an honor," he agreed.

"Of course, I'll have to stay in the background, you understand," Boz explained.

"I understand," he again agreed.

"However, you'll be able to call on us for support," the Boz said. "We're not without influence."

"I understand," Chip echoed. "I recognize it will be an uphill battle, but we're determined to make the President accountable, maybe not for what he did, but for how he did it. That was unconscionable!"

"My sentiments exactly!"Boz emphasized. "So, what's your plan?"

"At the appropriate time, I will ask the Speaker to be heard," he began. "If he refuses to acknowledge me, my group will start demanding I be heard. We'll have tipped off reporters who cover Congress to be sure to be there. We feel the Speaker will have to allow me to take the floor. We think he will feel confident he has enough votes to kill the motion I will make about allowing the Judiciary Committee to conduct an impeachment hearing. That's where it gets tricky."

"Smart strategy," Boz commented. "That might be where we come in. I think I can cash in some political IOUs to force a vote. Vance probably will ask for a voice vote so he won't embarrass his colleagues. He'll declare the motion defeated although it will have been seconded. The way I figure it, that will be only Round One. I'll bet the reporters will make a big thing out of it, and force a 'reconsideration.' Maybe Vance will try to table the motion, but that won't work. At some point, he'll have to give in. His Plan B will have the Committee voting down the Article of Impeachment. We'll try to make sure the vote goes the other way. You're into hard-ball politics, son. Are you willing to step into the batter's box?"

Chip's eyes glazed over. He forced himself to pause before saying, "I'm ready, sir!"

"Good! Good!" Boz declared, reaching over to punch Chip's shoulder. "Now, let's get to the prime rib!"

* * * *

The two were so engrossed with each other that they never look around at the other tables. If they had, they would have seen Diane having dinner with a fellow reporter who covers the Pentagon.

"What do you suppose the ex-Secretary of Defense and the leader of the 'Young Turks' are plotting?" Diane asked.

"Whatever it is, I don't like it," he answered.

"I think it was Charles Dudley Warner, a friend of Mark Twain, who said, 'Politics makes strange bedfellows,'" she asserted.

* * * *

Luckily, Diane had Alicia's cell phone number.

"Sorry to bother you so late," Diane said, "but I think this call is worth it."

"I said you could phone me at any time," Alicia replied.

"This is just an alert," Diane began. "Your name is not attached to any story I do on this. What would you think if I told you former Secretary of Defense Bosworth was having a cozy dinner with the 'Young Turks' leader Congressman Bascomb, Jr., at the Prime Rib this evening?"

Alicia replied, "I would wonder how you knew this."

"I was there and saw them," Diane responded. "We were too far away to hear what they were talking about. Besides, the noise level was too high. I can tell you this. Young Bascomb was beaming! My guess is Boz was making him an offer he could not refuse."

"That's usually the other way around," Alicia explained.

"Whatever," Diane remarked. "I thought you ought to know."

"That's very considerate of you, Diane," Alicia replied. "Is it alright if I tell the President you are the source?"

"It couldn't hurt," Diane said. "Ordinarily I wouldn't have bothered you with this, but it was so weird I don't know what to make of it."

"Me neither," Alicia replied. "I can't help but feel the President might be able to figure it out. I owe you one, Diane."

"No, I don't work that way, Alicia," she responded. "I think you and I understand each other and respect our mutual professionalisms."

"Thank you," Alicia said.

* * * *

Alicia felt Jared should know first. He suggested they both report it to the President.

"Well, isn't that interesting!" the President asserted. "That's something I'll keep in my hip pocket."

"Mr. President, I have to ask you something," Alicia said. "How much headway do you think will be made in the House on a request for an impeachment hearing?"

"Good question," he answered. "I'm a bit surprised at the way

Vance is handling this. From what I gather – sorry, Alicia, but I also have my own sources – he made a mistake of challenging Bascomb. Sometimes you are wrong in predicting which way the wind will blow in the House. I say that as the former Speaker. Jared and I have worked out a strategy, but don't be offended if we don't share it with you just yet."

"No offense taken, Mr. President," she commented.

"By the way, Alicia, I'm very impressed at the connection you have made with Diane Bana," the President said. "I'm equally impressed you can keep this on a professional level. And, I'm impressed by that little thing on your ring finger."

Alicia actually blushed when he asked to see it up close. "I don't have my loupe handy, but I'd say Tim must have saved up a lot of money for the ring. Jared and I wish only the best for both of you. Oh, yes, when the meeting takes place at the Bardon Foundation, I expect you to attend."

* * * *

What Diane did not tell Alicia was that she snapped a photo of the two Bs with her smart phone. There was enough light so she did not have to use the flash. "You just never know when that might come in handy," she commented to her dinner partner. She reviewed it to make sure it was clear.

CHAPTER 50

Any Story Is Better Than None

BOUCHARD TOOK NOTE of how much air time Diane was getting with what was going on in the House. He finally determined it was time to go with the Dr. Rodriguez story.

He mulled over what impact, if any, that would have on the growing(?) calls for an impeachment hearing. He concluded it all was part of that disappearance of Air Force One. He tested Jorge to see if there was any angle he had missed, but to no avail. All the Press Secretary said was he would appreciate a heads-up when the story would run.

Ambassador Vandergriff suddenly was not forthcoming with any information on President Borochenkov's grandson, which surprised Bouchard. He could not evenget the child's name. That would diminish the impact of the story.

He went back over his post-interview notes to refresh his memory. He really had two stories – the Dr. Rodriguez one, and the President's non-reaction to the potential impeachment hearing in the House. He decided Diane had usurped him on the latter; that left the former. But, he did not have a solid lead for that story. That made him change from a possible dead-bang lead to almost a second-day story. He finally decided on a type of lead he had not used in years:

"The secretive nature of the Air Force One flight to Moscow had two purposes, not one, according to what has been made public.

The one President Merriwether had explained centered on global warming, and its effect on air pollution. The other was a humanitarian one involving the grandson of Russian President Andrei Borochenkov."

The body of the story was the revelation of Dr. Rodriguez and the purpose of her presence on the flight to Moscow. He included a side bar on her background.

He knew it would not win a Pulitzer Prize by any stretch of the imagination, but at the moment that's all he had. He would keep trying to reach Ambassador Vandergriff.

Meanwhile, he included a lot of background on the illness itself, quoting the Progeria Foundation and the Mayo Clinic. He even made reference to Rabbi Kushner's book. At least it made for good reading, Bouchard concluded.

CHAPTER 51

The Decision Is In – Or, Is It?

THE BARDON FOUNDATION EVENT was a huge success, as was the press coverage. There were many photo ops of the three Presidents and of just Presidents Borochenkov and President Jiang. Bouchard noted President Merriwether allowed the other two to be center stage most of the time.

When Bouchard saw Ambassador Vandergriff in the background, he hurried over to him and asked for an update on the Russian President's grandson. "I'm not here to discuss that," the Ambassador said curtly." Did that mean no news is good news, he wondered?

There were public and private discussions. The Presidents pledged to meet again, first in Russia, and then in China.

There was so much activity and such a crush of news media that Tim and Alicia barely had time for a passionate kiss out of sight of reporters.

* * * *

Chip and Vance had reached an understanding that the matter of impeachment hearings would wait until the Bardon Foundation event ended.

With the summer over, and the following year being an election one including that for President, Vance agreed to a date for the House Judiciary Committee to begin the process of deciding whether or not to approve an impeachment "indictment" to be sent to the Senate for a "trial." In announcing this, Vance also said he would not vote under any circumstances "because of a perceived conflict of interest."

The first of a series of votes was to determine whether the Committee should proceed with the process. A simple majority agreed. Next, Vance proposed a Resolution allowing the Committee to begin a formal inquiry into the matter. That, too, passed quickly. The inquiry was pro forma, and another Resolution was approved for a full House debate.

The visitor's gallery was packed, as television cameras recorded the voting.

After the Committee voted, the matter went to the full House. Vance, as Speaker, then recognized Chip to make the motion to approve an Article of Impeachment of President Merriwether to be forwarded to the Senate. There was a second, and then the "Young Turks" one after another argued for passage. The only charge was that the President overstepped his authority in ordering Air Force One to vanish. As Chip put it, "This was an abuse of power." No one else spoke on behalf of the motion, which surprised Chip. A Sergeant At Arms aide passed a note to the leader of the "Young Turks" from Boz, who was in the visitors section, stating, "The vote is in the bag. With the election coming up next year, your fellow lawmakers know where their campaign money is coming from."

The first lawmaker to represent the opposition was Majority Whip Frances Markey. "Mr. Speaker," she began, "The charge of 'abuse of power' is obtuse and arcane, and therefore lacks specificity. Impeachment on that basis makes a mockery of the American system of justice in which an accused is presumed innocent until proved guilty beyond reasonable doubt. Just because there are those who allege and/or believe the President abused his authority is insufficient evidence of wrong doing.

"The President of the United States has specific and implied authority in many ways. Did the President intend to abuse his authority, or was he merely perceived to have done that? That is the key to this vote.

"I strongly urge my Honorable colleagues to quash this witch hunt here and now, lest there be innuendos this motion is politically motivated. Mr. Speaker, I yield the floor."

There was an uproar from the "Young Turks." "Mr. Speaker! Mr. Speaker!" Chip shouted. "I ask to be heard to refute the insinuation the Honorable Majority Whip stated!"

Vance replied, "If there are any others who wish to be recognized, they will precede you." None did, so he was allowed to speak.

"Mr. Speaker," Chip started, "the House allows difference of opinion but not political diatribe. The remarks by the Honorable Majority Whip are an affront. My motion simply is whether an impeachment finding is warranted. A political rationale is not a legal rationale. I call for a vote on my motion."

Vance stood up, and announced: "If there is no objection, this will be a voice vote." Chip and his colleagues had a Plan A and a Plan B at this point. If the voice vote was inconclusive, they would demand a roll call vote. There was some confusion because Members began milling around the floor. Vance banged his gavel, and called for 'the ayes and nays." He announced, "The vote is tied."

Chip was livid! "How can you determine that! I demand an electronic vote!" he shouted. As the votes were tallied, there still was a tie.

"This is unheard of!" someone next to Diane shouted.

"Well, Chairman Vance can break it!" another declared.

Diane turned around, and commented, "Did you forget the Speaker said he would not vote 'under any circumstances?' A tie vote means the motion did not pass!"

There was pandemonium in the visitor's gallery, and angry shouting by the "Young Turks."

Chip yelled, "What the hell just happened?!"

A colleague responded, "We've been had!"

"Mr. Speaker! Mr. Chairman!" Chip yelled. "I wish to be recognized!"

Vance banged his gavel asserting, "Order! Order! Order in the House!"

Finally, the Sergeant At Arms and his aides urged Members to return to their seats. Only some did.

"The Chair recognizes the Honorable Charles Bascomb Jr." Vance announced.

"Mr. Speaker, I call for a recount!" Chip pleaded.

The Speaker ordered the Clerk to take a second count. The total remained the same.

"Mr. Speaker," Chip persisted, "I respectfully request you cast the tie-breaking vote!"

"Mr. Bascomb," Vance replied, "I am on record as saying I would not vote under any circumstances because it could be perceived as a conflict of political interest."

"Mr. Speaker," Chip continued, "this then is a victory for the President!"

Vance did not respond, but banged his gavel several times.

"Mr. Bascomb," the Speaker remarked, "your comment will appear in the Congressional Record unless you exercise your right to amend it."

Vance banged his gavel again and adjourned the session. As the crowd dispersed, Boz shouted an obscene word, and stormed out.

* * * *

Chip spent the night going over Robert's Rules of Order trying to find a way to change the vote. The phone rang.

"Yes, Mr. Bosworth," he said. "I'm trying to . . . yes, sir. Oh, is that right, sir? That's for sure! No sir, I don't doubt your word. Yes, I understand. First thing in the morning once we're back in session. Thank you so much, sir."

* * * *

No sooner had the Chaplain of the Day finished his invocation than Chip approached Vance.

"With all due respect, Mr. Speaker, your reluctance to break the tie vote yesterday has cause great chaos," Chip said. "I seek reconsideration. Before you say no, please consider this. Only someone from the prevailing side can ask for reconsideration. However, there is no prevailing side in a tie. I checked with the Parliamentarian, and she agrees. Therefore, I respectfully submit you can determine reconsideration is in order. I know my motion will be seconded. I ask the vote be an electronic roll call."

Vance said he would check the rationale on his own. When Chip's interpretation was confirmed, the Speaker said he would allow it "only one more time."

When the roll call finished, the Clerk tallied the result. Before handing it to Vance, she checked it twice. The Speaker gaveled for order and announced, "The motion to reconsider the motion for impeachment of President Lincoln Merriwether is affirmed . . . by one vote!"

The "Young Turks" shouted for joy. The Progressive House Members were stunned. One finally asked, "Who the hell changed his vote?!" When they discovered who it was, he could not be found. Once he had cast his vote, he slipped out a side door, and entered a private limousine that sped them to the nearby Monaco Restaurant.

Once in a cozy table near the rear, Boz ordered the lawmaker a drink, which he refused. "Mr. Congressman," he said, "you struck a blow for democracy in the House. After you finish your term, you will find there are bright horizons elsewhere. There will be an executive position waiting for you at one of the firms I owned before I became Secretary of Defense. It does mean relocating, but your starting salary will be double what you made in the House. I know your two daughters want to go to a good college, and we'll take care of that."

"Mr. Bosworth," the Congressman responded, "that is very

generous. But, in the meantime, I'll have to face my fellow lawmakers, the media, and certainly my constituents."

Boz replied, "You can explain you changed your vote because it weighed heavily on you the angst suffered by that reporter who was supposed to be home that evening for an anniversary dinner with her husband, who suffered that fatal heart attack."

"Mr. Bosworth, you may not believe this, but that is how I felt," he countered.

"Well, there you go!" Boz beamed. "You're not telling a lie. You just had a conscience pang. I've helped you financially with your campaigns, and was glad to do so. You're a fine young man. What you did was the right thing!"

The Congressman had a press release distributed using the words Boz suggested. His colleagues would shun him for the rest of his term.

* * * *

Diane made a bee-line for House Minority Leader Schoenfeld, and asked for an explanation of what just happened.

"I'm as surprised as you are," she replied.

* * * *

Bouchard called the President for comment, but uncharacteristically circumvented Jorge.

"What type of 'no comment' would you prefer for your story?" the President joshed.

"No comment would do, sir," Bouchard replied, quickly adding, "unless you wish to expand on that."

"Nice try, but no cigar," President Merriwether commented. "However, I would prefer you go first to Jorge from now on. It's not fair to the other reporters."

"Thank you, sir," Bouchard said.

CHAPTER 52

Testing, Testing – One, Two

THE PROGRESSIVES NOT SURPRISINGLY wanted to delay a hearing in the Senate, while the Conservatives wanted the matter expedited. The impasse was broken when Jorge told reporters at the next briefing "the President wants the matter to be resolved as soon as possible." Even Bouchard did not know the underlying reason for that until the next briefing when the Press Secretary announced, "President Merriwether will be going to Bethesda Naval Medical Center for his annual physical examination. He will be given the usual array of tests."

At first glance, Bouchard did not attach any significance to the timing. He checked his notes, and affirmed it had been a year since the last exam. Reporters' attention would shift to the facility north of the District.

Many of The White House press corps had noticed that the President looked tired lately. They attributed that to a combination of the long Air Force One trip, and the Bardon Foundation conclave. While he did spend some weekends at Camp David, that did not seem out of the ordinary.

Normally, a President will arrive at the medical facility in the morning, and by late afternoon the results will be announced. Sometimes, a President will remain overnight. The case of the shooting of President Reagan was an anomaly since his recovery took longer.

Reporters were a bit surprised when Jorge announced "the President has decided to go to Bethesda this evening instead of tomorrow morning." They duly reported his arrival and planned return in the morning. By afternoon, there still was no announcement concerning the results of the examinations. It was 7:00 p.m. (after the early evening news programs were off the air) when Dr. Frankhauser appeared and announced:

"We did find a few abnormalities that require additional testing. For example, there were some dermatological problems, which means that we need to determine if they are cancerous. The President has been under a lot of stress, and we want to make sure this will not cause any future problems. Please do not read anything more into that – we like to make sure there are no surprises. I want to change his diet a bit because his cholesterol level could be lower."

When he paused, that gave reporters a chance to have their turn.

Question: "Dr. Frankhauser, how much longer do you expect the President will remain here?"

Answer: "Another day should do it."

Question: "Is he conscious?"

Answer: "If you mean does he know you're all here to ask questions, yes."

Question: "Seriously, doctor."

Answer: "Sorry, I did not mean to be flippant. Yes, of course he is fully awake. I really would like him to have an uninterrupted night of sleep."

Question: "Will he be given a sleeping pill?"

Answer: "The only pills I have ordered are vitamins."

Question: "While he's here, can he continue to function as President?"

Answer: "I would assume from that implication you might be concerned he would have to transfer his authority. I do not see that as being the case. Even when he's asleep he's the President."

Question: "When do you expect the President to be ready to leave here?"

Answer: "If you would ask him, he probably would say he's been here too long already. The extra time has to do with certain tests. If any treatment is necessary, like to do it immediately so he does not have to return."

Question: "Is that normal?"

Answer: "He's here only as long as he needs to be here."

Question: "Are you the only one examining the President?"

Answer: "Of course not. There are specialists who are involved, and that is routine."

Question: "Can the President come to the window, and wave to us?"

Answer: "I think the television cameras would do better tomorrow in daylight. However, I'm not a specialist in that field."

Question: "Can we get the names of those specialists?"

Answer: "I think we can have that tomorrow for you. Thank you."

* * * *

Upstairs in the room where the President was lying in bed, he said to Dr. Frankhauser, "I think you made my Press Secretary jealous with the way you carefully answered those questions."

* * * *

It was not until mid-afternoon that President Merriwether was wheeled out to his limousine – standard procedure at a hospital – for the short ride to the helicopter pad. He got up quickly, smiled, and waved at the gaggle of reporters. The first question was: "Did you enjoy your hospital stay?" The President chuckled and replied, "If you mean did I enjoy being prodded and poked, and awakened in the middle of the night for you-know-what, hell no!" Even the reporters and hospital attendants laughed.

Jorge distributed the medical documentation they asked for. Dr. Frankhauser said, "A couple of tests have been delayed, but that is no reason for the President to remain here."

President Merriwether could not resist interjecting, "Doctor, if you want patients to limit their hospital stays, keep serving that same kind of food I had."

With that, the limousine door closed, and the security caravan whisked him away. He and other Presidents used a Marine helicopter to avoid creating traffic jams, but he always complained how noisy it was. When reporters' attention was focused on the President's departure, Dr. Frankhauser quickly went back into the hospital.

CHAPTER 53

Good News, Bad News

The only advantage Bouchard seemed to have over the hard working White House press corps was the Dr. Rodriguez angle. He decided to keep calling the Moscow hospital where she and the Russian President's grandson were. Without Ambassador Vandergriff's help, it was difficult getting past the reception desk attendant. She had become tight-lipped and spoke mostly in Russian.

He concluded his only alternative was what was called the "back door" approach. This meant again phoning Rico.

"What, de nuevo?" he asked.

"Yes, again," Bouchard replied.

"We must stop meeting like this," Rico chortled.

"Get a new routine," he responded. "I really need your help." He recounted his difficulties with Moscow, and asked, "Could you check with the family to find out if Dr. Rodriguez has been calling them? Make up any excuse you can, like I'm doing a feature story on the wonderful work she's doing. You're good at mierda de toro."

Rico burst out laughing and remarked, "Can't you use polite words?"

Bouchard retorted, "Just remember, you taught me. Enough of that. The only way I can save my ass on this story is to find out such things as when she is coming home, what's the child's condition, and so forth. Hey, wait. I just thought of something else. She got a free ride to Moscow. Who's paying her return carfare?"

"Good point, mi amigo," Rico responded.

"If you have to sweeten the pot, I can scrape together some dineros," Bouchard offered.

"Yo comprendo," Rico replied.

"Muchas gracias," Bouchard said.

* * * *

Bouchard did not expect the return call so quickly. "No, she hasn't written to her family," Rico said.

"Shit!" Bouchard snarled.

"But, the news gets better," he added.

"What?!" Bouchard reacted. "I thought you said she hasn't written to her family."

"She hasn't," Rico responded.

"So, how do you know . . .?" he began.

Rico interrupted, "She called."

"Listen, you jerk, don't play games with me!" Bouchard replied angrily.

"OK, OK," Rico responded. "It seems she has to remain longer than she expected because the boy is not responding to the medication she brought with her."

"How long . . .?" he began.

"No telling," Rico answered. "The Russians said she could remain as long as she wanted. Dr. Rodriguez told her family the boy was too far gone by the time she got there. She and the Russian doctors wondered whether the medication would be effective when a patient is very young and the disease is detected early. She also said the Russian President was impressed with her, even though she doesn't hold out much hope for the boy."

"By any chance, did she say how she was returning?" Bouchard asked.

"As a matter of fact, she did," Rico answered. "The Progeria Foundation was going to pick up the tab, but the Russians insisted on paying for her return flight."

"You done good, Rico," he said. "Thanks."

"De nada, mi amigo," Rico responded. "What are friends for?"

"Maybe when she gets back I can do a phone interview with her," Bouchard suggested.

"I'll run it by the family and let you know," Rico replied.

* * * *

As a courtesy, Bouchard phoned Ambassador Vandergriff to give him the gist of the article he planned to use. "Did you speak directly to Dr. Rodriguez?" Ambassador Vandergriff asked.

"No, sir," Bouchard answered. "I was able to reach her family in Puerto Rico and got the information from them."

"Let me get back to you shortly," the Ambassador said.

"Fine, Mr. Ambassador," he said.

Half an hour later, the call came. "You've done an accurate job of writing," Ambassador Vandergriff responded.

* * * *

Bouchard's article for his morning edition was picked up by most of the White House press print and electronic correspondents.

* * * *

Three weeks later, Bouchard was flabbergasted to receive a call from President Borochenkov. The news was sad. Unfortunately, the boy has passed away. He explained "I phoned President Merriwether to thank him for making such a humanitarian effort. This proves our nations can help one another regardless of other differences. I told the President I look forward to further such cooperation! Dr. Rodriguez will return home tomorrow on one of our regular flights to Puerto Rico with our sincere appreciation of her efforts. She told me the Mayo Clinic has offered her a full time position to continue her research with funding from the Progeria Foundation, which she has accepted. I also told President Merriwether I very much appreciated the efforts of Ambassador Vandergriff in facilitating Dr. Rodriguez's and his long journey to Moscow."

President Merriwether called Ambassador Vandergriff to thank him for suggesting to President Borochenkov the goodwill gained in making those calls. "Da! Spasibo!" the Russian said.

CHAPTER 54

It's Enough To Make One Ill

SATURDAYS USUALLY ARE THE SLOWEST NEWS days of the week. Many of the White House correspondents take the day off, to return on Sunday.

Because of that, the helicopter that took President Merriwether back to Bethesda Naval Medical Center departed unnoticed.

Dr. Frankhauser was at the landing pad with a vehicle to take the President and a small security detail, headed by Whiz, to the main building. He had revealed to the President the results of some of the tests.

"I want to redo some of the examinations," he explained. "Your cancer has returned, and metastasized, although we had removed the prostate gland. Your body is not responding to treatment the way I had hoped."

"Doctor, don't hold back anything," the President said.

"OK, Mr. President," he responded. "I suspect it is beginning to spread to the surrounding lymph nodes. That's not a good sign. We'll have to do a bone scan. I'm very pro-active, President or not. Let's see, that prostate cancer surgery was about 20 years ago. You did not have radiation or seed implants. Probably scar tissue has formed in the urethra. Are you having trouble urinating?"

"More than I used to," he answered. "And, it's painful."

"You never told me about this condition," Dr. Frankhauser said. "What kind of patient is that?"

"Now you're coming up with all these side issues," the President complained.

"All right, Mr. President," he replied. "I guess I should tell you that Jared called me to say you had not looked well since the last exam, which was not all that long ago. Let's do some more tests and we'll talk more."

"The sooner I can get back to the White House, the better," he remarked.

* * * *

"Well, I've confirmed the cancer is spreading," Dr. Frankhauser explained.

"That's not exactly the diagnosis I wanted to hear," the President replied.

"Even though it is spreading . . . ." the Doctor began to say.

"What happens then?" the President asked again. "How much time . . .?"

"If we've caught the spreading early enough, we can begin chemotherapy. The side effects can be . . . well, pretty rough. I'm going to do some more tests."

"You haven't answered my question!" the President insisted.

"With luck and treatment, maybe a year," he responded hesitatingly. "You're just not going to be able to hide your condition too much longer. Well, you told me not to hold back."

* * * *

It was dusk by the time the helicopter flew back to the White House. Jared already had received the medical report. The President recounted the diagnosis, and looked sad.

"I suggest spending the next weekend at Camp David," Jared said. "Let's assume Dr. Frankhauser's prediction is premature, and you can beat this!"

"No one else is to know!" the President responded despondently.

* * * *

The helicopter flight would not appear on his schedule.

CHAPTER 55

Rush To Judgment

THE "YOUNG TURKS" URGED CHIP to make sure the House decision was not delayed going to the Senate Judiciary Committee.

Diane and the others who covered Capitol Hill rushed to interview not only members of the Committee, but also as many Senators who would be willing to comment. Of course, the "Young Turks" boasted about their "victory" openly.

As with the House procedure, the impeachment "trial" in the Senate would have to begin in the Judiciary Committee. Counting Senator Cummings, there were eight other Progressive Party Members and eight Conservatives on that Committee. Reporters concluded it would be unlikely there would be a tie vote. But, considering what happened in the House, this was not taken for granted. Senator Cummings would not say so to reporters who hounded him, but he hoped he would not have to vote. He wanted to stay above the fray. "After all," he muttered to himself, "who knows what can happen if the President is impeached?"

* * * *

Diane beat Bouchard to the punch when another possibility presented itself to her. She discussed it with her bosses, who bumped it up the corporate chain to the top. The word finally came back, "Go with it!"

First, however, she contacted Chip. He promised to return her call once he checked with others, including the Attorney General's office. She did not have any idea one of the others would be ex-SecDef Bosworth. Chip returned her call an hour before she went on the air with:

"With all the turmoil on Capitol Hill these days, one aspect seems to have escaped lawmakers. If President Merriwether should be impeached by the Senate, the spotlight might be turned on Chief of Staff Jared Winston. Legal authorities, and others with knowledge of the matter, have confirmed for me there could be a charge of conspiracy involving abuse of power against Winston because he certainly knew about

Air Force One vanishing. Congressman Charles Bascomb Jr. has indicated he is considering sponsoring a Resolution to that effect to the House Judiciary Committee. Accusing the Chief of Staff is one thing; having the House vote the way it did against the President is another matter. Keep in mind the Senate has not yet acted on the House Resolution. Furthermore, there is nothing in the Constitution specifically designating who would preside over a similar hearing for the Vice President! However, if Winston had been approved for Vice President, this could have resulted in him as President of the Senate having to preside over his own impeachment! That's one for legal scholars to scratch their heads over.

"This is Diane Bana on Capitol Hill."

CHAPTER 56

More Than Bouchard Expected

BOUCHARD WAS FURIOUS. "Yes, the hearings take place on the floors of the House and Senate, but damn it, the President is my turf," he growled!

He hurriedly called Rico yet again and demanded, "Why haven't we heard from Dr. Rodriguez?!"

"Keep your shorts dry, mi amigo," Rico retorted. "You must be sick – I mean, psychic. I just got a call from her family. She arrived an hour ago, but she's too tired to talk. Because I have such a – how you say it? – disposition dulce, she made you – through me, of course – an offer you cannot refuse."

"And, what might that offer be?" he asked annoyingly.

"She said she can arrange a flight to Mayo with a change of planes in Washington, DC," he began to explain. "You can interview her at the airport – I'm not sure which one it is – and then she flies to Minneapolis, where a vehicle will take her for a one-hour ride to Rochester."

"Well, mi chico, you have redeemed yourself!" Bouchard remarked. "Let me know the date, time of arrival, and which damn airport!"

"So, mi amigo, am I no longer un culo del caballo?" Rico asked tauntingly.

"No," Bouchard answered. "You've done a great job! And, you may have saved my culo."

* * * *

Rico had a photo of Dr. Rodriguez sent to Bouchard so he could recognize her when she arrived at Thurgood Marshall International Airport in Baltimore. Since she was flying first class, courtesy of the Mayo Clinic, they were able to use the VIP Lounge.

After the usual pleasantries of small talk, he said, "Please start at the beginning of your involvement in the Air Force One situation. Would you mind if I recorded this interview? My shorthand is not very good."

"Yes, that's fine, Mr. Bouchard," she replied.

"I was surprised to receive a call from Dr. Frankhauser," she began in near-perfect English. "He said he had read the paper I had written on the research I was conducting on progeria. I was getting ready to try it out on children with that illness. At best, there are several hundred children in three dozen countries with it, and I was hoping to find enough of them to begin testing a drug formula I had developed consisting of herbs found only in my region.

"The Doctor explained that word had come to President Merriwether that a grandson of Russian President Borochenkov was one of them. By coincidence – but in hindsight, perhaps by design – the President was coming to Ramey Air Force Base. The President wanted to know if I were available to join him on a secret flight to Moscow, and bring with me some of my formula. Of course, I said I would be honored!

"To anticipate your question, Mr. Bouchard, I did not have any way of knowing Air Force One would disappear from radar, causing such a political chaos. I merely boarded the airplane, only to have the reporters tell me we were returning to the Washington, DC area. I was confused, but then I thought there would be another flight from there to Moscow.

"I think it was only an hour – no more – into the flight when I heard the reporters ask Press Secretary Umberto why we had changed course. I do not know how they knew that, but there were angry words between them and him. He would not say anything more. I found an opportunity to speak with him in Spanish, and he explained President Merriwether did not want anyone to know the trip had to be secret for what he called 'national security reasons.'

"Shortly afterward, I was summoned to the President's quarters, and introduced to him. He explained another reason for secrecy is that the American Ambassador – I think his name is Vandergriff – arranged for the two Presidents to meet in Moscow. The plan was that while they were talking there I would be with his grandson, and that Dr. Frankhauser would be there, too.

"My immediate examination of the child indicated the disease had been rapidly progressing. I mentioned that to the attending physician and Dr. Frankhauser. I told them I feared I was too late to be helpful. The Russian physician said he had explicit instructions from President Borochenkov at least to try my medication. I did so several times, but felt it was too short a time to determine any result. I was asked to remain after President Merriwether boarded Air Force One to return to America, and stay as long as I desired to determine whether the medication would have any effect.

"I was surprised to see the Russian President arrive at the hospital after Air Force One left. Since Dr. Frankhauser suggested I bring extra clothing for the trip, I was able to stay for two weeks, constantly checking on the child. I did see a few encouraging signs, but just a few. President Borochenkov came every day to the hospital. One thing I did notice that also surprised me was the very strict security procedures in force. I finally came to the conclusion the President wanted to keep his grandson's illness from the public. I am not interested in politics, only in medicine, so I merely accepted the situation at face value.

"I guess President Borochenkov understood my frustration, and said to me one day, 'You are welcome to remain as long as you wish, but I understand it may be too late.' He told me he heard about the offer from the Mayo Clinic, and that they expected me to come there within a reasonable amount of time. He said I would be welcome to return to Moscow to continue experimenting with my formula. I told him I only had a limited supply, but I would be glad to leave what I had with the attending physician if he would keep careful notes on any reaction. But, the reality is the child could not survive. If my medication has even a short term effect, I will feel I have accomplished something. The President mentioned the death of his only grandson would end the direct male descendancy of the Borochenkov name.

"I must add the American Ambassador also came to the hospital every day. He told me the Russian President said his country would be happy to contribute to my research in any way possible as long it did not become a public matter. He explained the time might come when that would not be a secret. It was not my place to learn why it had to remain a secret. As I said, I am not into politics.

"My relatively short experience in Moscow had instilled in me a strong will to do everything I can to find some way to deal with progeria even though it affects such a small number of children. I am not married, and therefore do not have any children of my own. Right now, my life is dedicated to medicine and to concentrate on progeria. I am so grateful to the Mayo Clinic and to the Progeria Foundation."

"Dr. Rodriguez, I'm curious," he said. "Why all the fuss about this disease when it affects so relatively few children?"

"Mr. Bouchard, I am not offended by your question," she answered. "But, you may not realize I had another purpose in agreeing to the flight."

Bouchard was completely caught off guard. All he could manager was, "Come again?"

"Have you ever heard of the Cockayne Syndrome?" she asked.

His quizzical expression clearly indicated to her he did not.

She continued: "Both progeria and Cockayne are the result of mutated genes. The similarity stops there, for the most part. My desire was to determine whether I could learn something from Cockayne that could be applied to progeria. I had never seen a child with either. Cockayne hits 2 newborn children out of

1 million in the United States and Europe alone. Progeria occurs only once in 4-8 million babies. Both are always fatal.

"To answer your question, pose it to President Borochenkov and the parents of the child. Who is to say the mutation of a gene, while miniscule now, cannot literally explode? We do not know what causes the mutations. The Cockayne gene has been identified; the progeria one has not, yet. Some of the symptoms may confuse doctors into diagnosing the two illnesses as belonging to other medical conditions."

"What are some of progeria symptoms?" he asked.

She replied, "Slow growth; below-average height; narrow face and sharp nose; loss of hair, eyelashes and eyebrows; tight skin; head larger than face; thin lips; large eyes; small lower jaw; high-pitched voice; unusual formation of teeth; problems with body joints; dislocated hip; resistance to insulin; and an irregular heartbeat. It can be any combination of those."

"And, those of Cockayne?" he asked, surprisingly interested in such details.

She responded: "Short stature, stunted growth, very small head, slow nervous system development, hearing loss, eye abnormalities, severe tooth decay, and changes in the bones and brain."

"This is a lot more than I bargained for," he admitted.

"Mr. Bouchard, we cannot dismiss an illness just because it is limited to a small number of children. And as with medicine in general, a discovery for one ailment can lead to applications for others."

Bouchard did not know what to say, which was almost unheard of for him.

"Perhaps I have bored you with this overlong story of my role," she asked.

Bouchard replied, "Absolutely not!" But he kept the recorder on in case she might have other insights.

"By the way," she said suddenly. "I am current with the news reports of the outrage concerning what is called 'reporters being held prisoners on Air Force One.' I can tell you this because I was alone with President Merriwether several times. He agonized over the deception."

"What did he say?" Bouchard asked, because the term 'deception' intrigued him.

"That was a private conversation," she quickly answered. "I never would violate that. I would prefer we only speak about my work, if you have any other questions."

Bouchard decided he would not pursue that angle any further, but he would keep the word "deception" in the back of his mind for possible use in the future without any reference to her.

"Is there anything you wish to add?" he finally asked.

"No, I don't think so," she replied. "I do want to repeat how grateful to be in the right place at the right time. I feel honored to have met two Presidents, and an American Ambassador, who impressed me greatly with their obvious compassion for the situation. And now, I have to get ready to pass through security for my next flight. Mr. Bouchard, if I can save even one child, I will feel rewarded. Can we prevent this illness? That is a goal for the future."

Bouchard turned off the recorder, stood up, shook her hand, and responded, "Oh, by the way, where was Dr. Frankhauser during the flight?"

"Why, he was doing tests for the President's medical condition," she answered matter of factly. Did she see his jaw drop, Bouchard wondered?

* * * *

Bouchard knew the interview would make a great story, but that could wait. The last remark Dr. Rodriguez innocently made could result in a block-buster exclusive news story, and he needed to get hopping on that.

However, he realized he had a dilemma. She asked him for confidentiality, and he agreed. Did that cover her last remark, he pondered? It took him agonizing minutes before deciding on an approach that would resolve both concerns.

He phoned Dr. Frankhauser, and said he was doing a wrap-up story on the flight.

"Sir," he began, "I've been checking my own notes, rereading the stories, and recalling the television newscasts. I do not recall anyone asking you what your function was on Air Force One during the flight to Moscow?"

The fact that the Doctor paused significantly convinced him he had confirmed what he believed was the real reason, no matter what he said.

"Mr. Bouchard," Dr. Frankhauser answered finally, "you will have to get that information from the White House." His next words almost stunned Bouchard: "This is a case of doctor-patient confidentiality."

What the Doctor meant to say, but did not, was that he was the White House physician. As such, the President technically was a patient of his.

Bouchard did not want to put the Doctor in an embarrassing position, and he knew there would be a quick call to the White House. He decided discretion was the better part of getting an exclusive. "Of course," he finally said. "Yes, I will check with The White House. Thank you."

He could have tried to beat Dr. Frankhauser's call, but he had been admonished to go through Umberto first, and not try to reach the President directly. He decided to wait about half an hour before calling the Press Secretary. That way, he thought, Umberto might believe he was merely making some routine calls.

Bouchard recounted what he knew as facts. First, Dr. Frankhauser was on the flight. Second, he is the President's physician. Third, Dr. Rodriguez revealed something no one else seemed to know, even the press pool on Air Force One – that Dr. Frankhauser was conducting some kind of medical tests on the President.

Umberto politely responded, "Those are your facts, not mine." That was it.

CHAPTER 57

Self Q&A

SELF: AREN'T SUCH TESTS normally done at Bethesda Naval Medical Center?

Conclusion: The President did not want anyone to know tests were being done.

Self: Why did the President want that kind of secrecy?

Conclusion: He may have an illness never before revealed.

Self: What type of illness could this be?

Conclusion: It could affect his presidency.

Self: Would this justify the ruse of Air Force One vanishing?

Conclusion: The risk of backfiring was so high the apparent illness must be of such a nature this justified the vilification that has ensued.

Self: Isn't that a stretch?

Conclusion: Maybe, but it was very clever, and the President was willing to risk it.

Self: Didn't the President just have his annual physical exam done at Bethesda and got a good report?

Conclusion: It would seem a conflict, so I'll have to review what Dr. Frankhauser said there.

Self: Why hasn't the President begun campaigning yet?

Conclusion: Either he is confident of winning another four years, or . . . . maybe he has decided not to run.

Self: If the latter, is that connected to his medical condition?

Conclusion: It is plausible, and would answer the way he is conducting his presidency.

Self: Ergo, is it now clear the deception of Air Force One had two goals other than meeting with President Borochenkov regarding global warming?

Conclusion: Absolutely! The timing was incredible to have Dr. Frankhauser and Dr. Rodriguez on board with different missions to be accomplished simultaneously. The President is more clever than most people think.

Self: Is there any doubt Winston knew every facet of the flight?

Conclusion: No! He is too close to the President not to know.

Question: Do any Members of Congress have any inkling of the real reasons behind the flight?

Self: Doubtful, or else he would have been pilloried at the hearing. The President . . .
Self: Is the President certain he will not be impeached by the Senate?

Conclusion: No, and yes. Nothing is certain. The House vote was emotional. The odds are the Senate will be more civil. (Boy, I could beat Diane on that story.) Chief Justice Whittingham-Stern will have more control over the Senate hearing.

Self: Will the charge of "abuse of power" hold up?

Conclusion: I'm not a lawyer, but my guess is this is one of the issues the Chief Justice will focus on. Maybe the President abused his judgment, but what power did he abuse?

Self: Will the issues of global warming and the Russian President's grandson override his ruse of sneaking off to Russia?

Conclusion: That's the BIG question to be answered in the Senate.

Self: Can I get the President to confirm he has some kind of illness that could govern whether he will run next year?

Conclusion: I'm not hopeful. Why would The White House want to do that anyhow?

Self: If he does not run, will Winston seek the office?

Conclusion: No. I think he would have accepted the vice presidency only to make sure there would be a smooth transition if something happened on the flight.

Self: Am I biting off more than I can chew?

Conclusion: Somehow, I've got to end up with an exclusive story.

Self: And, how about the Dr. Rodriguez/progeria story?

Conclusion: That's the whipped cream on the sundae.

CHAPTER 58

The Moot of All Evil

CONGRESSMAN BASCOMB COULD HARDLY WAIT for his turn to propose a Motion for the House to consider accusing Winston of "conspiracy to commit abuse of power." Of course, one of his "Young Turks" seconded it.

House Judiciary Speaker and Judiciary Committee Chairman Vance said this time he would cast a vote in case of a tie. He had prepared a response in advance by acknowledging Majority Whip Conway as the discussion began.

"Mr. Chairman," he said, "the Senate has not yet conducted a hearing on the approved House Resolution that there was reasonable cause to bring an impeachment charge against President Merriwether. Mr. Chairman, I respectfully submit that without a Senate finding leading to impeachment, there is no foundation for the House to consider a conspiracy allegation. That is like putting the cart before the horse. Therefore, Mr. Chairman, I move to table the Motion by the Honorable Congressman Bascomb until such time the Senate makes a determination. It if does not approve impeachment is warranted, this Motion then will be moot."

Before Bascomb or any of the other "Young Turks" were recognized, Vance received a second. "All those in favor say 'aye;' those against say 'nay.' By voice vote, the Chair determines the Motion to table is passed."

Chip was at a loss for words, and embarrassed that his zeal caused him to skip due diligence. A growing number of his colleagues were having second thoughts about him.

* * * *

The "conventional wisdom" on Capitol Hill was that even further complications would arise if the House also "indicted" Winston, and the matter would be sent to the Senate. The original "impeachment" issue had to be settled first.

House and Senate Members had legal experts scouring law and history books for guidance. President Merriwether already had taken that action, including contacting law professor Howard Stern, the now divorced husband of the Chief Justice. He also asked for an opinion from the Solicitor General at the Department of Justice.

After absorbing all the opinions, and discussing this with Winston and Alicia, the President came to the conclusion there was no conclusion. This was an historic first!

Stern's report caught the President's attention:

"There would have to be conclusive evidence power was abused. Exactly which power was abused? The President did not order the pilot of Air Force One to do something illegal. There is a wide latitude of powers granted to the President, who also is Commander in-Chief of the Armed Forces. There was not 'personal' gain outside of his 'power' as President. The question of 'political' gain is moot.

"The dictionary definition of 'abuse' includes: misuse; hurt or injure by maltreatment; force sexual activity; reviling.

"To protect yourself, Mr. President, you should know there is one more definition that your opponents might bring up, but it is described as 'obsolete' – to deceive or trick. That goes back to any 'harm' done as a result of deception or trickery. Respectfully, assessing 'harm' on those bases would be extremely difficult at best.

"Because action in the Senate would be akin to a trial, the burden of proof is on those who support the Motion to Impeach.

"Anticipating a question you might ask, you would have the right not to 'testify.'

"Much depends on the wording to support the allegation of 'abuse of power.'

"As to the issue of Chief of Staff Winston, that certainly is moot pending the outcome of the only consideration of the Senate at the present time. The House has the option of considering a Resolution; again, that could be easily ruled moot because there is no adjudication of the matter now before the Senate.

"There could be other 'legal' issues, but this seems to be a situation of first things first. I cannot find a precedent in American history where a President and a Chief of Staff could be charged for the same act."

CHAPTER 59

(Dis)Order in the House

DIANE HAD NOT BEEN IDLE. Unlike Bouchard, she concentrated on what was swirling around Congress. She duly reported Chip's efforts and Vance's maneuvers. She kept calling Alicia for comment, but none was forthcoming. Her only alternative was to explain the whole impeachment progress and to include editorial comment:

"To impeach or not to impeach, that is the question," Diane began.

"Forgive me, Mr. Shakespeare, but that is what this Capitol Hill fandango is turning into. In simple terms, the House returns an 'indictment,' and the Senate holds a 'trial.' However, it really is not that simple.

"The House of Representatives has to go through a lot of formalities before an Impeachment Resolution is reported to the full House, which was done involving President Merriwether. The sole 'charge' against him is 'abuse of power' in secretly diverting Air Force One to Moscow after scheduled stops in Miami and Ramey Air Force Base in Puerto Rico. To say the House 'expedited' the 'indictment' is an understatement.

"Technically, the Speaker appointed what is called 'House managers' to present the Resolution of Impeachment to the Senate. The Senate has not even scheduled a hearing. By law, the Chief Justice of the United States would have to preside over that 'trial.' And, she was appointed by the President, who is the 'defendant.'

"If that is not confusing enough, along comes a charge of 'conspiracy' against Chief of Staff Winston regarding alleged 'abuse of power' by President Merriwether in the Air Force One situation. The House is at a stalemate on this because of the delay in the Senate.

"In the realm of conjecture, no one knows if and when both matters will be heard in the Senate, or whether the President and/or Winston will 'testify' in their own behalf.

"If all this were not so sad, it could be funny. In fact, it could rival the old comic routine by Bud Abbott and Lou Costello called 'Who's on first?' For those not old enough to remember one of the all-time belly laughers, straight man Abbott is trying to describe a baseball game to Costello.

"Funnyman Costello wants the line-up of players and asks, 'Who's on first?'

"Straight man Abbott answers, 'Yes.' He means the first baseman's name is Who, but Costello thinks Abbott is posing a question.

"Then, Costello asks, "What's on second base?

Abbott again replies, 'Yes.' I think you get the idea.

"Stay tuned for the next chapters of Who's Being Impeached Now? What's Being Done About It? I Don't Know. This is Diane Bana at Confusion Central."

* * * *

Alicia was the first to call Diane after she signed off.

"The President needs you to come up with material for the next White House Correspondents Dinner," she said.

Diane burst out laughing and responded, "Well, that's an offer that's hard to refuse. But, I will consider it."

"I'm sure you understood the risk you took with that over-the-top material," Alicia continued.

"Yes, I and my bosses did," Diane replied. "They really tried to talk me out of it. I could not think of a better way to capsulize what is going on here. I heard a saying some time ago. I can't remember who said it, and maybe I don't have the words right. But, my decision to go with the Abbott and Costello reference amounted to this: It will offend some, confuse others, and confound the rest."

"I'm sure the next time you try to contact House Member from the Conservative persuasion, you will either be put on hold forever, or the other Party will put a quick end to the call," Alicia commented.

"Worse – or better – than that, can you imagine the response I would get from one of the 'Young Turks?!" she asked.

"Seriously, President Merriwether wants you to know the factual portion was very much needed," Alicia remarked.

* * * *

The second call came from Bouchard. "This may surprise you, but I do not laugh often," he said. "There are those around here who sometimes refer to me as a 'joke.' Your piece was a gem!"

"Coming from you, that's quite a compliment, and I truly am grateful," she replied.

* * * *

The third call came from Congressman Bascomb, Jr.: "You think this is all funny?!" he literally roared. "Let's see who laughs last!"

She withheld the smart-ass reply she would have liked to have said.

Other calls naturally ranged from laudatory to threatening.

* * * *

Diane thought she was entitled to a breather; then, one of her sources called.

"I thought I would give you a heads-up that the Senate has set a date for the impeachment hearing," the caller said in a hushed voice. "It will be a week from tomorrow."

Diane did some quick calculation, and determined that would be the first week of November, plenty of time before the Thanksgiving hiatus. Before she went on the air with the "Breaking News" banner, she checked with two other reliable sources who confirmed the tip.

CHAPTER 60

In The Eye Of The Beholder

BOUCHARD WAS ITCHING to go with the story of the President's health, but he could not find a "hook" on which to comfortably hang it. "Hook" or no "hook," he had to counter Diane with his health story.

As a matter of courtesy, he alerted Umberto. While he trusted the Press Secretary not to leak that to other White House correspondents, he knew Umberto would immediately notify President Merriwether, who in turn would alert Jared.

"Just thank Bouchard for the advanced notice," the President told Umberto, which the Press Secretary did without further comment.

Headlined "Analysis," the story began:

"President Lincoln Merriwether has remained tight-lipped over what some call a 'blatant deception' regarding the Air Force One incident. He also has been silent about his health. The two may be connected.

"According to a source very knowledgeable about what went on in Air Force One on its mystery trip to Russia, the President was going through a series of medical tests conducted by Dr. Justin Frankhauser. The White House physician, and head of the Bethesda Naval Medical Center in nearby Maryland, was aboard Air Force One for the first time. The nature of the tests is not known, but the President only recently underwent his annual physical checkup there. While the report seemed routine, a careful reading of what was told to reports left room for speculation.

"Why is the President's health of such great importance now?

"For one thing, he is serving out the first term in the White House under horrific circumstances. The incoming and outgoing Presidents and Vice Presidents – along with many others – were killed by explosions during the Inaugural. At that time, President Merriwether was Speaker of the House, second in line to the Oval Office. Although he was not elected President, he might only be able to serve one more term. The 22nd Amendment states in Section 1: '. . . no person who has held the office of President, or acted as President, for more than two years of a term to which some other person was elected President shall be elected to the office of the President more than once.'

"For another, and this connects to the Air Force One incident, President Merriwether may already be receiving treatment for some kind of illness. A source with knowledge of this confirms that Dr. Frankhauser has made a number of unannounced visits to Camp David when the President was there.

"It seems clear now that meeting with Russian President Borochenkov on global warming and drones with nuclear warheads may not have been the only reason for the way the flight was conducted. If so, between the visits to Camp David, the stay at Bethesda, and what transpired on the flight, there may be a direct connection. That is why the question of his health is of great importance.

"Coupled with that is the matter of potential impeachment, now in the hands of the Senate. Whether his health will be an ancillary, but not legal, consideration is another matter, on which reporters surely will follow up on.

"In hindsight, the health issue may be further connected with the now defeated nomination of Jared Winston, his Chief of Staff and long-time personal and political confidant, to be Vice President. If something happened to the President on that flight, Winston could have become acting President, assuring a smooth continuation of government. However, there still is no current Vice President. That leaves the Speaker of the House Vance next in line to the Oval Office.

"Congress, as well as the country, deserves to know the full story of the President's health."

* * * *

Diane immediately contacted Alicia and asked if she could interview the President. The answer was a polite "not at this time."

She wanted comments first from Progressive Party members like Senator Cummings. An aide said, "He is not available."

Then, she contacted Senate Majority Leader Winters. He replied: "We feel it would be in everybody's best interest if the Senate acted on the impeachment matter in an expedited way."

On the House side, she reached Speaker Vance who responded, "We have done our work on President Merriwether. The issue of the President's health no longer is of our concern."

"Mr. Speaker, if the President is impeached, and there is no Vice President, you become the next President," Diane asserted.

"That's what the law says," he responded curtly, and ended the call.

Next on her list was Congressman Bascomb, who roared, "Let the chips fall where they may!" She did not have a clue what that meant, and went on to reach Conservatives.

Senate Minority Leader Amaroso echoed what Winters had said.

House Minority Leader Schoenfeld was not reticent in commenting. She declared, "If the President is ill enough that he might not be able to effectively serve our country, he should make that known immediately. But, he has been so smugly secretive about that Air Force One business that chances are he will be as secretive about his health. Winston would have been nothing more than a straw man for the President."

Diane included all of the responses, but did not offer her own comment.

CHAPTER 61

The Political Pot Boils Over

SENATOR WINTERS CALLED the President and asked, "What should we do, since those two stories have been published and aired?"

"I never have lost sight of the fact that the President also is head of his Party," President Merriwether began. "But, it would be improper for me to have any say so in the proceedings in your chamber. Let your duty be your conscience."

Bosworth was putting pressure on Chip to start the impeachment mechanism against Winston in the House. Vance was adamant about waiting for the Senate to act.

* * * *

Boz suddenly encountered a problem of his own. The Congressman whom he farmed out to one of his companies to keep his mouth shut called him bitterly complaining about his situation. "You promised me a good position at double the money I was making as a Congressman!" he asserted. "I had to move my family, sell my house, and change my life! That's bullshit! I was given an office without anything to do except read manuals! I'm not invited to meetings. We can't find decent housing; we're living in a motel! You lied to me! My wife's threatening to divorce me, and take the kids home!"

Puffing on a cigar, he calmly responded, "You made your bed. Now, lie in it. I did the best I could."

"You lying bastard!" he shouted. "Do you think I'm going to take this lying down?! Hell, no! I'll go to the papers and TV stations, and nail your hide to the wall!"

"Listen, son," Boz said firmly, "don't make threats! Your reputation will go into the toilet! I can see to it that no one will ever hire you! Just take the pay, and make it to retirement!"

"But, my wife . . . ?!" he pleaded.

"She's your wife, not mine!" he declared. "I got enough trouble with mine as it is! And, don't ever call me again!"

* * * *

Winters decided he was proverbially between a rock and a hard place. He had hoped for some direction from President Merriwether, but now he was on his own.

He wondered just how ill the President was. Maybe his fellow lawmakers would sympathize with him, and vote down the impeachment without openly saying so. What would the public reaction be to that?

Is there some kind of "deal" that could be worked out with the White House? If he could stall the hearing until the Thanksgiving break, that would give him a good six weeks to figure out what to do.

Most of his fellow lawmakers who were up for re-election, along with all the Representatives, were more anxious to get campaigning than dealing with impeachment. Now that the President's health has become an issue, how would that affect those campaigns?

He had a thought. "Alicia, this is Ansel Winters," he announced.

"What can I do for you, Senator?" she responded.

He explained his dilemma and asked, "Is there any way the President can give me some guidance on the health issue?"

"I understand you already spoke with him," she answered. "I honestly would feel very uncomfortable talking with him now."

"This does not bode well for the Party!" he asserted.

She thought for a moment and said, "Let me try to approach Jared about your predicament."

"That would be great!" he replied hopefully.

"Senator, I cannot promise anything," she explained. "I will try, and let you know."

* * * *

True to her word, she did talk with Jared. "It's the President's call, Alicia," he explained. "To be honest, he really has not said much to me about the health issue since he had his last treatment with Dr. Frankhauser. I have to admit I'm concerned that after all these years he's keeping this pretty much to himself. If I get an opportunity to bring it up, I will. The argument about how this might have a negative effect on the election for our Party, and that might persuade him to make a decision."

No sooner had she left his office than Umberto called him. "I'm getting a lot of heat from reporters about the Bouchard and Bana stories," he said. "I'm not sure how long I can hold them off. I don't feel comfortable going to the President with this right now."

That convinced Jared he needed to speak with the President.

* * * *

"Linc," he said – something he had not called him since he became President – "we need to talk."

"If it's about the health issue . . ."

Jared interrupted, "Yes, it is, and you can't shut me out after all these years!"

"Jared, don't tell me what I can or can't do!" he declared uncharacteristically.

The President did not say anything more, and Jared finally left. He only told Alicia there was nothing more the President wanted to say on the subject. "You'll have to come up with some excuse for an excuse," he said. "Sorry, but that's the way he wants it."

Jared returned to his office, and told his secretary he did not want to be disturbed. This was not unusual when he wanted to make private calls. Unbeknown to her, he did not make any calls, but stared out his window for almost half an hour.

* * * *

Alicia apologized to Diane and Winters. echoing Jared, "That's the way the President wants it."

* * * *

Cuddling up in Tim's arms that evening, all she said was, "Mostly, I love my job and its challenges. Then, there are times like today when I hate it!"

* * * *

Senate Majority Leader Winters called House Speaker Vance and said, "We've got to meet." Winters had an unmarked private room off the Capitol Rotunda.

"The President is playing us like we're puppets," Winters said. "I'm not sure I can stop the impeachment process. If the President continues to play cagey, we're going to lose what little edge we have in the Senate. Does he realize that? Why won't he let us use the health issue?"

"Beats the hell out of me," Vance agreed. "There's something funny about this I can't put my finger on."

"Wait a damn minute!" Winters blurted. "I just remembered something! Didn't President Fairchild try to hide her breast cancer? Didn't she have Dr. Frankhauser in on it?"

"You've got something there," Vance agreed. "If I didn't know better, I'd be willing to bet that is weighing on his mind. He's concerned reporters will remember the same connection. Maybe we should talk with Dr. Frankhauser. I suspect he would pull that doctor-patient confidentiality excuse. By the same token, he's probably told Jared to zip his lip, too. So, where does that leave us? Any thoughts about how a vote would go?"

"As they say, I'm firmly ambivalent," Winters joked. "If it came to a vote, I'd have to sell my soul to keep the Progressive majority solid. That should be enough to defeat the Resolution."

"If you can do that, the one in the House regarding Jared would fall apart," Vance added.

"Apropos of nothing, what's going on with Bosworth?" Winters asked.

"Why ask me?" Vance answered.

"The way I hear it, Boz bought off that one vote you guys needed, and sent the poor boy off to Siberia," Winters explained.

"Hey, maybe he's the one who's been trying to get hold of me with what he says is dirt on Boz," Vance realized. "Maybe I should take his phone call."

"That's all we need is Boz sticking his bulbous nose into our business," Winters remarked. "Remember, he paid dearly for calling a meeting of ESRG without telling General McCormick.'"

"I've got enough problems as it is with that pain-in-the-ass Chip Bascomb!" Vance declared.

"Junior," Winters added sarcastically.

"Well, if you guys deep-six the impeachment of Merriwether, I'll cool his jets good and proper," Vance retorted.

"There's got to be a way to get the President off the pot," Winters said. "Maybe that Bouchard guy will build a fire under him. He's already got some sparks going."

"Let's keep that in mind," Vance responded.

"Apropos of nothing else, and I'm hesitant to even bring it up because of your long relationship with the President, but I'd like your take on something that has bothered me for a long time," Winters remarked.

"What's that?" Vance responded.

"Well, President Merriwether and Winston have been without wives for many years," the Senate Majority Leader began. "Each was the best man at the other's wedding. That's been a close bond for a long time. Neither remarried . . ."

Vance interrupted, "Don't even go there! Yes, they're close, but not that close."

"I just was wondering why some scandal sheet never made up anything about it, that's all," Winters explained.

"I'll pretend I never heard what you said, and never bring it up again!" the Speaker admonished the Majority Leader."

* * * *

When the Speaker returned to his office, he put in a call to his mentor, but was puzzled when the President would not return it. That had never happened before.

CHAPTER 62

Privacy Issue

After Jared left the Oval Office, the President stared at the Great Seal embedded in the carpet in front of his desk. Finally, he had his secretary call Dr. Frankhauser.

"Yes, tell him I can be at Camp David this weekend," he said.

Then, President Merriwether personally dialed a special number.

"Yes, Mr. President, I can arrange to be at Camp David this weekend," the other person responded.

* * * *

The President told Jared he would be at Camp David for the weekend "to rest up a bit. Hold the fort until I return."

That arrangement was not unusual, although the President normally would have some others there to keep him company. This time, it was obvious to Jared he wanted to be alone. He did not have any way of knowing there would be two others there.

CHAPTER 63

Procedures and Ponderings

DIANE DECIDED TO DO a background piece on impeachment:

"The procedure for impeachment in the Senate, once it has received the proper documentation from the House, is much like a court trial. However, there is an odd set of convoluted procedures involved.

"Once the Resolution to impeach President Merriwether was adopted in the House by a simple majority, a Resolution was passed allowing Speaker Vance to select what are called 'managers' to act as sort of prosecutors to present the case to the Senate. As 'lead manager,' a sort of district attorney, Vance chose Majority Whip Conway, explaining 'Merrill is confident enough to even chastise me on occasion.'

"Next, the House passed a Resolution notifying the Senate of what it had done. The Senate, in turn, adopted an Order notifying the House it was ready to accept the 'managers,' who then appeared before the Senate, and officially presented the Article of Impeachment. This done, the 'managers' returned to the House, and made a report to the House.

"Where it stands now, the Senate Judiciary Committee has announced a date for the so-called hearing/trial to begin. That is what Majority Leader Winters was trying to delay, much to the dismay of Senator Cummings, Judiciary Committee chairman. If the Judiciary Committee agrees there is sufficient cause to present the matter to the full Senate, the House 'managers' make their case for impeachment. At this point, the Chief Justice would act as presiding judge. The President would have the right to defend himself personally, or have someone else do so. Each side could call witnesses, who would be subjected to cross-examinations.

"Once all testimony is given, the Senate would deliberate in private, much like a jury. A vote of two-thirds of the Senate would be required for 'conviction.'

"Impeachment of government officials is easy to begin, but difficult to accomplish. Only three Presidents have faced impeachment. The one involving Andrew Johnson came when he succeeded Republican President Lincoln after he was assassinated. Johnson, a Democrat, faced a Republican-dominated Congress. Without getting into the continuing legislative battle between the two, the House passed 11 Articles of Impeachment against Johnson, generally dealing with Reconstruction of the South after the Civil War. By the time the full Senate deliberated, they were down to 3. He was acquitted in 1868 on each count by one vote.

"In 1974, the House voted for three Articles of Impeachment against Richard Nixon: obstruction of justice; abuse of power; and, contempt of Congress for failing to produce required documents. He resigned before the full House could vote.

"During 1998-99, Bill Clinton faced four Articles: perjury; 'perjurious, false, and misleading testimony' in a civil case related to the Monica Lewinsky scandal; a cover-up involving evidence in the scandal; and, other similar charges. He, too, was acquitted.

"Could President Merriwether be the fourth to face Senate action?

"This is Diane Bana on Capitol Hill."

* * * *

After watching Diane's report, Bouchard felt this now was a reportorial challenge. As he pondered how to really push the President's health angle, his phone rang. It was his "spy" who tracked vehicles heading for Camp David.

"It's that Doctor somebody again," he said.

"So, what's new?" Bouchard countered smugly.

"What's new is that there was a second vehicle," he continued.

"So what?" Bouchard countered.

"So this one had diplomatic plates, that's what!" he retorted.

"What?!" Bouchard shouted.

"Is there something wrong with this connection?" he asked jokingly.

"By any stretch of my imagination, I don't suppose you got the numbers on the plates?" Bouchard asked almost pleadingly.

"This will cost you," he answered.

"If it's worth it, hell yes!" Bouchard responded irritatingly.

As he put the "spy" on hold, he quickly checked with a source he kept on file. "What the hell?" he said. "It's from our State Department!"

Bouchard finally got back on line and said, "Yeah, you deserve a bonus! Good job!"

He quickly called the press office at State, identified himself, and asked, "Could you tell me why a high level State Department official would visit President Merriwether at Camp David?"

"I don't have that information handy, but let me check and get back to you," the press aide said.

"I'm on a deadline," Bouchard lied.

Five minutes later, his phone rang. "Sorry to say, it certainly was not the Secretary," the aide reported. "He is right here in his office. Is there some question you want to ask him?"

"I've got one for you," he answered. "I have a license plate ID that indicates the vehicle is one from the State Department. If it's not the Secretary's, whose is it?"

"I don't have that information handy, but let me check and get back to you," the press aide repeated what Bouchard thought must be a recording.

Again, five minutes later, his phone rang. "That is not the Secretary's plate. All I can tell you is that vehicle is used to transport high-level State Department personnel."

"Thanks for your promptness," Bouchard said, hanging up.

What the hell is going on here? he mused to himself. If it's not the Secretary, who is it? He decided this was a dead-end because it would take forever to try to find out, and maybe he would be stone-walled anyhow.

What's the connection between the two visitors? It does not make sense there is one. There's the White House physician, who's either examining the President, or giving him some kind of treatment, and then there's a mysterious and obviously high-level State Department somebody. Damn, I hate answerless questions.

Almost as a last resort, he went to Umberto's office to try to solve the mystery. "I honestly don't have a clue about the State Department visitor," Jorge responded. "I don't have to justify Dr. Frankhauser's visit."

His frustration rising, Bouchard tried contacting Jared. "Mr. Bouchard, the President does not confide in me who he has visiting him at Camp David, so I honestly don't know anything about a State Department official going there," Jared explained.

Bouchard began to scratch his head. Now, instead of one unanswered question, he had a second one. Since when doesn't Winston know who's visiting the President there?

CHAPTER 64

Concerns

WINSTON WAS UNNERVED by Bouchard's question. Not only has the President – his long-time friend – stopped taking him into his confidence, but a mysterious visitor shows up at Camp David when President Merriwether was supposed to be alone.

Just then, Alicia stopped by to ask him something. Before she could speak, he said, "Come in, and shut the door." She did so, but could not suppress an air of uneasiness.

"You know the President and I go back a long way," he began. "There's no one else I can confide in, so let me ask you, Alicia. Have you noticed a change in the President lately?"

She was surprised by the question, and had to hesitate before answering, "Well, he has looked a bit tired. And, concerned. Yes, that's the word. Why, Jared?"

Now he looked concerned. "This is in strict confidence, Alicia," he responded. "I've noticed a disturbing change, but I cannot fathom why."

"What do you mean?" she asked.

Now he hesitated before replying, "He snapped at me the other day. In all the years we've known each other, he has never done that."

"Jared, that could be because he's concerned about what the Senate could do to him . . . and what the House and Senate could do to you," she reasoned.

He looked up at the ceiling as he rocked back in his chair, remaining so for a minute or two. Finally, he sat upright and responded,

"That would be the minimal explanation. I think there is something more than that occupying his mind. It's just that he won't discuss it with me."

"Maybe he's worried about his health becoming an issue . . ." she offered.

Jared interrupted by asserting, "I don't want to go there!"

That surprised her. She knew she had to drop that subject.

"The President is at Camp David for the weekend," he began. "What's not out of the ordinary is that Dr. Frankhauser is there, too." She was about to say something, but he continued, "What is out of the ordinary is that someone from the State Department – a high official, from what I gather – is there, too. And, I do not know who, or why."

She was not sure whether he expected her to share her thoughts with him, so she did not offer any and waited for his next remark.

"Alicia, I'm very frustrated, and even hurt," he said. "I never thought I would say that where he is concerned. You know, I really owe my life to him. If not for him, I would be a nobody."

"But sir, you are a somebody!" she replied quickly. "You are making a difference!"

"I appreciate that, Alicia," he responded. "That's not what I'm getting at. Something is brewing, and I don't know what it is. I'm not there to help him if he needs it. Look, I know full well had I become Vice President, that was to be just an insurance policy. I'm no more qualified for this position – and God forbid the presidency – than anyone else. I can think of other people who could do this a lot better. I'm just a caretaker."

She realized he was wallowing in self-pity, but he thought so much of the President that he could not help but agonize.

"If I knew who that State Department official was, I think I could figure out why he was there," he said. "I would feel better about that. Alicia, what I am trying to say – and not doing a very good job of it – is that I am scared at the prospect of something happening to the President and I would not be at his side."

Alicia decided on what she wanted to say: "Jared, wait for the President to return, and maybe things will get back to what they were. If he wants to share what went on at Camp David over the weekend, let him take the lead. Everything may well work itself out."

Jared surprised her by smiling. "I always knew there was something special about you," he said. "Thanks for being a good listener. You're right. Maybe I worry too much."

When she returned to her office, then she began to worry.

* * * *

"Jared, come see me in the Oval Office," the President said Monday morning. "I have something to share with you, and someone for you to meet."

The Chief of Staff smiled. "Everything may well work itself out indeed!" he said to himself. "Alicia was right." But, once inside the Oval Office . . . .

CHAPTER 65

Announcements

UMBERTO ALERTED THE REPORTERS not only in the White House, but also those covering Congress. There was not enough room in the briefing room. It being a nice day, the President's appearance would be held in the Rose Garden.

"Ladies and Gentleman of the press, and Americans everywhere," he began. "I have two very special announcements to make.

"Trying to find someone to take on the responsibilities of Vice President presents a unique challenge. I have selected someone who not only is qualified in the broadest concept of politics and government, but who also should not have a problem earning Senate confirmation. That person is . . . Ambassador Preston Vandergriff."

He suddenly appeared as if out of nowhere. Actually, he had been standing to one side next to Jared, but none of the reporters noticed.

"We have a copy of his resume available, and I'm sure the media will report on that in detail. Why a career diplomat, you may ask? He has risen through the ranks of the State Department with increasing ability to deal with problems in an efficient way, while earning respect from world leaders. Most recently, he was responsible for arranging the meeting in Moscow with Russian President Borochenkov. That was no small feat. When I notified President Borochenkov of my decision, he tried to talk me out of it, offering to trade us Russia's Olympic medals if I would change my mind. (Laughter.) The President had the highest praise for Ambassador Vandergriff, as have leaders in every country he has served in. That is good enough for me.

"The second announcement will be brief." He paused (for effect, naturally) before adding slowly, "I shall not seek, nor will I serve, a second term as President of the United States." Reporters knew those words were uttered by President Lyndon Johnson.

There was a collective gasp! By the time reporters recovered, the President and the nominee had walked back inside. Alicia was frozen in place. So was Bouchard. Then he smiled, and sought out Diane.

"We both have been scooped by the President!" he said.

"In all honesty, did you know about this in advance?" she asked.

"If I would have, you would have read about it!" he asserted.

"So, what do you make of this?" she asked, and then realized he was not about to share his next analysis with her.

Bouchard grinned, "It caught me off guard, so I'm not sure. I'll have to think about it."

"Same for me," she replied.

"To each analysis," Bouchard said, raising his hand as if there were a glass in it.

"Skoal!" she replied.

He decided not to share his revelation of "now I know who was in the other car."

* * * *

Also caught off guard was Umberto, who shared his frustration with Fountaineau. They could not get back to their offices fast enough to begin dealing with a deluge of questions for "amplification" of the President's twin announcements.

When Alicia returned to her office, she went through the list of calls. The first one she returned was from Tim.

"Boy, you guys know how to grab headlines," he said.

"So, former news guy, what do you think of the announcements?" she asked.

"Well, I'm more interested in what the President did not say than in what he did say," he answered.

"Run that by me again, my bashful beau," she replied.

"If I were back in the news business, that's what my lead would read," Tim began. "First of all, this kills the impeachment business in the House. Second, by saying he won't be around for a second term should do likewise in the Senate for him."

"You're not only good looking, you're smart!" she asserted.

"Wait, you might change your mind, because there's a third," he remarked.

"And, that is . . .?" Alicia asked.

"Why isn't he running for another term?" Tim asked.

"Good question," she responded, "for which I don't have an answer. Look, honey, I wish we could talk more, but I have a ton of calls to return and make. See you tonight?"

"Wait for my announcement," he joked.

* * * *

Vance and Winters came to the same conclusion as Tim regarding the impeachment actions.

"That was about as clever as I can remember in all the years I've been here," the Speaker commented. "He killed two birds with one stone."

"What do you think of the Vandergriff nomination?" the Senator asked.

"You're the one that's going to have to deal with it," Vance responded.

"I can't see how we could turn that down after all that's been going on," Winters replied. "That should sail through without a ripple."

"Well, the good news on my side of the Rotunda is I won't have to deal with Chip anymore," the Speaker said. "He'll have to find another windmill to tilt at."

* * * *

When Congressman Bascomb phoned Bosworth, he refused to take the call.

* * * *

When the onslaught of calls subsided, Jared asked Alicia to come to his office. "Alicia, for a while there, I thought you'd be my permanent replacement," he said.

"Not a chance, Jared," she said. "You're too good at what you do. But, I do have a question or two. I spoke with Tim about the announcements, and he made a comment that got me to thinking. If I'm poking my nose where it does not belong, tell me."

"You've got the floor," he responded.

"Tim said as a former news man he was more interested in what the President did not say," she began. "For example, why do you think he is not going to run?"

"Since we're off-the-record, I can confide in you because I trust you to keep this to yourself, and that means not sharing this with Tim," he explained. She nodded yes. "In two words, his health."

"So, there is substance to the rumors I've been hearing," she commented.

"I now know he's been getting treatments from Dr. Frankhauser," Jared continued. "There's no need to get into specifics. He has a type of cancer that has spread. He ignored it for a while, and that made it more difficult to deal with now."

"That's why Dr. Frankhauser was aboard Air Force One," she realized.

"Yes," Jared replied. "That's why he comes here to The White House, and why he goes to Camp David. The prognosis is not good. I think he was apprehensive about going public because President Fairchild also had cancer, albeit a very different kind."

"And, Ambassador Vandergriff?" she asked.

"That was a curve ball to me, and I'm swinging wildly on that one," he admitted. "When the President called me into the Oval

Office after our meeting, the Ambassador was there. Actually, I was relieved when the President laid out his scenario. I doubt Vandergriff will have any trouble getting confirmed by the Senate. And, allow me to let you in on a secret. He will get the Progressive Party nomination to be the next President. I'll bet anything he'll make it. In fact, if Linc leaves before his term is up, and Vandergriff becomes President, that might well get around the Constitutional limit. That could be an interesting development."

Alicia was taken aback by what she just heard. "Do I infer the President had this planned out?" she finally asked.

"Well, it was a combination of things," Jared answered. "Ambassador Vandergriff had heard about President Borochenkov's grandson, and called President Merriwether with the plan to have Dr. Rodriguez on Air Force One. The Russian President really likes the Ambassador, and readily agreed to the plan. He even laughed at the ruse involving Air Force One."

Alicia interrupted, "So, the business about global warming was a phony one?"

"Oh, no, that's very real," Jared replied. "The President is committed to it. Of course, so is Ambassador Vandergriff."

"Let's get back to the President's health," she said.

"To be honest, Dr. Frankhauser does not know how much time the President has," he began. "That being the case, he came to two conclusions: One, I should not become President. I'm not offended by that. Two, he wanted a new Vice President who could succeed him. That's how the deal worked out. The President hides the pain he is suffering from, but it only can get worse, not better."

"Jared, what about your future?" she asked.

"Thanks for asking," he answered. "Ambassador Vandergriff already asked me to stay as his Chief of Staff when he becomes President. And, I'm positive he will want you and Jorge to stay as well. As for me, I'll leave with Linc. When that happens, you might well be the front runner for Chief of Staff. The President still has sources on The Hill, as I'm sure you have discovered. He told me on more than one occasion he was not surprised at the high regard lawmakers and their staffs have for you. He knows it has not always been easy because of him – especially the Air Force One gambit – but, you came through with your reputation intact."

"I'm embarrassed," she admitted.

* * * *

She could not wait to phone Tim, and promise him "an evening you won't forget. And, don't complain that you have a headache."

* * * *

Bosworth called a press conference at his home "for a very special matter."

When the reporters were settled in, he announced:

"I actually have two announcements. The first is that I am changing my political Party affiliation to Conservative! Second, I will be a candidate for President on the Conservative Party ticket!"

Question: "Why do you think you will be a viable candidate?"

Answer: "I have been a successful businessman, and a high government official."

Question: "Weren't you only sixth in line to the Oval Office?"

Answer: "Next question."

Question: "What prompted you to announce just after President Merriwether's press conference?"

Answer: "It was – I mean – it is the reason. There is no doubt Ambassador Vandergriff, who does not have any managerial experience in government, is being groomed to succeed the President. His expertise is in the diplomacy, and he should remain there."

Question: "Isn't diplomacy expertise a plus for a President?"

Answer: "You're missing the point. The President is the chief executive of the United States. He is supposed to run the country.

Think of him as the CEO of a huge corporation. That is how I operated the Department of Defense."

Question: "Why not just challenge the Ambassador for the Progressive Party nomination instead of switching to the Conservatives?"

Answer: "I feel the Progressive Party is too sneaky. To allow Air Force One to disappear on a presidential whim, and throw the country and the Congress into chaos, tells me all I need to know."

Question: "Who will be your running mate?"

Answer: "As the old saying goes, 'that's for me to know, and you to find out.'"

Question: "It has come to our attention you manipulated the House vote on impeachment of the President."

Answer: "Is that a question? Where did you hear such drivel?! I won't dignify a rumor by addressing it! Next question?"

There weren't any.

CHAPTER 66

Adieu

BOUCHARD HAD BEEN PART of the press corps at Boz's news conference. As usual, he did not ask any questions. However, he had some for President Merriwether via Umberto.

When Jorge heard them, an idea formed in his mind. He first went to Jared, who suggested Vandergriff – who had enough time to retire from the State Department – be included in a strategy session, along with Alicia.

After there was consensus on a plan, Jorge called Bouchard and thanked him for his eagerness. "You can scoop your colleagues by announcing the President will give one of those 'fireside chats' he modeled after President Roosevelt tomorrow evening in prime time," the Press Secretary said.

Diane could not understand how Bouchard got the jump on such a major story.

* * * *

"My fellow Americans, I want to amplify the announcements I made about the nomination of Ambassador Vandergriff as Vice President, and that I will not seek another term.

"There has been much speculation about both. They are interconnected, but let me begin with the Office of the Vice President. Mr. Winston has been my Chief of Staff not only in The White

House but also in the House of Representatives where I was honored to be elected Speaker. When I originally nominated him, I was on Air Force One. The flight from Ramey Air Force Base in Puerto Rico to Moscow took nearly 12 hours. A lot can happen in that time, as well as during the trip back to Andrews Air Force Base. Should I have not been able to fulfill my duties as President, I wanted to make sure a Vice President was in place. I should have nominated someone much earlier, and I apologize for that delay.

"I am not implying the next in line to the Oval Office – House Speaker Vance – was not capable of fulfilling that role. However, I confess the nomination was more of a stop-gap measure than a full time appointment. My plan always was to select a full-time Vice President. I honestly did not have anyone in mind until I met Ambassador Vandergriff in Moscow. Almost in an instant, I knew he fit the bill. Yes, there are those who say he does not have experience in government operations because he is a career diplomat, or any experience with Members of Congress. I decided that was a plus, not a minus.

"Turning to my decision not to seek another four years as President, the unvarnished truth is because I have a medical condition in which the progress is not positive. I will try my best to finish out my term, but I am comforted in knowing I have a most capable Vice President.

"This brings me back to why I chose Ambassador Vandergriff. I have given a lot of thought to the role of President of the United States. The federal government is somewhat like a huge corporation. A successful corporation has a board of directors, a president or chief executive officer, and another top executive. Think of Congress as the board of directors, the President as the CEO, and the Vice President as the other top executive.

"My view of that is the CEO, like the commander of a ship, sets the course. His immediate subordinate carries out the orders. To use another simile, the head of the corporation sets the policy and his subordinate takes care of implementing it.

"We are in vastly changing times – an era of electronic communication. Your sons and daughters, and their sons and daughters, will live a much different life than we have had. With that in mind, we should change the way our government operates to be in sync with the new era. To do that, it is my firm belief that future Presidents should continue to make final decisions, but they should delegate the implementation of those decisions under the direction of the Vice President.

"For that reason, I see in Ambassador Vandergriff a model for the transition to the new era from our present one. He does not have to personally run the government, but he does have to possess what I call 'global vision.' We are so interdependent on countries other than ours that such vision and experience is crucial.

"I don't know of any university that has a course in how to become President of the United States, nor Vice President, nor to be a Member of Congress. One way to look at it is that government employment starting with The White House consists of on-the-job learning.

"I honestly believe a brighter future for America starts with better and more efficient government. Federal workers should be proud of their work, as should every American. While I am not up to the task, I hope the appointment of Ambassador Vandergriff is a new beginning, which I also hope will carry over to his becoming the next President of the United States.

"Keep in mind I was not elected President, but ascended to The White House and the Oval Office only because of a horrific turn of events during the Inaugural massacre. Here is my mea culpa. I have not felt comfortable because of that. I never expected to be sitting where I am this moment, but I am unabashedly grateful for the opportunity to hopefully make a difference.

"Thank you, and good night!"

* * * *

Ironically, both Bouchard and Diane led off their reports with the same word – "WOW!"

He reported that some believed the "chat" was nothing more than a self-serving commencement type oration." Diane noted others who said they were reminded of Vice President Harry Truman who became President only because Franklin D. Roosevelt died shortly after being elected to a fourth term, and often was called the 'accidental President."

Many people wanted to know the exact nature of President Merriwether's illness. The standard answer was, "This will be revealed at the proper time." Of course, that meant after he passed away.

* * * *

Tim and Alicia decided to make reservations at the romantic L'Auberge Chez Francois Restaurant in the northern Virginia community of Great Falls. Unhurriedly picking away at a luscious and calorie-laden dessert, she said, "As much as I thought I knew Merriwether, I really underestimated him."

"Me, too," Tim replied. "You know, it took a lot of political balls to pull off that Air Force One disappearance act, knowing it could end his career. And yet, he believed what he did would be justified in the grand scheme of things."

"He had the whole scenario planned out, even to the impeachment," she mused.

Tim laughed, and she asked, "Did I say something funny?"

"No, sweetheart," he answered. "I was thinking of New York Yankees catcher Yogi Berra who mangled the English language. One of his convoluted sayings was, 'It ain't over till it's over.' It was his version of what a sportswriter once observed about a game in which the score kept changing – 'The opera isn't over until the fat lady sings.'"

Now she laughed.

"So, do you have a date reserved for our wedding?" he suddenly asked.

She stopped laughing. She was not sure if he was serious. Then she responded, "I'll check my calendar and get back to you on that."

That night, not a word was said during their intense love making.

CHAPTER 67

Coda

VICE PRESIDENT VANDERGRIFF, with Mary Ann McCormick as his running mate, soundly defeated Secretary of Defense Bosworth and Senator Cummings in the November election. House Majority Leader Conway was elected Speaker, and House Whip Hudak became Majority Leader.

* * * *

President Merriwether, too ill to remain for the Inauguration, said goodbye to the White House staff privately in the Oval Office the following week. Winston joined him on the walk through the Rose Garden toward the Marine One helicopter for the short flight to Andrews Air Force Base. Once there, Winston helped the President climb the stairs of Air Force One. They stood at the cabin door, waved to the onlookers, and then entered the plane.

* * * *

At the funeral a month later, Winston gave this eulogy: "President Merriwether was a modest man. All he wanted said was something his mother remarked in her failing days: 'I don't want flowers on my casket because it's too late to smell them.' To him, it meant, if you have something good to say about another person, do so when they are alive and can appreciate it."

Among those attending the funeral were Russian President Borochenkov; President-elect Vandergriff; many Cabinet officials; Speaker Vance and Majority Leader Winters; Drs. Frankhauser and Rodriguez; Tim and Alicia (she was named Chief of Staff when Winston left); Whiz and Frankie; and . . . . . Bouchard.

* * * *

At the White House Correspondents Dinner, Diane and Bouchard announced the awards they had won "really belong to the reporters on the Air Force One mystery trip to Moscow."

Diane still had the photo from the Prime Rib dinner, something she never would share with Bouchard unless she could use it.

The End

Cast of Characters

Amato, Paul – Secretary of Homeland Security
Anderson, Tim – Bardon Foundation
Bana, Diane – Capitol Hill correspondent
Bartlett, Gerry – Associated Press correspondent
Bascomb, Charles (Chip) Jr. – Congressman
Borochenkov, Andrei – President of Russia
Bosworth, Jeremiah (Boz) – Secretary of Defense (SecDef)
Bouchard – White House correspondent
Chapman, Melanie – Aide to Dr. Justice Frankhauser
Conway, Merrill – House Majority Whip
Cummings, Christopher – President pro tempore of the Senate
Doerner, Charles – Congressman
Fountaineau, Greg – Deputy Press Secretary
Francene, Palmer – Air Force General, Deputy Chairman of the Joint Chiefs of Staff
Frankhauser, Dr. Justin – Admiral, Head of the Bethesda Naval Medical Center
Hudak, Asher – Congressman
MacAfee, Martin – Colonel, Air Force One chief pilot
McCormick, Mary Ann – National Security Advisor to the President
Merriwether, Lincoln A. – President of the United States
Norman, Christine T. – Solicitor General of the United States
Pearlstein, Constance – Senator
Peckinpaugh, Admiral, Commandant of the Coast Guard

Perez, Enrico (Rico) – Miami News reporter
Ridgely, Haley – Admiral, Chairman of the Joints Chiefs of Staff
Rineheart, Alicia – Director of Congressional Liaison in the White House
Rodriguez, Dr. Inez – Puerto Rico medical researcher
Schoenfeld, Martha – House Minority Leader
Simpson, Bobby Joe – Congressman
Sperling, Victor – Director, Central Intelligence Agency
Stern, Joyce Whittingham – Chief Justice of the Supreme Court
Stern, Howard – Law professor
Umberto, Jorge – White House Press Secretary
Vance, Marshall – Speaker of the House
Vandergriff, Preston – U.S. Ambassador to Russia
Wiscznewski, Henry (Whiz) – Head of White House Secret Service detail
Winston, Jared – Chief of Staff, the White House
Winters, Ansel – Senate Majority Leader

About the Author

David H. Brown was born, raised, and educated in Cleveland, Ohio. After earning a bachelor's degree in Journalism in 1950, he began his nearly 15-year newspaper career with *The Cleveland Press* as a copy boy. After three years in the private sector, he became a reporter for *The Circleville Herald,* then state editor of *The Columbus Citizen,* and returned to *The Press* as a general assignment reporter.

In 1967, he began his federal government career as assistant director of information with the Department of Justice. He transferred to the Federal Aviation Administration to become the press officer for the original Anti-Skyjacking Task Force. In a consolidation, he joined the News Division of the parent Department of Transportation. In 1974, he became the first professional public affairs officer for the Government Printing Office. In 1976, he founded and was first president of the National Association of Government Communicators.

During his government career, he served on the Mass Communications Committee of the Agriculture Department Graduate School, where he developed and taught classes in media relations. He conducted programs for the Public Relations Society of America/New York University. He also was the part-time national capitol correspondent for *O'Dwyer's Newsletter,* the largest public relations publication.

After retiring in 1991, he became an adjunct professor of speech at Montgomery College, where he also taught Journalism classes, for seven years.

Drafted into the Army in 1944, he became an infantry rifleman with the 97th Division, which saw combat in Germany. The unit later was on its way to Japan as one of the first amphibious assault troops on Honshu Island when World War II ended.

In 1950, he was commissioned a 2nd Lieutenant with the Army Reserve's 83rd Division. In 1966, he became a mobilization designee with the Office of the Chief of Information in the Pentagon. In 1968, he also became adjutant, and later executive officer, of an Army Reserve Unit. When he retired in 1978 as a Lieutenant Colonel, he was awarded the Meritorious Service Medal. Among his other decorations were the Combat Infantry Badge and Bronze Star Medal.

In the University Heights suburb of Cleveland, he served on its Civil Service Commission, Board of Zoning Appeals, and Planning Commission before becoming a City Councilman. In Rockville, MD, he was rotating chairman of its Board of Appeals. A civic activist, he was given the Montgomery County Civic Association's Community Hero Award in 2002.

He has been a public speaker for more than half a century.

This is his ninth book.

Other Works by David H. Brown

Nonficition

I Would Rather Be Audited by the IRS Than Give a Speech

Airline Passenger Screening has Become EMA-Type SNAFU

Full Body Scam: The Naked View of Current Airport Security

Life is Just a Bowl of Memories: A Memoir

Nine/Eleven

Fiction

Operation Red Herring

The Decoration/Memorial Day War

Murder at 250 Center Street

Next in Line to the Oval Office